Praise for

THE FINE COLOR OF RUST

"Delightful, laugh-out-loud funny, and unforgettable. I love this book."

—Toni Jordan, author of *Addition*

"I adored *The Fine Color of Rust*. It's funny, irreverent and highly entertaining. I was sad to finish it, and I still miss Loretta!"

—Liane Moriarty, author of *The Husband's Secret*

"Loretta is one entertaining, compelling narrator, funny and self-deprecating, with an acerbic wit and occasional histrionics that belie a deep love of the people around her, whether she likes them or not. . . . A truly moving surprise at the end reveals O'Reilly's point all along, that there is value in things that don't cost anything and true beauty in a pile of junk."

—*Booklist* (starred review)

"O'Reilly's tale of a backwater Australian town seen through the eyes of Loretta Boskovic, who struggles to make ends meet and do good for her community, is hilarious and tenderly moving."

—*Publishers Weekly* (starred review)

"A story about love: where we look for it, what we do with it, and how it shows up in the most unexpected packages."

—*The Big Issue* (Australia)

Also by Paddy O'Reilly

The Fine Color of Rust
The Factory
The End of the World

THE
WONDERS

A Novel

PADDY O'REILLY

W

WASHINGTON SQUARE PRESS

New York · London · Toronto · Sydney · New Delhi

WASHINGTON SQUARE PRESS
A Division of Simon & Schuster, Inc.
1230 Avenue of the Americas
New York, NY 10020

First Washington Square Press trade paperback edition February 2015

WASHINGTON SQUARE PRESS and colophon are trademarks
of Simon & Schuster, Inc.

For information about special discounts for bulk purchases,
please contact Simon & Schuster Special Sales at 1-866-506-1949
or business@simonandschuster.com.

The Simon & Schuster Speakers Bureau can bring authors
to your live event. For more information or to book an event,
contact the Simon & Schuster Speakers Bureau at 1-866-248-3049
or visit our website at www.simonspeakers.com.

Interior design by Leydiana Rodríguez

Manufactured in the United States of America

10 9 8 7 6 5 4 3 2 1

Library of Congress Cataloging-in-Publication Data

O'Reilly, P. A. (Paddy A.)
    The wonders : a novel / Paddy O'Reilly.—First Washington Square Press
paperback edition.
        pages ; cm
    "Washington Square Press fiction original trade."
    1. Fame—Fiction. 2. Reality television programs—
Fiction. 3. Satire. I. Title.
PR9619.4O74W66   2015
823'.92—dc23   2014018895

ISBN 978-1-4767-6636-2
ISBN 978-1-4767-6637-9 (ebook)

The soul is still the same, the figure only lost;
And as the soften'd wax new seals receives
This face assumes, and that impression leaves;
Now call'd by one, now by another name;
The form is only chang'd, the wax is still the same . . .

Ovid, *Metamorphoses*, book 15
tr. John Dryden et al. (1717)

Who has not asked himself at some time or other:
am I a monster or is this what it means to be a person?

Clarice Lispector, *The Hour of the Star*

1

L EON WAS TWENTY-SIX when the true fragility of his body revealed itself. He died for the first time. There was no flying, no tunnel. He didn't see a light. He died, and a few minutes later he regained consciousness on a gritty carpeted floor under a pair of small hands pounding his breast as a female voice counted aloud. He opened his eyes. A male face loomed over him, so close that all he could see were stubby black mustache hairs sprouting from the pores of an upper lip and the rose-pink flesh of the mouth. The man was pinching Leon's nostrils shut, about to give him the kiss of life.

Leon felt a grunt of exhaust wheeze from him as if a knee had pressed into his rib cage. He sucked desperately to get breath into his chest. Every cell right out to his skin lit up, an instantaneous electric surge through flesh and bone.

The owner of the rosy lips fell backward onto the floor, muttering, "Jesus fucking Christ."

The firm's first-aid officer, the woman who had been pumping his chest, shot out a laugh.

"My god, he's back." The armpits of her green cotton blouse were dark with damp. Clear snot trailed from her nose to her lip. "Leon? Leon?"

He moaned and rolled his eyes toward her, still unable to speak, and she laughed harder, as though the laughing was an expulsion of something trapped inside. She wiped her nose on her sleeve, rubbed her hands down her skirt and rocked back on her heels, staring at the ceiling, laughing that seesaw braying laugh Leon had never heard from her before. His head lolled to the other side, and he saw his work colleague, the one who had been breathing spent air into his body, kneeling with head bowed as if in prayer.

He had died and been brought back to life in an office. He remembered a phrase: *Death be not proud, though some have called thee mighty and dreadful.*

"The ambulance is on its way, mate." Leon's colleague punched himself in the chest, a frantic gesture of relief. "Jesus, you gave us a fright. Fuck."

The next month he died again. Seven months later, again. Each time less mighty, less dreadful: his deaths were becoming modern and mean. Life tethered to the medical industry had begun. In a year's time, when his ailing heart muscle had given out, they transplanted a new heart inside him, a heart removed from a healthy young woman whose brain had been unwired by a fall onto concrete. After an uneasy truce, his recalcitrant body began its assault on the invading organ. No quantity of immuno-suppressants would convince his body to make peace with the muscular pump that could save it. His body and the heart battled on together in their bad marriage until he could barely walk.

By then he was living with his mother in the country. His sister traveled up from the city with her two children. The boy, his nephew, barreled out to the backyard and began tearing around the garden. The cat had bolted as soon as he arrived. Leon's five-year-old niece came and sat next to him while his sister perched on the arm of the couch, her legs twined, hands resting in her lap.

"So how are you, Leon? Mum says you're improving a little."

He stared at her, amazed. "I'm dying, Sue."

"Oh, Leon, always the pessimist. Let me get a cup of tea first, then we can chat."

Once she had gone into the kitchen, his niece lifted her wide eyes to him.

"Are you really dying?"

He nodded.

"Where will you go when you die?"

He guessed it must be time to think about that. He didn't believe in heaven and choirs of angels, or a sulfurous hell with eternal punishment. He didn't believe he would be reborn into another body. He was perfectly confident in what he did not believe and unable to fill the resulting void with any positive belief. Which left nothing.

"I think I stop being. I won't be here anymore but I'm not sure I go anywhere."

She lowered her gaze and played with the hem of her dress. He was sorry to disappoint her.

"Maybe I'll go to heaven." That was what people did to children. They told comforting lies. His mother had told him the same thing, except he had never believed her. She had described it in the same singsong voice the third-grade teacher used to recite the times tables, as if something repeated enough times must surely be true.

"It's okay if you don't go anywhere," she said. "It's only that I wanted to visit you."

Two weeks later he was bedridden, unable to eat, breathing with the labored effort of an aged man. The hospital still had no suitable donor. They rushed him in, implanted a pump beside his failing heart to keep him alive and sent him home again to wait and hope for a new heart.

It seemed there was an epidemic of heart disease. The waiting list was longer than ever. Leon had drifted to the bottom because this was to be his second heart. His body had already rejected one. New kinds of hearts were being grown in laboratories and artificial hearts that could last thirty years were at trial stage but not close enough. Preparing to die was his most logical course of action.

Until the call came.

He had to choose. One choice was risk, it was illegal, it was madness. His other choice was waiting for an impossible donation while he was being eaten up with fear and rage. And then dying anyway.

2

A YEAR LATER, LEON returned to a town near his childhood home in the old goldfields. He rented a flat with high ceilings and arched windows facing a grassed courtyard. From the window he could watch the weather taking shape in the morning sky and magpies stalking the lawn after rain. His benefactors had deposited enough money in his bank account for a year's rent and expenses, saying he would need that much time to recover well enough to return to normal life.

As he convalesced, his life cemented into a routine. Cereal and tea for breakfast, an apple and coffee for morning tea. He walked laps of the sports field every day, surrounded by yapping dogs, groups of tracksuit-clad women pumping their arms and chattering breathlessly, fathers urging pairs of chubby children to greater effort. He couldn't help picturing them as the blood cells and platelets that swim the channels of the circulatory system, repelling invaders and carrying oxygen and nutrition. A year of studying the body to understand what was being done to him had painted the whole world in the lurid imagery of illustrated medical texts.

In the evenings he prepared a meal and ate it while watching the news. After dinner he read a book or watched television or a film or sat at the computer, learning about the healing process of the body. He'd joined the bridge club but quit when the members' time spent on bitter disputes about club politics overtook the playing. No one visited. The people at the local supermarket recognized him, nodded, moved on.

Heroic efforts by a surgeon and an engineer had resurrected him but one year on, to his shame, Leon was less alive than when he had collapsed to the floor of the office with no heartbeat at all. Physically he had healed. The pain around his cavity was gone. He had stopped hurrying to the mirror first thing each morning to stare at his metal heart as if that would ensure it kept pumping. But something else inside him had changed. He was dispirited, a monk who emerges from his solitary cell to find that over the years not only has he lost the knack of being in the world but his faith, the core of his being, has withered.

When his original prescriptions finally ran out, he was forced to visit a local doctor for more immunosuppressants and antibiotics.

"I can't just prescribe these medications for you, Mr. Hyland," she said to Leon, who sat hunched in a question mark on a straight-backed chair beside her desk. "I need to refer you to a specialist, and to do that, I have to examine you."

He had no choice. He swore her to secrecy. The moment he left the surgery she called her husband. They kept silent for a week, until one of them, or someone they had told, got on to the local paper. Then bedlam. There was no more hiding away: his secret was out, and life was forcing its way in.

Reporters chased him down the street as if he was a slum landlord or a dodgy car dealer. He locked himself in his apartment for two weeks before hurriedly relocating to a cheap flat on the outskirts of town and changing his phone number. But he was tracked down again. The rumors spread further. Celebrity agents appeared. They courted him, treated him to lavish dinners, teased him and winked at him and tried to be friends, all so he would open his shirt. *So this is how a woman feels*, Leon thought wryly one night after the gaze of his dining companion, a mustached promoter with a big gut and a fat wallet, kept dipping to Leon's chest.

His suitors name-dropped about their other clients. They promised wealth, fame, a sensational new life. One of the agents offered so much money Leon was close to signing, but when he was told what kind of appearances and events he'd be asked to do—live talk shows, interviews with journalists, parades through the marquees at horse races and fashion shows and movie premieres—he balked.

"What will I talk about?"

"Yourself, of course. How you got that magnificent heart. The medical process. The emotional journey. Your favorite food. Whatever you like. We'll train you to be media savvy."

It sounded to Leon like those excruciating school speeches where you had to talk about your hobby or your most exciting vacation. Stammering red-kneed boys with spittle in the corner of their mouth, girls crossing their legs and twirling their hair as they ummed and gazed vacantly at the ceiling, the teacher tapping a pen on the desk in exasperation.

This particular agent had traveled to Leon's town on the high plain northwest of Melbourne. The two of them sat in a small dark café with rows of CDs behind the tables and jazz music playing softly. Leon used his fork to push a cube of luminous white sheep's cheese around his plate. He had always been a careful thinker, one who needed to disguise his long deliberations with sleight of hand. He lifted some oiled rocket leaves and decorated the cheese with them.

"I haven't got that much to say."

"Mate." The agent put his knife and fork down on his plate of pasta ragout and leaned forward. He had the lined handsome face of a retired movie star, and he wore a tan jacket of leather so fine it creased with the softness of cotton when he moved. "Mate, they all say that. Once you get started you won't be able to stop." He put on a mock falsetto. *"Oh, I couldn't possibly talk about myself all the time!* Then you can't shut them up. Trust me, you'll love it."

It was the sneering imitation of his own clients that put Leon off. Would the agent end up talking about Leon like that?

Rhona Burke, American entrepreneur and touring agent, called the next day.

"I'm not asking you to say yes or no until I give you an idea of my show."

Everyone else had been talking strategies, coverage, media saturation. Rhona began with advice.

"Don't tell anyone the story of how you got that heart. I don't know how many people were involved or who has seen the heart already—don't spread it any further. Have you told the story to anyone else who wanted to book you?"

"Not really. No details."

"Don't. No matter who you end up with. It's worth much more than you realize. You need to hold on to it until the crowd can't stand the wait any longer. Then you make them wait a little more."

"A tease?"

"Not a tease. A performance. I can explain better in person."

He would meet her. If nothing else, it would mean a trip out of the small town that had so abruptly become known in the media as "the home of the man with the metal heart."

3

THE TRAIN TO Melbourne traveled through a series of worn mountains with flat tops called the Pentland Hills. They looked to Leon as if some giant had taken to them with a sword and sliced off their peaks, leaving them as dining tables for his guests. They stretched to the horizon, floating in the sky, and the train swayed on the track across them like a chariot above the clouds. Humming to the rhythm of the train and tapping his fingers against the glass, Leon felt bubbly and shy, like a kid on the way to his first job interview.

Once the train had passed through the Pentland Hills, it started to travel downhill toward Melbourne. It stopped at Bacchus Marsh, then moved into the bleak uniform plain of Melton, where plastic bags fringed the wire fences and piles of boulders marked the sites of failed enterprises and building projects. In the distance, a yellowish dome of smog enclosed the city of Melbourne. As the train approached the city, the dreamy optimism that had lifted Leon through the hills sank into a flat pragmatism.

He had begun to think that this Rhona Burke person was most likely a swindler, an American hustler come to exploit him and make him into the Elephant Man of the modern world. Leon was no performer. He couldn't sing or dance or even make a decent speech without turning to jelly. What else could this woman mean but to put him in a sideshow?

If the train had stopped at that moment, Leon probably would have jumped off. Instead he sat smoldering with humiliation, picturing himself being jeered at by teenage thugs, pitied by women.

"Oh, the poor, poor fellow," he imagined one sideshow visitor whispering in her English upper-class accent. In Leon's vision everyone was wearing Victorian clothes and carrying canes and umbrellas. Ladies caught their horrified gasps in gloved hands and looked away delicately.

What a shock, then, to meet Rhona at the station in Melbourne. She was waiting to greet him when he got off the train, wearing cowboy boots and rhinestone jewelry. Titian-red hair. A big white handbag studded with fake rubies. Leon had been stewing in indignation about how he was to be displayed as a monster, gawked at by strangers, until he stepped onto the platform and found himself staring at Rhona as if she was the exhibit. Around him the other travelers were staring too.

"Mr. Hyland, a pleasure to meet you," she said in her big American voice, stretching her hand out to shake. "Geez, honey, they told me that Aussies always shut their lips tight to keep out the flies."

Only then did Leon close his mouth. He shook the short woman's hand and observed her more closely. Under the glitter of the gold and rhinestones, and behind the jeans and cowgirl attitude, Rhona Burke was older than she first seemed. He guessed from the downy skin and the softened jawline that she was in her sixties. She was clearly manic, though, he could already tell: one of those people who hurry through each day not to get it over with but to make sure that every morsel of everything good is sucked out of it and savored.

"Come with me, hon. We'll have lunch. Or just a coffee if you want." She took Leon's arm and urged him along the cold busy road to a taxi. They bent into the warmth. Once they were settled in the backseat, she handed Leon her card.

The business card sported her name in raised red lettering, shining like nail polish dripped onto the white surface. Her trade name, *The Penny Queen,* was spot-varnished copper underneath a stylized stroke of the brush that evoked a big-top tent. Leon stared at the card, leaning his cheek against the cool glass of the taxi window. So this was what she wanted. In the space of this single morning he had been thrilled at the idea of working, furious that he might become a sideshow freak, charmed by Rhona's sassy style, now flung into despair again by the idea that she wanted him for a circus.

"And what would I do for you?" He waved the flimsy business card. "After all that talk you only want me for show-and-tell? I'm not the bloody Elephant Man."

The driver glanced at Leon in the rearview mirror, quickly shifting his head out of the line of vision when he caught Leon's eye.

"Leon, darling, don't be such a drama queen. I've already signed one drama queen for this troupe, and a small team cannot last if it contains two drama queens."

No one had called Leon darling since he'd left hospital after his first organic heart transplant when the nurses, who were too busy to remember anyone's name, called the patients darling and sweetheart and love, and the doctors, also too busy, called them Mr. Um or Mrs. Err before launching into medico-talk. Now this stranger, this cowboy-suited exploitative charlatan, was darling-ing Leon like a condescending teacher.

"Forget it." He tapped the glass window behind the taxi driver's head. "Would you please let me out at the next intersection?"

The driver shrugged and began to ease the taxi into the left lane of traffic. Horns tooted behind them. A cyclist rode by shaking his gloved fist. Rhona put her hand on Leon's knee. Her heavy gold and silver rings rested in a row of knuckle-dusters on the fabric of his trousers above his kneecap. They were menacing but beautiful at the same time, and curiously warm.

"Not a sideshow exhibit. Not a freak the way you're thinking. Hon, you're going to be like Elvis. You're going to have women screaming and fainting over you. Not with fear or horror, but with passion. You're going to be whoever you want. It's not just people staring at you. You're going to entrance the people who come to see you. More than a weird body, more than a trick, you're going to give them a story, a life, a legend. The rubes want to feel they're getting to know you on a personal basis even when they're forty deep crushed against the stage. I can make you into a celebrity everyone loves. The one everyone wants."

It is the skill of the entrepreneur to recognize what people desire and provide it for them. Leon could feel the loneliness and longing etched into his features. It was a map for a pro like Rhona.

Rhona waited while Leon gazed out of the taxi window at a tram trundling by, loaded up with bored commuters on their way to lunch, staring at their phones or nodding off with their leaning heads leaving oily prints on the windows. He had begun to believe he would be alone for the rest of his life, a miserable hermit with a mutilated body. He was sure his broken-open chest and his scars and his breathlessness meant that no one would be able to overcome their distaste enough to hold him, let alone love him.

"More money than you've dreamed of, Leon. Fans. Adoring fans. You'll be a rock star."

"Right. Me. A rock star."

His gut told him to say no. He could move to Sydney or Brisbane, travel to distant suburbs for medical treatment, use false addresses and post office boxes to keep his anonymity, try to build himself a normal life again.

But Rhona had ignited hope in him, and hope can make fools of us all.

4

TWELVE WEEKS AND six thousand miles later, Leon stood outside the door to his new life. His third life. Behind the door were his future business partners.

He knew little about these people except that Kathryn Damon was an Irish woman whose gene therapy for Huntington's had cured the Huntington's but left her covered in wool. He had a vague memory of seeing her on a current-affairs show a year or two ago. Or he could be thinking of someone else, that girl raised by dogs in Romania maybe. Christos Petridis was a Greek performance artist who had somehow transplanted metal wings onto himself. Kathryn had been recruited months before. Christos had arrived last week. Leon was the last. Tomorrow they would relocate to Rhona's country estate Overington, in Vermont, to begin intensive training for the show.

The next few months, perhaps years, of his life would be spent with these people if he chose to stay. He waited at the rust-colored timber panels and pearly white handle of the door and he made himself a promise. *If I hate these people*, he told himself, *if I can't get on with them or I find them too creepy or disgusting to look at or I feel they are reacting that way to me, I will walk away.*

No matter that Rhona had provided enough money up front to pay for his medications and living expenses and any trifles and trinkets he might want for the next few months. Nor that she assured him he would have accumulated in three years a fortune large enough to fund a dream retirement. Nor even that she had committed to keep him safe from the biotech and pharmaceutical companies that had pursued him with terrifying ferocity since his clockwork heart was revealed. If he got the heebie-jeebies for any reason, he would politely say "Thank you anyway, Rhona," as he had been taught by his mother, and he would pack his things and fly home.

He went to grasp the doorknob. Too late. On the other side, Rhona had already twisted the handle. The door swung open. Three people stood inside waiting for Leon to cross the threshold.

And that's where he stopped. At the threshold. Stupefied by the sight of Kathryn Damon.

Rhona stood beside the open door to Leon's right. Christos was there too, further back, statuesque in the light of the floor-to-ceiling window that looked out across a paved sandstone courtyard flanked with urns and marble benches. The courtyard was so large it was difficult to believe the house was in the middle of Manhattan. And then there was Kathryn.

Leon was trying to step through the doorway, but his legs had turned to pillars of rock. Kathryn was overwhelming his consciousness. A moment later, a panicky sensation streaked through his body, a shot of adrenaline, and he began to tremble.

Seeing this woman, this human inhuman animal, was like confronting a shape-shifter forged by a capricious god.

In the seconds while Leon teetered back and forth on his immobile legs, Rhona backed away and lifted a tiny camera, peering into the viewfinder, and panned across the scene. Immediately, Christos came to life. He strode across the room and placed his palm flat against the lens of the camera.

"No filming, please," he said. "I do not want to be recorded without my express permission."

Christos's voice snapped Leon out of his stupor. How regal he sounded. He was a lord, a commander. His English was fluent and natural, if somewhat formal, but the hint of Greek accent, the deep voice, the pauses and hesitations before words he wanted to stress gave him an impressive gravitas. He had a voice that caused you to listen as if whatever he said would certainly be important and worthy.

Leon returned his attention to Kathryn, who was observing him from her position next to a bookcase. In her hand was a book, a photography monograph with tropically hued greens and reds shining from the open pages. The bookcase beside her had a stepped effect, a kind of tumbling of colorful spines and classic dull crimson and blue hardcovers down to the large-format books and magazines on the bottom shelves. Leon shifted his focus to the ripples of spine in an attempt not to stare at Kathryn.

"Go on, then, have a good look. This is me, all of me." Her voice was not what Leon expected, even though he would have been hard put to explain what he had expected. Perhaps something otherworldly. High and thin, ethereal. Instead she had a warm mellow voice with an Irish lilt. "Get it over with."

He let out the breath he had been holding.

Kathryn closed the book, which came together with the slap of hand on flesh, inserted it into the bookcase and lifted her arms. She twirled a couple of times with her arms held in ballerina position, dropped a quick curtsey. "I've been hiding away so long I don't know what to do with myself when someone's staring at me. I suppose I'd better get used to it."

"You sure better, all of you. You're going to be looked at in ways you've never been looked at before." Rhona returned to the doorway, patted Leon on the bottom and told him to come inside like a good man. "And thank god you're not drooling like the security guard when he caught sight of her through the window. That stylist did an amazing job. We're going to have to really make sure there's no sexiness at all in Kathryn's act or we'll be accused of performing pornography."

"Charming, Rhona." Kathryn flopped into the armchair by the bookcase. "Very classy."

Leon was trying to look at Kathryn with a noncommittal gaze, but he had never seen anything so desirable. She could have been a voluptuous showgirl zipped into a skintight costume of black astrakhan. Her pale face and ears were framed in black twists of lamb's wool, and yet she had normal female features, a wide red-lipped face. Her long wool-clad legs ended in bare feet shod in stilettos. The wool finished in neat cuffs at her ankles and wrists. Two bright pink nipples. Leon couldn't understand exactly what it was about this hybrid creature that made her more womanly than a woman, but she was. She was luscious. And although he had never been religious, the word that came to mind was "sinful."

When she lifted her leg to cross it in the armchair, the whole room was eclipsed momentarily by a glimpse of pink. Of course, she was naked. There was no wool down there. Leon groaned inside.

"Okay." He moved his leg forward, began walking into the room to draw attention away from his suddenly swelling crotch. "Where should I sit?"

"Somewhere with a cushion for your lap, I think." Christos sniggered as he lifted a bentwood chair from behind the piano and placed it beside Kathryn. "At least with me you can be safe, Kathryn."

"Not by any willpower of your own, you big fag."

"Don't be nasty. I thought you said you'd be my fag hag."

Leon caught sight of a young dark-haired man with thick curly lashes sitting in the corner of the room. The young man smiled sweetly at Leon's nod. That would be Christos's young Russian boyfriend, Yuri. Rhona had invited everyone to bring a spouse or lover or family member. Only Christos had come with someone.

"Leon, come on. You've come a long way to be here and we might as well get to know each other. I showed you mine and Christos's wings have gone ahead to the estate. Your turn to show us yours." Kathryn winked.

Rhona nodded, so Leon began to unbutton his shirt. Usually he wore an undershirt beneath his shirt. Without the extra layer, the hole in his chest cast shadows on the fabric when he passed near a light source or stood in sunlight. Today he had come prepared and underdressed, knowing that his fellow freaks, as he had already begun to think of them, were expecting to see his heart.

Kathryn clapped a slow clap and started to hum the stripper's tune. As Leon reached the last button he hesitated. For all the amazement his visible brass heart engendered in observers, how could it even compare to the phenomenon that was Kathryn Damon, that woolly sex bomb stretched out languorously on the armchair in front of him?

"Show us your tits," she hooted with her hands cupped around her mouth.

Rhona's cowboy boots had spurs. They jingled musically as she came to Leon with her hand out, ready to take his shirt.

"You are magnificent. Believe me, Leon. You three are all different, and all magnificent."

Leon dropped his shoulders. The shirt slid down his arms, and he caught it with the fingertips of his left hand as it drifted toward the rug. Cool air flowed through his chest.

"What the feck!" Kathryn used the arms of the low chair to push herself up. "Oh my god. Oh my feckin' god. Now that is a proper spectacle. Can I come closer?"

He nodded. She lowered her woolly scalp to Leon's breast. The backs of her naked ears were pale and shot through with faint blue like old pen markings. A fragrance drifted up from her, a grandmothery cozy scent that Leon realized must be lanolin.

"Do you ever touch it?" She raised her eyes to him, still bent toward his chest.

"You can touch it if you want." He had never said that to anyone before. He hoped she would say the same to him and that he would be permitted to cup the tight black curly wool cropped close to her skull. Or the breast. He willed himself not to think about the breast. "I mean, you can touch the metal part. Be careful of the joins."

He released the clasp that held the titanium rib section in place across the fist-sized hole in his chest, and swung open the door of silver bones. Kathryn peered into the cavity.

"Holy shite, I can't believe I can see right through you! The scarring in the hole looks so ancient, like bog-man skin." She shifted to see from a different angle. "So that's your blood going through the tubes out of the heart. And the struts—"

"Ceramic, to hold the heart in place," Leon interrupted, not pleased to be called a bog man. He was having second thoughts. He didn't want anyone touching the heart, possibly knocking out a synthetic artery or dislodging a strut.

"May I touch it too?" Christos asked. "I also have mechanical devices in me. It is vexing that I can't see them without a series of opposing mirrors or examine them properly with my fingers. You are a lucky man."

The absurdity of that statement struck them all at the same time. Kathryn guffawed.

"Let's talk about what's going to happen now." Rhona intercepted the possibility of Leon's heart being handled by passing out electronic schedules. She was shaking her head and muttering about discreet coverings for Kathryn.

"The trouble with this new style is that it's revealing when you move a certain way. We could have a camouflaged G-string thing made for you. No one would even know it was there."

"Oh, great. Underpants, the ones monkeys wear in the circus. I could get big striped bloomers. Do you want me to wear a matching pillbox hat too? Should I have a little organ strapped to me that I can grind while you take the hat around?"

When Rhona had described Kathryn and Christos to Leon, she had mentioned that Kathryn was a little spiky. In their months together before Leon and Christos arrived, Rhona said, she and Kathryn had settled into a pattern of communication where Rhona, by nature the excitable one, would back down in the face of Kathryn's withering commentary and wait for the fury to fizz out of her in odd interjections and mutterings before the conversation could continue. "It's her way back," Rhona had told him. "Her way back to herself."

"I know." Kathryn was talking rapidly. Her Irish accent was much stronger now. "What about a bikini, then? Hot pink with

— 21 —

spangles, maybe. And a costume I can rip off like a stripper. Pasties for my nipples, right?"

Leon directed his gaze resolutely at Rhona. Anywhere but at Kathryn. Occasionally he would glance at Christos or Yuri and widen his smile to indicate amusement or agreement as if he was engaged in the conversation. It was imperative that he not look at Kathryn's nipples.

In high school this kind of thing had happened to him every day. The hot flush of lust, the guerrilla erection, the schoolbag draped across the groin. At thirty-one years old, he should have had at least a touch more control, but no. Clenched between his thighs and crushing his balls down into an impossible squeeze, his semihard cock pulsed each time the image of that pink cleft flitted through his mind.

Rhona picked up a folder and tapped it against the arm of her chair. "We have tentative bookings starting in summer and I haven't done a bit of promotion yet. It's word of mouth. The rumors are flying. I've given you a paper copy and an electronic copy of what we'll be doing up until the launch. What I want you to do is check whether there's anything you aren't comfortable about. I think you'll be fine but—"

"Comfortable, that's what I need, sure. I could wear a nappy. That would be different. Sexy sheep chick in nappy. Oh yes, that's right. With a dummy. And a comforter. Oh, kinky."

Rhona waited for Kathryn to finish speaking before going on as if she had heard nothing. To prepare the group for performance, she said, media training would begin immediately: posture, facial control, body language, pacing answers, deflection and targeting, voice modulation. Learning how to deal with questions and the "rubes who think you're a toy." The coming weeks would be intensive and intense. Back to school. Leon had learned little the first time around. Perhaps this would give him some of the social skills everyone else seemed to have absorbed naturally.

"Life is short," Rhona said. "Fashions change, tastes change, laws change. Let's get you out there before they make us illegal."

5

IN THE WARMTH of the limousine after the airplane ride to Vermont, Kathryn fell into a deep sleep, her head tucked into her shoulder and her face half-covered by the high collar of her velvet cape. Christos and Rhona talked in low tones that stopped and started like the rumble of a faulty engine while Leon stared out the window at the snow-covered fields and the spindly trees. It was spring. Although the trees seemed bare, they had a greenish haze in the sunlight that must have been the beginning of new leaves. Having never traveled farther than Sydney, Leon had only ever experienced this kind of landscape as the backdrop to a movie. And here he was, a character in the movie. In this new surreal existence, Santa might come riding over the hill in his red uniform and sleigh.

Rhona reached across the divide between the limousine seats and tapped Kathryn's knee.

"Wake up, honey, we're home. Boys, welcome to Overington."

Leon swiveled to face the front as the driver pressed a button on the leather dashboard of the car, and the steel and timber gates in front of the car swung open, only to reveal another pair of steel and timber gates. A wall of thick cypress hedge, six feet high, grown up and around metal posts and rails, formed the outer fence. Curls of rusty razor wire crowned the inner fence of cyclone wire. Between the two fences was a no-man's-land of melting gray snow and stony ground, and beyond the fences stood a copse of pine and spruce. Farther to the west, a long tiled roofline with upturned corners, reminiscent of a Japanese temple, rose above banks of white snow.

The second gate began to open as soon as the first had closed.

"The double perimeter is for the animals." Rhona nodded to the two men patrolling the inner fence. "I told you I give sanctuary to retired circus animals?"

"They never try to escape though, do they." Kathryn was looking at the razor wire.

How did she feel being part prey animal, part predator? Leon wondered. Surely she would smell different from other animals. Not human, not sheep, but something in between. How did the circus animals behave when they scented her?

"They might," Rhona said. She made a mock tigerish growl. Her yellowish teeth were one of the few giveaways of her age. She had obviously never bleached them, unlike everyone else Leon had met since he arrived in the States. "I'm joking. It's paradise for them here. And they're not dangerous animals anyway. The fences are to stop people from getting in."

The second gate groaned shut behind them, and the car eased into a driveway flanked by newly dug flower beds. Straggly thin trees arched over the path to form a shadowy tunnel. Though the car windows were closed, the white pebbles crackling under the tires made the sound of wealth—limousine pulling slowly down a long, manicured driveway.

Rhona sighed. "I still love Overington. I built it twenty years ago. I had a crazy dream that one day it could be a retirement home for some of my old friends. Never again. Give me a wild animal over a greedy human anytime." Rhona leaned forward to peer through the window. "Here it comes. I hope you'll love it too."

The limousine swept around the last curve and the house came into view. It was two stories with a long roof, pitched low despite being in Vermont, where, Leon had heard, in winter the snow fell for days on end. Ribs of blond beam framed the stucco walls. The same blond timber surrounded the windows and doors. At the top of the walls, under the roofline, hung long wooden louvers, silvered with age.

"The louvers open and close over the course of the day to let in light. If you look from above, the building is shaped in the form of a cross. Four wings extending from the central shared space. Four fully self-contained apartments, plus a communal kitchen, dining room and living area. Gymnasium, sunroom, massage room, that kind of thing. What do you think?"

"Why all the cameras?" Christos asked.

Leon had noticed them too, hanging from corners of the building, fixed at regular intervals to the fence.

She told them the cameras had been installed for the animal sanctuary. When the animals were first brought in eight years before, the landscape designer built discreet wire fences covered in vines and wild grasses around the enclosures. One morning in the third week after its arrival, an aged lion, doped up on pain medication for arthritis, was found by the animal keeper stabbed fourteen times and left to bleed to death on the rocky mound at the center of its enclosure. The next month an elephant was shot in the thigh with a homemade bow and arrow. The tip of the arrow was steel, filed so sharp it could have pierced brick. The boy who did those things was caught, but a year later two of the five chimpanzees were kidnapped, and a video of them cowering in the corner of a student dorm was posted online. They were later dumped at an animal shelter and returned to Overington.

"I should have realized earlier—the animals would stay in, but I had to keep the humans out. Don't ever underestimate the cruelty of the public. Especially you three, you need to be prepared."

"Kids are kids." Christos shook his head. "They do silly things without thinking. Most of them don't mean to hurt anyone."

Leon agreed. "I've never met a bad kid. My niece is a sweetie." He could remember the moment she first saw his metal heart, her terror mingled with delight and laughter, the way she ran screaming to her mother, then rushed straight back to have a closer look. "She calls me See-Through Man."

Rhona shook her head. "Not all kids are good kids. We've ruined some. You give them too much, they forget their humanity. I'm not joking. They don't care about anything or anyone. It's all sensation to them."

After the incidents, Rhona had built the double fence around the perimeter of the estate. But fences were not enough. Fences were mere passive protection. A year later a young woman climbed the fences and tried to cuddle the chimps. The two chimps who had been traumatized by their last encounter with outsiders turned on the intruder and bit her savagely, after which she brought a lawsuit against Rhona's estate that dragged on for a year. It had become clear that the animals, of whom only a few were left, needed aggressive protection. So Rhona installed electronic surveillance and trip alarms, and hired a security firm to carry out regular patrols.

When the limousine finally pulled up at the front door and the four of them stepped onto the driveway, Leon couldn't help staring at Kathryn and Christos stretching and yawning and examining their surroundings. Together they were three problematic creatures, part human, part something else. Surely as curiosities for young delinquents they would be worth more than a few old circus chimps. Not for the first time since he had left Australia, a spasm of apprehension rippled down his spine.

6

THE DAY AFTER their arrival at Overington, more staff were brought in: a security overseer whose name, Hap, was as neat, solid and reassuring as the bulky man himself, and a marketing director, Kyle, very high energy and known for the success of his viral campaigns. Rhona had decided she'd taken on too much. She would remain as the personal manager of the group and hand over the bulk of the marketing to someone else.

"It's all changing so fast. Publicity used to be schmoozing and boozing and press releases and freebies. That's what I'm good at. Now it's social networking and crowd-sourced campaigns and smatternet, whatever the hell that is. We need someone to take care of the new markets."

From his first morning on the job, Kyle changed things. While she was introducing him, Rhona mentioned she wanted to call the show Überhumans. It was the first Leon had heard of the name, but then he was not yet fully participating in conversations and decisions. This new world had thrown him off-kilter. More than ever he had fallen into the role of watcher and listener, the silent student: orienting himself, steadying himself in the face of monumental change. He had been the same as a boy, collecting his self-help books at home, reading, studying and thinking but slow to act. Despite cramming *The Popular Teenager* he had still failed to be picked for sports teams or clubs—to his parents' deep disappointment.

"Überhumans?" Kyle said incredulously. "Like, you mean, some German thing?"

"No, sweetheart." Rhona turned to the three überhumans and rolled her eyes. "I mean, like, better than human. Über—it sounds sexy, don't you think?"

"Sexy if you're a university student, maybe. I mean, how long is it since you ran a show, Rhona? Audiences don't want to think, they don't want to be educated, they want to be entertained. I'm sure that hasn't changed."

"Listen, sonny, I have three shows still touring that I set up fifteen years ago. Quality doesn't go out of fashion."

Kyle shrugged. "Sure, but, Rhona, trust me. Überhumans? No. You're paying me to know what works now. What about Superhumans?"

"You think that hadn't occurred to me? They're not superheroes."

They settled into an energetic argument about what the show should be named while Leon pushed himself off the chair and went to continue organizing his new apartment. Überhumans? More like unterhumans. That was the German word for "under," wasn't it?

He picked a few more books out of the box beside his bookcase. He examined each one, flipping open at a random page to read a paragraph or two, before lining up the volumes on the shelves he had marked for war history, arranging them loosely in alphabetical order between the medical texts and the shelves for his childhood books. Überhumans; what a joke. His own ravaged body put him in mind of an old man in a bathrobe shuffling out to the mailbox, looking up and down his lonely street, shuffling back to the cup of tea and burned white toast with a scraping of butter waiting on the kitchen table.

That night Rhona convened dinner at a local Italian restaurant. She had booked the whole place out. The three future celebrities could still move around freely—only Kathryn's physical difference was evident in normal clothes, and she could easily disguise it by dressing in pants and a long-sleeved blouse topped by a bohemian arrangement of scarves around the head and neck—but without strangers in the room they could relax. They drank an aperitif in a private room while their meals were laid out next door. Once everyone was settled in front of their plates in the dining room proper and the doors were locked, Kathryn unwrapped herself and stretched out.

Kyle curled strips of creamy linguine onto his fork, which he then rested on the side of the plate. It was clear from his bent head and frown that he was formulating a speech. After a few moments, as the rest of them were eating, he raised his face and spoke.

"Well, everyone, I love it already. I love Overington and I love your whole setup. I know it's normal for the incoming person to be toasted but, you know what, I'm going to jump in and toast you." Kyle rose from his seat and lifted a glass of champagne from the table. "I've been in marketing all my adult life, worked across the States, even Europe. You could say I'm a workaholic—my ex-wives always do. I've seen a lot of crazy things and run a lot of top campaigns that gave people a mighty surprise. You'll soon find that I'm no *normal* marketing guy." On the word "normal" he'd hesitated and his tongue had tripped. N-normal. He recovered in an instant. "That's funny, me saying to you three that I'm not normal. I guess I'm trotting out my usual spiel. You've caught me out! I'll have to be more original in the future."

Leon expected Kathryn to be listening with her usual impassive expression, but she was smiling. Everyone got Kyle's charm except Leon. Kyle was forty-three, twice divorced, supporting three children in California, but he could have passed for twenty-five. His skinny frame and his thin sandy hair and his assured manner for some reason bothered Leon. His words were too shiny, like bright lights that blind you to what waits in the shadows behind. One of the women at the office where Leon used to work had lived in another country for five years. She said she had learned to speak the day-to-day language easily, but the nuances, the origin of phrases, the irony implicit in a word or a missing word were beyond her. She described it as living with a child's comprehension in a world of complex adult conversations. Leon felt the same way with Kyle.

Kyle loosened his thin black tie before he spoke again. "Phew, that's better. I will never get used to the noose, no matter how long I live." He rubbed his throat. "Now, what I'd like to do is toast each of you. Firstly, Rhona, for having the good taste and good sense to hire me. Then you three, Kathryn, Christos, Leon. You've come a long way already, but I'm here to make sure the whole world gets to know you. And a toast to Yuri too, because we all need support. I understand there are a lot of other staff behind this project and I'll be getting around to meet them later. But tonight, I want to celebrate you three wonders of the world and assure you that I'll be working my ass off for you." He lifted his champagne glass.

Rhona lifted hers. "To the new wonders of the world."

"The wonders of the world," Kyle chimed in.

7

AND SO IT was decided. They would be called the Wonders, Rhona announced.

Leon laughed. The Wonders sounded like toys, or a game show.

"The big wonder is that any of us is still alive," Kathryn said.

He'd already noticed how quick she was with a joke. Afterward she would fold into herself, return to reading her book or quietly leave the room. This time she stayed, giving her full attention.

They had gathered to watch Yuri demonstrate the insertion of Christos's handwings, in case for some reason Yuri was unavailable and someone else would be called on to manipulate the unwieldy frames into the sockets in Christos's back.

Christos stood with his feet apart and knees a little bent, hands on hips, visibly bracing himself to support the extra weight. He was naked from the waist up. The scaffolding implants that would hold the triple-jointed metal wings were clearly visible between his shoulder blades, on either side of the spine. They were ceramic, ivory colored, and shaped like arum lilies. Inside the sockets, he had told them, were wet joins where nerves and tissue were protected by a valve that opened when the handwings were inserted into the scaffolds.

He turned his head to speak to Rhona and Kyle as Yuri lifted the left wing from its case.

"'The Wonders' is a good name," Christos said. "It has charisma. Also, Yuri and I have discussed it and decided that, yes, I will accept Seraphiel as a stage name for this project."

Yuri took a deep breath, then lifted a handwing from its case and grasped a joint at the end between his thumb and forefinger. He folded the wing into a concertina shape that would be hidden from view to anyone in front of Christos. Leon moved around to see more clearly. The handwing was beautiful, wrought of multiple bronze-colored metallic strands with tiny joints at elbows, wrist and fingers—the insect-like skeleton wing and hand belonging to a new creature fused of metal and flesh.

Christos bent from the waist, his back muscles tensing in ridges. The moment Yuri fixed the second wing in place, sweat beads balled on Christos's upper lip. At least Christos sweated. Leon had been starting to think that Christos was inhumanly fit as well as inhumanly handsome and inhumanly vain. Christos straightened his back and opened the wings. They unfolded upward from the first elbow then outward from the second until they arched above him, fingers curled at the tips.

"Can you move them around?" When Kathryn stretched out her hand, one of the long spindly handwings extended slowly over Christos's shoulder. Light pulsed through the transparent tips at the ends of the handwings. The three-fingered hand grasped Kathryn's fingers, and she let out a giggly breath of astonishment.

"It's like a bird taking my hand with its beak. And the fingers, what is that, electricity?"

"It is the passage of current through the nervous system. The metal strands are nanoengineered metal with optical conductive strands inside." Christos spoke with effort, frowning, eyes squeezed shut.

"You'll have to learn to work those things with your eyes wide open, Christos," Rhona said from the other side of the room, where she had retired to perch on a steel and leather chaise longue and observe. "The rubes want eye contact. It makes it real for them. It makes *you* real."

Kyle stood beside Rhona, ash-blue eyes narrowed as he observed Christos. "It would be better if it looked easy. Right now it looks like a whole lotta hard work."

"Yes, yes. It's practice. I haven't had enough practice yet." The sweat from Christos's face was dripping in dark splotches on his blue cotton shorts. Yuri pulled a wipe from his gym bag and dabbed Christos's forehead.

Across the room, Kyle pulled out a recorder and began talking softly into it. "Sweat, posture, effort," he muttered. "Angel mythology, how to work it in. Revisit strategy for graphic work."

As Rhona circled the room, inspecting Christos from different angles, Leon shivered with a surge of nostalgia for the days when his surgeon would do the same to him, checking to see how his body was holding up, cupping her hand around his shoulder as she leaned in to examine his cavity.

"We might have to get those sweat glands on your face closed up. It's not very attractive when you're dripping like that. There's some kind of laser thing they can do." Rhona peered at Christos's chest. "You've got no underarm or chest hair?"

"In my exhibition *Palliative Art Care*, many years ago, it was necessary to have smooth skin for the application of the texts. My chest and arm hair was permanently removed. Excuse me, Kathryn, would you please stop doing that?"

Kathryn let go of his wing hand, which she had been massaging with her fingers, separating one metal finger from the other, flexing the joints and pushing the fingers together.

"Marvelous," she said. "Splendiferous."

It sounded unlike the way Leon had heard her speaking so far. Was she was mocking Christos? Rhona seemed to be wondering the same thing when she asked sharply, "What do you mean, Kathryn?"

"I mean exactly what I say, Rhona. I'm rehabilitating words that have fallen out of use. Having just read P. G. Wodehouse, I think I'll start calling things 'marvelous.' I like 'smashing' too. And 'dandy.'"

"Hello?" Christos's voice reverberated through the room. "Are you finished with me? My wings are exhausting to wear."

"Sorry, darling. Yes, we'll close up those face pores. You'll still sweat from your back and underarms, so there won't be any health issues." Rhona touched a liver-colored blemish the size of a coin on Christos's arm as she spoke. "We have some work to do. Physical and mental. Not just Christos but all of you. You're fine specimens, but now you also have to learn what it is to be fine performers. Once Kyle has taught you a few basic tricks we'll bring in a proper performance coach."

Leon shrugged his shoulders and twisted his neck to release the tension in his back. His reason for joining Rhona's troupe was exactly that: they would be performers, not objects for passive exhibition—two-headed cows or giant pumpkins. However, what performers actually did was not clear to him. The night before, sleeping in his new bed in this new house, new country, new world, he had dreamed of Liberace and woken with a yelp. His pillow was slimy where he had obviously been open-mouthed and dribbling during his dream. Now Rhona was using the word "tricks."

8

RHONA LED A tiny woman wearing grimy checked pants and a chef's hat into the common room.

"This is our cook, Vidonia. I realize you each have some food issues, so Vidonia will plan out a diet for you and prepare your meals each day. She's a qualified nutritionist as well as a chef."

"Hi, Vee." Kathryn smiled and went back to reading her book.

Vidonia pulled a small notepad and gold pencil from her pants pocket. "I found some good recipes for your black rice, Kathryn. I'll try one tonight."

During the orientation tour of Rhona's property, Leon and Christos had been shown the main kitchen. It was industrial-sized with long stainless steel benches, saucepans and sauce pots, crepe pans and tureens, a six-burner stove and an oven that could fit a suckling pig. Vidonia seemed as though she would barely be able to see the top of the stove let alone lift a stockpot full of boiling soup off of it.

"Mr. Hyland, what are your requirements? Any allergies or dislikes?"

He'd prepared for this, for the day someone would have to know about his odd eating pattern. "I'm sorry, I do have a few things. They had to take some of my stomach away after an infection during my surgeries. It's a third the size of a normal stomach. And part of my duodenum is also missing."

Vidonia nodded, scribbling on her pad.

"I eat five small meals a day. I drink liquids between meals, never with them, because I don't have enough capacity in my stomach for both liquid and solid. Spicy foods give me indigestion, and offal can make me retch—it's dangerous for my stomach to react violently, so . . ."

His grandmother used to serve steak and kidney pudding on the third Thursday of the month. One evening when she asked Leon to help her with the preparation, he had to juggle the slippery kidneys from their wrapping to the cutting board. A particularly slimy one shot out of his grip and went splat against the fridge before sliding to the floor, leaving a trail of purple bloody material on the white surface. Later on, being wheeled in and out of surgery, he often recalled that dark meaty smear, the deadness and yet the fleshiness of it, the reminder that we are made of such mortal tissue.

"Anything else?"

"No," he lied. "That's all."

Leon was barely acquainted with the people who shared the house. Everything he said he measured first by what kind of impression it might leave on them. Besides his fellow performers and Rhona, Kyle and Yuri, there were the housekeeping staff; the security staff; the animal keepers and gardeners; the media trainer; a fitness coach; Kathryn's stylist, who came weekly to keep her coat shorn and neat. Coming out of a year of total solitude, he was a man of gaffes and blunders, still sleepwalking, the social equivalent of a dining companion with a long red crease in his face from sleeping on the pillow seam.

Vidonia kept scribbling. "I'm going to be around six days a week, so you can always change your order." She grinned, her teeth pointy but cute in a vampire kind of way. "And I'm a fabulous cook."

"She is." Rhona patted her own mounded hips with both hands. "I blame her for my great big ass."

Vidonia turned to Christos. "Mr. Petridis? Your special diet?"

Christos sighed. He turned on his side on the divan near the window. Yuri sat cross-legged on the floor beside him.

"I have"—he paused lengthily—"a number of requirements. My diet is restricted, like Leon's, because of surgical intervention. Also, I am allergic to shellfish, and I prefer to avoid pork. As for the weighting of protein, fat and carbohydrate in my meals—think of me as an elite athlete. I must carbo-load before a performance. I must have muscle mass and endurance. I will need energy bars available at all times. Drinks high in amino acids and mineral salts should be placed beside each machine in the gymnasium. Yuri can make my special shakes. I prefer him to do this. And he himself is a vegan. He must not have any animal products in his food. I don't understand it, but I respect it."

A dimple of pleasure appeared on Yuri's cheek. He was so in thrall to Christos that Christos gained even more stature when Yuri was around.

The first time Leon had met Christos it occurred to him that here was a man who deserved his own leonine name. Christos was a true lion of a man, shaggy haired, muscular. He moved with immense physical grace, the male leader of a pride padding around his dominion. When Leon was eleven, he had asked his mother why she had chosen Leon as a name. She told him that his father had chosen it and she never knew why, except that the manager at the department store where his father worked at the time had been named Leon.

"I'm sure it was more than that," she said, pausing to think, which was something she rarely did, preferring to set to a task rather than waste time "mooching about and getting maudlin," as she called it. "It was probably some relative of his. I don't think it was his grandfather." She stopped wielding the mattock long enough to look at the sky as if she would find the answer there, or as if Leon's dead father might be up in the clouds waiting for her to ask him a question.

He'd died when Leon was nine. It was a Saturday. Round three of the round-robin at the local church tennis courts. He and his mixed doubles partner had won the first two matches easily. The doubles partner had mentioned that to Leon's mother after the funeral. Leon was handing around sandwiches and suffering hugs from moist-eyed women.

"He didn't even raise a sweat in those first two matches. We won six–nil in the first and six–three in the second. We probably would have won the day."

"Another glass of wine?" Leon's mother replied in such an arch voice that Leon was instantly certain she had known about this woman and his father behind the tennis club rooms. On one occasion, Leon had been sent to fetch his father and had come upon them as they tripped out from the shrubbery behind the clubhouse. The woman's skirt had been accidentally tucked into her underwear. They were both flushed and laughing, but when they saw Leon the smiles dropped from their faces and they turned formally to each other and said good-bye and thank you for the game.

The woman kept talking as if her guilty secret was forcing inanities from her mouth to fill the yawning space of what she couldn't say. "Other people had training in first aid. He was flat out on the court. I couldn't help staring at the dead leaf caught in his hair. His mouth was opening and closing like a ventriloquist's dummy."

"I see," Leon's mother said, looking over the woman's shoulder at another guest at the wake and nodding hello.

"They gave him CPR for a long time."

"You'll have to excuse me." His mother handed Leon a plate of sausage rolls and walked away, leaving him standing beside this woman who knew he knew, both of them stiff as totem poles in the middle of the crowded room.

He never had a chance to ask his father things a teenage boy needs to ask. And he never believed he was living up to his name, unless he counted the lion in *The Wizard of Oz*, so timid he needs to drink a potion for courage. A weedy bookish boy should not have to grow up with the name Leon. He should have been called Egbert or Mortimer. When he joined Rhona's troupe and finally got the chance to choose a new name, Rhona decided his moniker would be Clockwork Man.

Even Leon sounded good after that. And what did she mean by it anyway? Was she trying to say something about Leon's character? That he was heartless, a mechanical man? How would she know? He spent the early sleepless hours of the morning during the first days at Overington thrashing and freestyling around the huge bed they had installed in his apartment, close to weeping at his own stupidity in becoming a part of this dubious venture.

Christos was still listing his dietary requirements. "I cannot eat tough meat; the membrane of citrus fruit; skins of fruits or vegetables; corn, celery, or sweet potatoes; chili or hot curry."

Vidonia led Christos and Yuri to the kitchen to show them where she kept the ingredients Yuri would need to make Christos's special shake each day.

Rhona turned to Leon. "Is there anything else I should know? Any other things you need?"

"I need something." Kathryn stretched along the couch and flexed her feet and arms before standing up and slipping the book she had been reading onto the shelf. "I have devoured your entire library. Haven't you got anything post 1940 to read?"

"Hell, I don't know. I bought someone's library and put it there. I only read business books. Leon can probably help. He brought crates of the damn things. We had to get a carpenter in to build more shelves in his apartment. I don't know why he doesn't throw them out and download books."

"I'm an old-fashioned girl—I like paper books too. Let's go, Leon." Kathryn walked off ahead of him toward his apartment.

His face heated up. He did read electronic books now. The physical books he had brought with him were from the old days. He kept them for comfort, for the spines that greeted him each day with their familiar typefaces and brand colors, their reassuring solidity. As well as his self-help library, which filled two long rows of bookshelf, he had books on the body, on biochemistry and surgery and prosthetics, and other medical texts he only partly understood but that had obsessed him as he underwent the surgery to implant his metal heart. He was a natural researcher, a habit that started when he was a child, hunting down every reference to the superheroes he longed to be. He had found solace in the joys of solitary study, in understanding the genesis, the history, the nature of a thing.

The top shelves were stacked with war stories and biographies of triumph over adversity. As a boy he used to lie on the bed with his *Guinness Book of World Records* or a history of the Peloponnesian wars pressed open beside him and his mind saturated with images of his heroic possibilities: Leon on horseback galloping through the low scrubby mountains toward Attica to deliver vital communications that would prove the turning point in the course of the war; Leon in a business suit dropping his ultimatum on the table in the boardroom, six gray-haired captains of industry begging him to save their reputations; Leon in the lab adjusting the fine controls of the electron microscope before calling over his busty and adoring lab assistant to point out to her with quiet pride that, yes, here it was before their very eyes, the cure for cancer.

This was going to be Kathryn's first real moment of getting to know him. He was convinced she would take one look at his library and crack up laughing.

"It's all very tidy," Kathryn said as she walked past Leon into his apartment.

He waited behind her, his reddened cheeks reflected in the hall mirror beside him.

"These books aren't what I read now," he said.

"Sure," Kathryn said. She moved to the wall of bookshelves and began to scan each row.

Outside the windows of Leon's apartment a man in overalls walked by with a chimp riding his shoulder. A blue jay fossicked in the leftover snow on the side of the garden bed while the sun spilled a trapezoid of light through the glass and onto the wooden floor. Leon skirted past Kathryn to the bench that divided the kitchen from the living area.

"Would you, um, like a cup of tea? I'm having one."

"No, thanks." She bent to look more closely at the bottom rows. "*Seven Steps to Self-Confidence?*" she read.

Leon switched on the electric kettle. The grumble of the heating element thrummed through the countertop.

"*You Can Be a Better Lover, Emotional Intelligence, Mood Therapy for the Introvert, The Power of You, Who Moved My Cheese?* So, Leon, have you found the power of you yet? And more important, are you a better lover?"

He felt a sudden urge to bare his feet in the trapezoid of light. The sun through glass licking his toes, heat rising through his body until he melted into an innocuous pool of butter.

"Oh jaysus, this is a good one." Kathryn stooped sideways to read the title. "*The Wounded Heart.* Could be written for you, Leon." She tipped the book out of the shelf.

The kettle was billowing steam beside Leon. It was supposed to turn off automatically but it seemed to have been boiling forever, clouding the air and dampening his face. He knocked the switch to off. The man in overalls walked past the window again, going the opposite way, this time without the monkey.

When Leon returned from the fridge with the milk, Kathryn was standing on the other side of the bench. *The Wounded Heart* lay between them.

"Oh Christ, Leon, forgive me. I shouldn't have made fun."

He had forgotten what many of the books were about. He picked up the book and read the subtitle: *Hope for Adult Victims of Childhood Sexual Abuse.*

He caught Kathryn's eye and held it. He should have been able to fake a sorrowful expression to hide his amusement, considering his long, mournful face, but his lips disobeyed and twitched into a curve.

"It came in a job lot from a church sale," he confessed. "I haven't even read it."

"You mean . . . you weren't?"

He shook his head, unable to conceal his smile.

"I ought to punch you, fella, making me feel like a mean witch."

"I just can't resist a book bargain."

Kathryn snorted. She slipped *The Wounded Heart* back into the bookcase and hoisted a tower of borrowed biographies into her arms.

"Buy a few novels, will you?" she said over her shoulder as she swung out through the apartment doorway. "They're better than that self-help shite."

9

THEY HAD BEEN working as a group for many weeks, learn-ing to tease without offense, complaining, arguing, joking, slumping into their beds after a day's training, getting up the next day to start again. Yet Leon was still intrigued by Rhona. She was as fleeting as the light off a spangle, all glint and glitter, then gone. One night, Leon found her dozing on the couch in the common room. He sat down quietly in the puffy maroon leather chair beside the fireplace, trying not to disturb her, and opened his book.

Even though he was itching to ask a question, Leon tried to read while she slept on the couch opposite him. Finally after fifteen minutes, when Rhona's crinkly eyes finally fluttered open, the question burst out of him.

"Why do you have the circus logo, Rhona? It makes me feel a real freak. Like I'm in a sideshow."

Rhona yawned, covering her mouth with her hand, and let her tired gaze drift over to him. "But you are a freak, honey."

"I mean, I'm not one of those freaks from the old circuses,

the pinheads and the dog men. I'm the opposite. I'm a medical miracle. Kathryn is too. She's cured."

Rhona laughed and rested her head on the arm of the sofa. She spoke with her eyes closed. "Leon, sweetheart, no offense, but there are more medical miracles than straight-up humans these days. And freaks too, like my daddy used to have in his sideshows. You go to some of those third-world countries where there's one doctor for every ten thousand people and you'll find unbelievable human specimens. Freaks are everywhere. That's not what I was looking for. The first time I saw Kathryn I found what I needed to make the most amazing show of the new millennium. She was a mess, but I thought I could save her. And then I would put together a show to give her back some dignity. For that kind of a show I needed people whose difference or mutation or disability, or whatever it was, made them more than human. And they had to be young and they had to be reasonably good-looking, otherwise it would be an ordinary old freak show and I'd have the PC police down on me in a second. I needed performers. I needed to make it a spectacle of wonder and prestige, not a damn sideshow."

Rhona jimmied herself up from the couch, where her short legs hadn't even reached the third cushion. She inched around until she faced Leon, eyes still bleary, her russet hair floppy as a rooster's comb.

"A few years ago, another troupe started up in London. You probably don't remember them, darling, they were only in the news for a week or so. They had some interesting specimens— a three-armed man, a pair of conjoined twins with full upper bodies each but joined below the waist, a torso woman. The show never went anywhere. It was far too much like an old-time freak show. They had no idea how to exploit what they had. And they had no idea how to read the world we're living in.

You have to give the people both what they want and what they can take, Leon. It's always changing and you need to have the intuition to read the times. I learned that from my daddy, the Penny King."

Leon frowned, disturbed that she had used the word "specimen." "Some interesting specimens," as if he and the others were not even human. Rhona hadn't noticed his unease. She was smiling to herself, eyes half-closed. She let herself relax into the couch cushions as she spoke.

"He really was a king, Leon. A king of men. I'd sidle along behind him in his spurred boots when I was a kid. Behind those boots scuffing the dirt or spraying mud or aiming a swift kick at whatever useless animal got in his way. That's why I was always behind, where a kick never landed, where his eyes never strayed. Always behind, watching and learning. From the age I could stand up and walk I wanted to be just like him, the Penny Queen."

Leon had never been to a real circus. When he was growing up, the traditional three-ring with lions and feather-crested ponies had fallen out of fashion, and his family couldn't afford hundreds of dollars for tickets to the new kind of circus, the glamorous spectacular with opera singers swinging through elaborate artist-designed stage sets.

"I was born in my mother's camper. She wasn't the kind to mollycoddle, so by the time I could walk I was exploring every part of my little world. I learned plenty as I trotted behind my father on his trips around the vans and the cages, the rings covered in sawdust, the vats of feed for the livestock, the tents and the booths. It was a different world, Leon. A world in itself. I saw the way he held the hands of distressed women, the money he slipped to men who were having a hard time. The whip he used on lazy workers. The cash that passed from his hand to the city council that granted him space to set up. The bone china he drank his breakfast tea from, the bespoke jackets with linings of silk, the hand-carved walking stick he used to beat my mother. He was strong and cruel and handsome, and I adored him."

"What about school?" The thing Leon had longed for most when he was a child was to escape the pitted brick walls and leering bullies of school.

Rhona coughed a little, sat up again and adjusted her skirt as if the memories were making her clothes feel tight and twisted. "They called me 'circus girl' when I was sent to boarding school after my father had lost everything and the show had closed down. We girls all lay in our beds in a row, soft farts and snuffles and whispering carrying through the night, the sounds of animals in the darkness. I felt oddly at home there, enclosed with all those bodies the way I had always been. The night cries and the whimpering were as familiar and comforting as the narrow bunk in our old traveling van and the roaring of lions in their cages. The regimen of the school, the closed circle of our days cranking around and around like an old merry-go-round, gave me the feeling I had never left home. And when the other girls, skinny muscular farm girls who loved to run and throw balls and the spoiled haughty daughters of diplomats, began to torment me, to call me names and leave pins in my bed and tear up homework and spit into my meals and do everything they could to make my life miserable, then I was sure I had found a home not so different from my old one at the circus."

"But what you do now isn't so different. If it was so hard, why make a career of it?"

"I don't deny it's a punishing life, the traveling circus. At six years old I was working the ring. Each night I did a five-minute cameo as a clown. Tiny and decked out in big shoes and a pink frizzy wig, I stepped into the ring and the whole crowd went *awww*. All I had to do was run around being chased by two clowns in a bull suit, with the audience screaming for my safety. A trapeze artist swung down from the sky and scooped me up to the cheers and shrieks of the children. That was my act. And that's the pull. That was where I learned what it is to be loved by the crowd. You'll soon understand it too, Leon. There's nothing like it. It's what sends the famous mad. The huge chasm between being the object of pure hysterical adulation and spending the rest of the time the same way as every other mortal, squeezing your pimples and being disappointed by the people you love.

"I knew when I set up the Wonders that it shouldn't be a circus, but I wanted to bring elements of a circus to it, the things missing from the entertainment of today—so flat and easy and fake. That's why the logo, Leon. I wanted to bring radiance, humor, aching tiredness and satisfaction and pain and mystery and the knowledge that the performers would have to do it all again tomorrow. Hard physical work makes humans sing. My father taught me that as well.

"When you sit on the wooden strutted seats in the audience at the circus looking up, mouth open like a flycatcher, what you see in the air above you, flying in bird formation, are tiny delicate trapeze artists in sparkling costumes. The girls standing on ponies that canter around the ring seem to be made of glitter and air. That is part of the magic. Get up close—these people are muscular and thickset and have bunions and bad teeth. They're sinewy but can bend themselves over backward without a thought. They've got unbreakable will. That's what you need to make it in the business.

"And that's the other thing, Leon. If you think about the ones I chose—you, Kathryn, Christos—what linked you wasn't only the bizarre transformation of your bodies. It was the immense pain, the long tedious recovery, the endurance and determination that kept you all alive. You may look fragile. I was never fooled. You three have gone through so much already—you are the toughest people I know."

She stretched over to the side table and picked up her phone.

"For a while I actually considered calling our show the Enchanted Circus, in memory of where I came from. Even now I can't see sawdust on a floor without my heart contracting. I'm an old woman, Leon, but I still miss the dirt and the aching muscles and the cowboys and trapeze wires and corny music and the sticky sweet smells. And my father. That cruel old bastard, I miss him still."

She switched on the phone and began downloading information. The conversation was over. It was the longest speech Leon had ever heard her give. It occurred to him that Rhona probably felt like a freak sometimes. She'd grown up in a world so alien to his that she might have come from another planet. Perhaps every human being was a freak. Hadn't he read that every person has at least a handful of damaged genes? That all humans embody a myriad of nature's mistakes?

10

LAUNCH DAY WAS approaching, and Kyle and Rhona had drawn up a list of questions that were not to be asked by journalists or interviewers.

"Members of the media will always try to slither around and pose a question you don't want to answer," Rhona told the three weary Wonders, who sat lined up opposite her like puppies at obedience school. One distraction and she could lose them. "I've seen it all in my time as a producer. You need a few techniques to divert the conversation. The reporters will be given these lists well before they meet you so they can prepare other questions. If they go off script, smile. Shake your head. Talk about how much you love the city you're in and how welcome they've made you feel. Or answer the question you wanted them to ask.

"So, the forbidden topics. Christos, as we discussed, we will not mention your age. You're still a young man, but you've got ten years on these two. You know, we all know, youth is what the public and the media love, so we'll simply avoid the subject.

You can get away with a few years anyhow with that olive skin. I also won't let the interviewers bring up anything to do with religion. I know the name Seraphiel will flush out a few religious nuts and the press will try to make something of it, but it's a good name, a powerful stage name, and we'll avoid all mention of religion to damp down any of that kind of thinking. Is that okay with you?"

"Yes, I understand. So can I go now? I need to rest."

"No, you can't go yet. You all need to know all the points because if the reporters can't get an answer from you, they'll try the others. So when I say don't talk about religion, I mean nobody talks about religion. You need to know every single point on the list, and never, ever answer a question that starts with 'I heard that . . .' or 'Rumor has it that . . .' They're fishing.

"Leon, obviously the number-one question they'll not be allowed to ask is anything about the mechanical heart surgery. Procedure, location, personnel, don't tell them anything. We'll do the reveal at a time and place to be decided by me and Kyle for maximum effect. You'd better not have told anyone yet, Leon, because that is the last bit of information we need. It's our final meal ticket.

"The second verboten topic is how you maintain your heart. We don't want you talking about medications or exercises or medical appointments. It makes you sound feeble. You're not an invalid, you're a Wonder. And the third one. No talk about your love life. You're not trained up enough yet to answer that one smoothly. You'll blush, you'll stutter, you'll end up with every single woman in the known world knocking at our door to propose marriage to you. Give it another couple of months, once you're better with the media, then we can drop this one off the list."

Leon shrugged, trying to seem insouciant. Strange women

proposing marriage to him? He'd only ever had two girlfriends and they didn't last. He felt the rise of blood to his cheeks as he remembered the second girl lying stiffly on the bed while he pushed into her, and the way she would roll off the bed and hurry to the bathroom, shielded in a sheet or a piece of clothing, as soon as he had finished. "Is there anything you'd like me to do for you?" he'd asked several times. She smiled and told him it had been lovely. After two months she'd said she didn't want to see him anymore because she was too busy at work.

"Look," Rhona said to Christos and Kathryn. "He's blushing already and no one's even asked him a question."

If only there was some treatment to stop a man blushing. It was as if shame was an essence carried in the blood.

"Kathryn has asked that we do not discuss her family or her ex-husband. I think we can all respect that. Family includes the possibility of children. We're not having some women's mag hack roll out the usual questions about kiddies and a family. Secondly, no talk about sheep."

Kathryn broke in. "Exactly. So, I'm woolly. I'm not a damn sheep. I never want to hear the word 'sheep' spoken about me again. Lady Lamb is a pretty name. Lady Sheep sounds like a car-seat cover."

"And these two probably don't realize, Kathryn, because they don't see the mail you're already getting, but there's to be no talk about animal protection societies, animal cruelty, animal liberation, other animal-related causes or organizations. They think that because Kathryn's got wool, she should be patron of the Save the Polar Bear Society of South Wisconsin. We have to keep the public on the other side of the privacy fence. And the media too. Big walls, that's what we want. Walls of silence and privacy, the public seeing only what we give them. Crazies keep out."

Leon looked up at the giant louvers outside the windows, which were folding with the grand and slow momentum of the sun. Outside, in the rambling estate with its green canopies and wandering animals, its replanted indigenous understory and its old enclosures now becoming overgrown, the birds and the ground dwellers were settling to roost and sleep as they did every night when the light dimmed to a dusky blue and the earth began to cool. They followed ancient trails and lived in ancient unchanging ways. Whereas inside the house, despite its calm aesthetic and rich furnishings, there was no old way. Everything was new and untried, even the bodies they inhabited. Leon's sporadic lurches of misgiving, like he was experiencing right now, may have been a reaction to the new place, the new life, the new sphere, let alone his new body. Or perhaps he was unnerved by the way Rhona and Kyle talked about the audience and the media as if this was war and they were enemies to be outmaneuvered, barricaded out or ambushed.

"So we are finished?" Christos curled forward in his chair and groaned. "My back is torturing me tonight."

"Ah," Rhona said, tapping her screen. "Nearly forgot the last one. Christos being gay. We don't talk about it."

"Because?" Kathryn asked. "Aren't you out and proud, Christos?"

"Because most of his fan base will be women, and we don't want to disappoint them."

Christos levered himself off the chair and pressed the heels of his hands into his lower back. "My sexuality is irrelevant to my art. There is no need to bring it up. Now I must go and lie down."

"Not irrelevant to the disappointed women," Kathryn remarked before she too collected her things and left the room.

Leon paused in front of Rhona on his way out. "Rhona, I've

been thinking. I'm not sure how good I'll be at this. I'm not like the other two. They're so confident—"

Rhona rapped her rings on the wooden arm of the chair. "Get with it, Leon. This is a job, and you're going to be paid a fortune to do it. If you're not worth the money, I'll have no hesitation in dropping you. There are other wonders out there, believe me."

When Leon was a boy, the human wonders of the world belonged in the category of men who performed amazing feats of strength, who ate metal and glass, who escaped from boxes chained underwater. Leon didn't do anything—he had been forged as a wonder by someone with far greater powers.

"Do you understand me, Leon?" Rhona pulled his attention back. She faced him, hands on hips. "You're a physical wonder all right, but I'll say it again. This is a job, pure and simple. You perform the job badly, you get fired and I hire another wondrous damn wonder."

"Yes, I get it."

"Well, you'd better. I think you're really sweet, Leon. You're a doll. But at the end of the day, this is a business."

An accident of fate had turned him into a wonder of the world while the person ahead of him on the waiting list for a heart transplant had probably died. The one risky decision he had made in his life had blown open the door to a new dimension. Again, he experienced that lurch in a part of his body that no longer existed.

11

LEON'S MOTHER AND sister and nephew and niece were packed and ready to leave. Already the day seemed brighter, the air clearer. He'd brought them over for a week because everyone at Overington expected him to, and realized his mistake the day they arrived. He didn't want them there. They would only have considered coming because they also thought it was expected. Curiosity had probably helped them decide.

The media trainer had suggested Leon's mother and sister act as audience for his press-conference training. How foolish and pretentious he'd felt, striding across the sprung floor of the rehearsal room, lifting his chin to speak, the trainer adjusting the angle of his limbs as if he were a mannequin. After three months of work, he still stuttered over occasional words when he caught sight of the red eye of the camera, still surreptitiously checked his reflection in the studio mirrors to see if he was standing or sitting straight enough.

During their stay the two women spoke in awkwardly formal voices with everyone. They tried to help the staff because they were unused to being cooked for and having a house-keeper make their beds. While Leon's nephew spent all day outdoors following the gamekeeper around, his niece had stared openmouthed at Kathryn for the entire first day, then started asking her question after question, then turned her attention to Christos and Yuri, then to Rhona. On the last day of the visit, as they exchanged their relieved good-byes, the girl threw her arms around Kathryn's waist, pushing her face between the folds of Kathryn's cloak and into the warm woolly belly. Kathryn went still. She had made it clear that she was not to be touched, ever, not to be hugged or to have a hand held or even to be tapped on the shoulder.

"Oh dear," Rhona said softly. "Oh, sweetheart, you shouldn't..."

They watched, amazed, as Kathryn bent her head and drew the girl in tight, kissing her swiftly on her crown before pushing her away and offering a polite spoken good-bye to Leon's mother and sister. She was shaking. The moment Leon's family turned to gather the suitcases, she melted from the room.

While the Wonders trained, Kyle had been doing ground-work for the launch. A filmed four-second clip of Christos opening his wings in a darkened room was set free on the net. For a couple of weeks Kathryn flew around the world in a chartered jet. She turned up at a club in Tokyo, a film premiere in Paris, a restaurant in Shanghai, the after-party of a location wrap in Berlin, the opera in New York. She was fully swathed, the image of a wealthy fashionable woman. At each venue, her instructions from Kyle were to go to the ladies' room and, while she was there, stand in front of the mirror. She was to shrug off her head and shoulder covering and give herself a quick finger massage of the neck or adjust her makeup. If anyone stared or spoke, she would yawn and make an innocuous remark, such as: "It's ex-hausting, isn't it?" or "These events really wear me out." Then she was to smile, pull her scarf up over her head and shoulders, and leave the venue. Kyle would escort her to a waiting car to hurry her away. He would have given her the go-ahead to perform as soon as the bathroom was populated with three or four of the important people he had targeted who had enough influence and talking power to become vectors.

For Leon, he commissioned a comic animated game called Clockwork Man in which the player had thirty different ways to assemble a mechanical heart and get it into the character before any number of silly disasters happened. It was addictive, and within a week it was the top-selling app on handheld devices.

Once that was all in place, and the buzz was happening, the Wonders were to appear together on the world's most famous TV talk show and launch with a bang.

Finally the day came. Training had begun in March and now, in July, they would be tested. They'd driven out of Overington, with the sun flaring over its flower-dotted gardens, down to a fetid New York and into a cool dry TV studio.

The cameraman came toward Leon, lens aimed at his breast as if he was about to pin a victor's ribbon on the chest of a race winner. *I am a winner!* Leon kept smiling as he tried to follow the mantras of the media trainer. *Think positive! A winning smile! Everyone loves you!* His self-help books had said the same things with the same exclamation marks. *Fake it till you make it! I say YES to life!*

When the close-up of the hole in his chest flashed up on the large screen behind the host, the studio audience screamed as one. Even Leon, catching a glimpse from the corner of his eye, was aghast at the woody topography of his scarred flesh with its new "healthy" tan magnified five hundred times. It could have been a gnarly medieval forest or the carved relief of an Egyptian battle. Only when the shot pulled away to reveal firstly his heart, tiny, snug and gleaming in its place, then his human torso, and lastly his strained face, did any of it seem real.

His heart, steady as it was, no longer told him he was afraid. It kept pushing through blood at the same regular pace without regard to his emotional state. Other parts of his body made up for the heart's equanimity. The adrenaline zinging through his bloodstream stung his fingertips and face in prickles of fear. He was dizzy and disoriented. His eyes watered, and his eyelids fluttered under the glare of white light.

"Settle down, ladies and gentlemen." Matt Karvos, the show's host, gestured for Leon to join Kathryn and Christos, who had already endured their own scream reaction, on a couch facing the audience.

As rehearsed earlier, Leon pulled on a loose shirt that a hand passed to him from behind the curtain. At last he could sit down. He stumbled across the studio floor snaked with gaffer-taped cables and leads, and sat down beside Christos and Kathryn on the couch. At the far end Kathryn lounged on the fat cushions with her legs crossed and her cape wrapped loosely around her body. She appeared relaxed, nonchalant, but Leon could feel the vibrations of the couch caused by her left foot, under the cape, jigging madly against the floor.

Medical examinations had been documented to validate the Wonders' authenticity before they were invited on the show, so the producers were happy. Rhona was happy because she had managed to keep tight control over the whole appearance. Hap was handling security. Kyle had negotiated the deal and coached them and checked and confirmed every detail until he was convinced nothing could go wrong. Kathryn and Leon were still wary. It was Leon's first time on television. Kathryn had appeared on television before, but only in guerrilla footage shot as she tried to run away or push shut the front door while a burly cameraman thrust a lens at her and a reporter tried to muscle his way inside. Christos was the only one with real camera experience. He had appeared on various shows in the past talking about his art. He had warned the others to be aware that the camera might shift focus to any one of them at any time.

"You think you are finished because someone else is talking and you let your face relax? Pow, they turn the lens on you and you come across to millions of people as a miserable party pooper."

"Thanks for the advice, Christos. I feel so much better now. Absolutely spiffing."

"No, Kathryn, I am not joking. It happened to me on the most important art show in New York. I watched the recording and there I am, thinking my part is over, rolling my eyes at something stupid I had said. But no one realized that. They believed I was rolling my eyes at what someone else had said. They never asked me back."

The regular guests of this program, a comedian and a "crazy news" reporter who entertained with offbeat anecdotes from the news or interjected sexual innuendo into others' stories, were relegated to a couch at the far side of the stage for this special Wonders edition of the show. Leon had met them in the greenroom, where they smiled like hyenas. "Do you do anything?" the comedian asked through his handlebar mustache. "Or are you just for looking at?"

Once the three were seated, Rhona appeared at the curtain where Leon had stood seconds before, on the mark where guests posed momentarily in the spotlight before bounding down the stairs to greet the host. Rhona may have been short and old and not particularly beautiful, but she soaked up that spotlight and reflected it ten times brighter. Even Leon and Kathryn and Christos began to clap as she raised one arm in a gesture of acknowledgment. She was back where she belonged—at the center of a three-ring circus.

"Rhona Burke, the Penny Queen," Matt Karvos announced, and the band struck up "Entry of the Gladiators," the circus clown music.

Rhona stepped carefully down the stairs on her high-heeled cowgirl boots and walked to the host. He kissed her on both cheeks, knocking against the felt brim of her hat. As the music came to an end, he held out his hand to escort her to her seat between the Wonders on the couch and him at the desk.

"Here." She pulled off the ten-gallon hat and gave it to him. "You can have this. It's a genuine Penny King hat from the Enchanted Circus of 1955. Only six left in the world."

"Miss Burke, I'm honored."

With lights flashing *Applause* and a man running up and down the studio floor in front of the audience waving his arms to make them shout louder, the cheering escalated to screams again. Kathryn gave Leon a look that said, "Get me out of here." Christos yawned a tight cat yawn of anxiety, which he hid with a hand gesture of smoothing his hair into place. Beyond the cameras on the stage floor Kyle was dictating notes, his head bobbing as he muttered into his recorder. When he caught Leon looking his way, he gave an awkward thumbs-up, like a parent on the sideline of his son's losing soccer team.

"Now tell us all about the Wonders, Miss Burke. Where did they come from? Are we looking at the future of the human race?"

It would seem logical that the host would be interviewing Leon or Kathryn or Christos. After all, they were the "talent," as they had been called backstage. A young runner with a clipboard had leaned in through the doorway of the greenroom. "Are you the talent?" he'd said hurriedly before pushing farther into the room and catching sight of Kathryn. "Oh yeah. You're the talent." He pulled his blunt head with its headphone and mic out of the doorway and raced off down the corridor, rubber shoes squeaking on the linoleum floor, his muttering voice a fading sound track.

"By 'the talent,' he means the guests," Kyle said, and patted Kathryn's shoulder.

"I said before I didn't like to be touched."

Kyle shrugged and raised his hands in surrender. "Sorry."

"No offense, Kyle. I didn't mean to be rude. But I don't like it."

"Got it." Kyle had crossed the room, lifted his recorder and spoken quietly into it as though he was noting this important instruction.

At that moment clipboard boy had come to collect the performers and guide them to the live-broadcast studio. Kyle followed slowly, watching Kathryn from behind as she strode along the carpeted corridor, her cloak wrapped tight around her.

Onstage Rhona was telling the anecdotes the group had agreed could be released at this point. She had decided Leon and Kathryn would be too nervous at the first gig and that she would set the scene at the launch herself. She was enjoying herself, chatting with the host, swapping repartee with the cohosts, who were trying to attract attention from their couch at the far end of the studio. She even posed a question to the studio audience.

"Aren't you glad I found these amazing people?" She nodded as she spoke.

The audience cheered a yes. Leon's innards were performing slow acrobatics somewhere around the region of his lower intestine. Christos was steady but tense, a professional, alert and focused. Kathryn sat immobile save for her hidden foot piledriving into the floor, a rigid smile on her face.

Last night from inside his hotel room, he had heard Kathryn and Rhona in the corridor. Kathryn told Rhona she was afraid.

"They'll tear me apart again," she whispered. "They'll make me out to be a monster."

"No, darling, that's exactly what they won't do. I've made sure of it. This is why we're here."

12

THREE WEEKS AFTER their first TV appearance, Kathryn described to Leon how she'd woken that morning from a nightmare. She had dreamed herself a victim of fly-strike, an infestation of maggots in live sheep flesh. Her voice rat-a-tatted out the words as if to shoot down the whole ghastly picture.

Although fly-strike was not a possibility in Kathryn's world, Leon knew from experience that fear is more often about the unlikely than the likely. If only he could reassure her in some way—but how can you reassure someone that their fears are foolish when they already know it?

"It's crazy, I know," she said, draining her glass of straw-colored wine. "Stupid, monumentally dumb to even imagine it. But I'm still aching with terror at that moment in the dream when I caught sight in the mirror behind me of the writhing mass of maggots, devouring me alive."

His fears were more prosaic: catching a cold or flu and sneezing violently or eating something bad and suffering convulsive vomiting that might shake loose the tubes to his heart. Even low temperatures bringing on a chilled shiver were enough to make him hurry to the closet and strap himself into the restrictive brace designed to maintain the stability of the heart during exercise. For Kathryn, the climate was irrelevant. Her wool kept her at an even temperature no matter what the ambient weather. Kathryn saved her terror for the diseases and parasites that belonged to the family to which she had become an unwilling relation: maggots, sheep lice, bluetongue, foot and mouth, pinkeye.

Before she married she was a lazy housekeeper, she had told him. She described the bathroom of her singles flat crusted in a rind of steam-baked dust. Her living room carpet sucked at the soles of her shoes with the same gluey squelch as the carpet at the local band venue. She lifted her cleaning game a little after moving in with her husband. But by the time Leon met Kathryn, she had become a hygiene obsessive. When she disappeared into the bathroom with a kit bag of wipes and disinfectants, no one said a thing. If a buzzing blowfly entered a room she sat immobile until someone smacked it down. Leon found it discomfiting to see tough Kathryn blanching at the sight of a harmless insect. She, like he, clearly lived in fear of the day when her body would betray her yet again.

Kathryn's other trouble, earlier on, had been that sheep's wool should be kept in prime condition by the lanolin secreted from the skin. Her skin secreted plenty of lanolin, enough to give her the supple skin of a teenager, but for the first year after her change she was shaving and washing herself constantly. Day after day she continued her obsessive attention to her skin and the wool as if she could make it less conspicuous, less bizarre. She ended up wreathed in scabs and rashes. Her regrowth was brittle. Every time she was caught in the rain she came down with terrible chills because the wool had lost its waterproof quality, and she stayed damp for hours. She was spending every

— 66 —

second day in the waiting room of her dermatologist. The hospital where she had the treatment that went wrong had provided no aftercare—they spent their time trying to deny culpability and ensure she wouldn't sue. Which of course she did, or at least her husband did in her name, and he profited bountifully from Kathryn's affliction.

Leon had read the articles about her husband and his exploitation of Kathryn's illness. He had sold photos of her that should never have been taken, let alone published. Kathryn barely mentioned him. Only Rhona referred to him, although never in Kathryn's presence. He was trying to profit again by pressuring Rhona for a cut of Kathryn's income. "I'm dealing with it," Rhona had told Leon. "My lawyers are going to take that asshole down."

It was a farmer who cured Kathryn's skin problem. He'd seen a newspaper report. She had already been exposed in the media when Rhona took over her management, but her fame was an ugly thing, a brutish perverted kind of fame where she was degraded and derided and she reacted with swearing and crying and shrieking when they chased her down the street, and so they slavered over her even more.

The farmer sent her a letter written in fine cursive handwriting. She showed Leon the letter, which she had kept with her ever since because, she said, it was the most respectful and kind letter she had ever received. It made her believe once again that goodness was possible in the world. The letter apologized for disturbing her and commiserated with her for the treatment she had experienced at the hands of the media.

I am ashamed to say that I saw you on television, the letter said, *because that is admitting that I continued to watch and did not turn it off as I should have.* It went on to explain that the letter writer was brought up on a sheep farm and had taken it over when he came of age, and he knew very well that when a sheep's lanolin is stripped from the wool by pest treatments or excessive washing, which can also happen when well-meaning people hand-raise a lamb, the sheep's skin will suffer terribly until the lanolin is replaced. *So I wanted to make a suggestion, if nothing else works, that you might want to give your own skin a chance to replace the lanolin, which I understand it does of its own account, and I may be wrong but I think that in a few weeks you will be feeling much better.* The letter signed off with a wish for her good health and a resumption of her privacy.

She was in good health now, but the three Wonders each relied on large daily doses of medication and regular medical attention. Rhona had originally planned to use a local private clinic as their main treatment center. She had drawn up a confidentiality agreement and arranged to book out the entire clinic one day a month. It wasn't enough. After three emergency visits to the clinic for Christos, whose emergencies had turned out to be little more than mild aches, and which necessitated the clinic shutting down normal operations and rescheduling other patients to ensure the Wonders' privacy, she threw up her hands and hired a full-time doctor. Dr. Minh Trang would live with them, eat with them, travel with them, and work to keep them in good health. A fully equipped doctor's office was established behind the kitchen, where the cool room used to be, and she was given the guest cottage in the garden, beside the elephant house, as her living quarters.

"And it's extremely odd," Rhona said as they watched the moving-van men unload the new doctor's boxes, "because when I introduced her to the elephants—and, yes, I had warned her about the animals before she signed up—Maisie did a back-leg stand and offered the doctor a plantain from the feed bin. Maisie's usually quite standoffish with strangers."

Kathryn was happy. "A woman doctor of our own! Splen-diferous. Thank goodness I won't have to rely on farmers and veterinarians for medical advice."

If Christos had made that joke, Kathryn would have retali-ated in kind. That she cracked the joke herself showed how far they had come since their early cautious courtesies while learn-ing to live together. They may have had separate apartments, but Leon, Rhona, Kathryn, Christos and Yuri saw each other every day. For a loner like Leon, it had been a trial. He knew he was changing when he found himself missing Christos or Kathryn if they were away for a few nights. He was discovering a different kind of loneliness, one that involved other people and what happened when they went away.

The day after she moved in, Dr. Trang called Leon to her office for his first examination.

"Welcome to Overington, Dr. Trang," Leon said from the doorway. He sniffed the air. A blaze of grief ignited in him for the surgeon and engineer who had saved his life, had transformed his body while he was dying, and had built and implanted the mechanism that brought him back. Even though he was certain he would never see them again, he always scoured the Australian news for any mention of a heart like his own, or a pioneering surgical technique, just in case. The hidden basement where he had spent a year in their care had smelled this way—sharp with antibacterials and the scorched dust of heating elements.

"Please call me Minh. It's a privilege to be here." Minh stretched out her hand, welcoming Leon into the room.

"Oh, we're just normal people except for our little oddities," he replied.

"I'm sure you are. The privilege is because of the enormous amount of money I'm being paid and the very little work I'll have to do."

Leon's cheeks and forehead simmered pink.

"Clothes off, please. You can leave your underpants on. I'll come in when you call." She was tall, long-haired, her face broad and open. Narrow from behind as she walked out of the room. Her band of black hair ended in a neat line at the shoulder blades.

He unbuttoned his shirt and slipped off his shoes. He'd been working out in the gym, but his chest and arms still showed signs of years without exercise. Hints of the spindly, slack, bony man he used to be.

The doctor paused at the doorway and inhaled a deep breath before she looked at his chest. When Leon first joined the Wonders, Kathryn was so spectacular he thought no one would be interested in looking at him. People's reactions proved he was a spectacle of an equal order. What he'd grown used to over the course of the surgeries and the year of recovery was so shocking to other people that they were usually left speechless. Even Rhona had been silent for seconds when she first stood before him and saw the tunnel through his breast. Not Minh though.

"How do I get to the heart?" She perched on a stool so that her head was at the same height as his heart. A couple of plucked eyebrow hairs were reemerging black and blunt above her eye, and the smoothness of her skin was a contrast to his own, lightly pocked from teen acne and further marred by open pores across the nose.

He showed her the hidden catch, and she swung open the titanium bars. There were only a few functioning nerve endings left in the scar tissue, but he could sense her fingers as they played across the surface of the cavity. She moved around behind him, and once again her fingers tickled his skin.

"A little dry here. I'll get some ointment."

Leon closed his eyes. She ran her finger around the inside of the cavity like a child skimming cream from a bowl. Her other hand rested on his arm, warm and firm. His breath slowed. He felt the tension from his thigh muscles draining through to the floor. The touch of her gentle fingers gave him the odd sensation that the knotty damage was being smoothed out, as if being touched in this most private place was bringing together his emotions and his physical being in a way he hadn't experienced since he had almost given up hope of life.

"I would so love to meet the surgeons who did this," she murmured, shining a light into the heart cavity and pausing to make notes on her recorder. "It's completely crazy. Why metal? Of all the materials they could choose from, they pick metal. Hard to manipulate, difficult to repair, inflexible, prone to fatigue. Madness." She stopped, took a pair of tweezers and tapped the surface of the heart once, very lightly. Leon quivered with fear, but she patted his arm. "Don't worry, that's all I'll do. Maybe it's not exactly metal. It doesn't sound quite right. Could it be that it's actually not a simple metal alloy but something else?"

He didn't answer. Leon had no idea what his heart was made of. While Susan and Howard were operating, manufacturing, measuring, doctoring, computing, he had tried to understand what they were doing to him by reading about pain receptors and blood cells and osmotic transfer. Learning a new language for his new body. Or when he couldn't face another chemical formula that seemed impenetrable, or another text on the cauterization of blood vessels that brought to mind the burning stench as Susan waved away the surgical smoke of his flesh, he played electronic games or pored over jigsaw puzzles or figured out cryptic crosswords. Sometimes he had returned to his favorite books: the war stories, the biographies. Anything to keep his mind off the pain, and the inexorable and visible perishing of his body.

What's more, although Minh was his new doctor, he didn't know enough about her to trust her. Already Overington had lost a housekeeper to the trash media. She'd sold her story of "working for the freaks." Leon could imagine the next article. *A doctor tells the gruesome medical stories of the Wonders.*

Minh and Leon stared at each other for a moment. Leon said nothing.

Minh broke first. "Okay, I understand. Rhona said you wouldn't answer questions about the mechanics of the heart. Doesn't make my job any easier though. It certainly would help if I could talk to your doctors."

All he knew of Susan and Howard was that Howard must surely have died soon after Leon left the basement. He had been in the last stages of cancer. When Susan had dropped Leon at the train station with his small bag of clothes and a bank account full of money, he experienced the panic of a child abandoned by his parents, left to fend for himself with no skills and no tools and no idea about how to live with his new heart. He had sent the weekly updates they'd requested on his health to the e-mail address Susan had given him in the six months that followed, until one day the e-mails began to bounce. He went to find her at the university only to discover she had resigned. There was no forwarding address. She had told no one where she was headed.

Since the TV debut of the Wonders, more universities and pharmaceutical companies had contacted Leon, offering inordinate amounts of money for the opportunity to examine him, to take scrapings of the titanium-bone cement, to do imaging of the inside of the heart and map its mechanisms as if he was a newly discovered island that explorers were desperate to claim as their own, driving a flag into the earth, a stake into the heart. Aside from Rhona's insistence that he keep the workings of the heart secret, Leon knew he shouldn't allow those people into his body. Their motives had nothing to do with his well-being.

Minh tapped around other sections of his chest. The sound reverberated through Leon's bones in minor quakes.

"I hope you don't mind me saying, but you have a face that looks like it belongs to another era," she said as she worked. "There are some famous and truly lovely illustrations in seventeenth-century books of anatomized bodies. Something about your face reminds me of them."

"Oh, great. I remind you of an anatomized body."

She laughed a strong rising laugh, melodious, a laugh that made Leon want to laugh with it. "I didn't mean that! Only the face, Leon, your lovely, long, melancholy face. Oh . . . sorry, I didn't mean so be so, um . . . Anyway, yes." She cleared her throat as she took his wrist in her hand and pulled a watch from her pocket.

As she moved her two fingers around the thin blue skin of his inner wrist, searching for the pulse, he waited for it to dawn on her.

"Oh." She sat down quickly on the stool behind her, as if she had no control of her legs.

"Please, doctor, don't make a zombie joke." The last physician who had discovered his lack of pulse had gone a little haywire.

"So it doesn't beat."

"If we turned off the machines in the room you would be able to hear a very faint whirring. Spooky, everyone says. It took me a long time to get used to not having a heartbeat."

After she had caught her breath, she drew blood into four small vials that she labeled for testing and placed in a rack on the bench. She took photos of the heart and the cavity from different angles. Next she rolled the sphygmomanometer stand to Leon's side. Leon watched her face as she wrapped the cuff around his arm and started the machine. The cuff swelled and squeaked against his skin. She released the valve and listened. A moment later she laughed and tore apart the Velcro panels to release his arm.

"I'm an idiot. Of course, your arterial pressure isn't like anyone else's. I have nothing to measure it against. That, together with no pulse. They certainly didn't teach us any of this in med school."

Susan had warned him about how he would have to learn to live with a new pitch of silence. "I can't imagine what it will be like," she'd said. "You will not hear the life beating inside you. I wonder how it will feel." She'd rested her hand on his head for a moment before turning her focus to her workbench, where she was screwing miniature titanium pins into fine silver branches.

"Are you making a sculpture?" Leon had asked, imagining a gleaming bonsai tree tucked in the corner of the room alongside the piles of technical drawings and metal parts tried and discarded by Howard over the past months.

"Yes, I guess I am," she had replied, looking down at the silver bone in her hand. "It's you."

After Minh ensured the titanium rib bone gate was fastened in place, Leon endured her measuring his reflexes, weighing him and pinch-testing his fat. While he filled out a questionnaire, she made more notes, and finally he went into the bathroom and came out with his urine sample in a jar.

"Nearly done," she said, taking the sample in her gloved hand and decanting it into two tubes.

"Why did you take this job? Won't it be boring, looking after only three people, no matter how medically odd we are?"

"I don't think you three will ever be boring. As you may have noticed, you have blown away my whole concept of 'alive.' A man with no pulse. Extraordinary." She snapped off the thin latex gloves and dropped them into a plastic bin under the examination table. "It's true though, I'm hoping the work here won't occupy me full-time, because I paint. I love to paint. My parents hated the idea that I might turn into an artist and so I went to medical school. Now half the doctors I trained with are in writing and painting and acting classes on the weekends. But don't worry, I am an excellent physician with some specialist training. You're in safe hands."

"I believe you." He did. Her calm confidence made him want to put his health, his body, his everything, completely and immediately into her care.

"I'll need to do some imaging of the inside of your heart, which will be tricky because it's probably metal. We'll have to either take you to a facility that has a special machine or get one transported here. It would be very expensive to do that though." Minh glanced around the room before fanning herself with the paper she had been using for notes. "I'm sorry, but what on earth is that smell?"

"It's elephant dung, near the window, probably. The keeper can move it for you," Leon said. "And I'm afraid I have to say no."

"No to what?"

"No imaging."

"But what if something goes wrong with your heart?"

"Are you an engineer?"

"No."

"Then you couldn't fix it anyway."

"But I could call people in. People who know."

"No."

This was Leon's third heart. When it failed, his time would be up. That's what he had decided. No more intervention. Next time death would have its way.

13

ONCE THE TV launch had catapulted the Wonders into strato-
spheric fame, Rhona began the program of intimate "meet
the public" dinners. It was time to start making real money.

The public wasn't public at all. No one in "the public"
could afford the fee required for a ten-guest dinner with the
Wonders. Leon couldn't believe anyone would pay that kind of
price but the requests piled up and had to be culled. In August
they met with ten gridiron players who were being rewarded for
a successful season. By the time the Wonders' show began, the
football players were so drunk they could barely speak. One of
them peed into the cleaner's closet, thinking it was the urinal.
Next was a fund-raising dinner put on by the Republican Party.
In England a few models and peers got together and flew the
Wonders over for a special showing in a castle in Kent. Two
months and several events later, they arrived at the actress Julia
Vickers's house in Los Angeles for a dinner engagement.

Walking through that house, it became clear what a million
dollars meant to movie people: nothing, a small tip, a mistake

when buying furniture, a diamond collar for the puppy. Leon was surrounded by so much crystal and polished silverware he joked to Rhona that he needed sunscreen. Three or four staff appeared every time someone lifted a hand and Rhona complained that she should have charged ten times the fee. Surely these ten wealthy guests, the paying guests, could never return to a normal life after experiencing this kind of opulence. Would he and Kathryn and Christos become the kind of people to pay a fortune to meet another celebrity even more famous than themselves?

Because that's how fast it had happened. Six months after Rhona had formed the Wonders and two months after their first public appearance, they were bright shiny celebrities, flickering presences in the lives of countless humans they would never meet. They were the topic of conversation across borders, across races, across classes, when they had done nothing but appear. Of course they were living in the era where if you appeared enough, if you paraded around in the right places like something worth seeing, you must inevitably become celebrated. Even if they had been fakes they would have been celebrities. And now they were hovering inches from the ground, already detached from the grubby earth trudged by ordinary people.

"I don't really know why I've come to this event." At Julia Vickers's dinner the woman sitting beside Leon, on the other side from Rhona, put on a mock-glum face. Her face displaced the air, opened the room with such perfect symmetry that even the glum expression could have sold magazines. Leon had been trying not to stare at her since they arrived, fully aware of the irony that *he* was there for the purpose of being scrutinized.

Behind the beautiful woman, the blinds on the window wall were pleated into an arrangement that kept drawing Leon's eye, something geometric that made them appear as if they had been hung sideways or that he was looking at them with his eyes crossed. All of the furniture in the house sloped and bent at angles that made him feel unbalanced, as precarious as an ornament teetering on the edge of a table.

The woman tilted her head. "I'm embarrassed. I mean, I think you're fascinating, and so are Seraphiel and Lady Lamb, but it's a bit pathetic, isn't it, that I'd pay to meet you?"

"Don't people pay to see you?" Leon was taking a guess, but it was likely in this company and with that face she made her money because people wanted to look at her.

"Yes, but I'm only a clothes hanger, a vehicle. For fashion, for a script, a product. For someone's idea of a joke. You are the thing itself. Clockwork Man."

"Or simply the vehicle for the heart."

Rhona nudged him to get his attention and asked loudly if he could see any butter on the table. There was no butter, which she knew full well, only shallow dishes of oil and balsamic vinegar and bowls of glistening rock salt in perfect shapely hills.

"I'm sure the waiter person will bring you some."

"It's the trendy thing I hate." Rhona was tearing her bread roll into pieces and mashing it into the oil dish. "What's wrong with a pat of butter, I say. One teeny scrape of butter, that's all I'm asking for."

"I haven't eaten butter since I was fourteen." The woman on his other side made her captivating glum face again. "I'm Maria, by the way."

"Do you have an allergy?" Leon asked.

Maria's velvety lips curved into a pouty smile. "Only to getting fat. I've been on a diet for sixteen years, since I started modeling. I'm past my use-by date, but no one's thrown me offstage yet."

He recognized her now, from advertising perhaps, or a film.

Her nickname was "Eleven," as in one better than a perfect ten, and she had established a hugely successful cosmetics business called Eleven.

"Lady Lamb is across the table so I can't tell her myself, but would you pass on a message for me?" Maria Eleven said. She was leaning so close that her silky words tickled his ear. Even her breath was perfect, warm and smelling faintly of rosemary.

She moved even closer. Was that her moist lip skimming the lobe of his ear? A quiver of desire passed through him. "Thank Lady Lamb for insisting there be no pets at the dinner. Ursula usually brings her nasty little yappy rat thing to parties and we all have to pretend we don't notice when it piddles in the middle of the room."

He would not mention that to Kathryn. She loved dogs and cats but some reacted to her by cringing or hissing or barking. The stipulation about no pets was written into a clause of the Wonders' contract, wedged somewhere in between the list of security requirements and the financial penalties for events that went over time. "Believe me," Rhona had said while Leon was flipping through the contract, "they won't want to go over time."

Once the hostess had introduced everyone and toasted the Wonders, the waiters brought out the entrées, slipping them in front of the guests silently and smoothly as a conjuring trick. The dish was announced as white truffle *soi tan*. Leon had no idea what *soi tan* was, but the chefs must have gone to exceptional lengths in order to feed all three of the Wonders with their difficult appetites as well as keeping the paying celebrity guests, who must have tried the most expensive foods in the world, satisfied that the food was exotic and rare enough to justify at least part of the dinner cost.

He needn't have worried. The models and actresses took

a couple of tiny scoops and pronounced the dish extraordinary and delicious before nodding at the waiters to take the rest away. The male guests devoured the whole serving in two or three spoonfuls, since it had been delivered in a dish the size of an egg cup. Leon ate his slowly. Inside was custard, warm and salty and rich, with a tiny flake of white fish resting on the bottom of the cup.

When he had finished his dish and pushed it aside, Kathryn caught his eye. "Hungry," she mouthed, and grimaced. In the world of high couture, high celebrity and high prices, the fashion of huge plates with tiny servings of food had never gone away. The wealthier that people became in this country, the smaller the servings of food on their dinner plates. The Wonders soon learned to have a snack before their events. Food was important to each of them, especially Christos, who used power grids of energy in the operation of his wings. The lean servings of the stars left the Wonders ravenous and cross, reminding Leon of the snappy tempers of hungry children at school in the late afternoon.

By eight thirty the dessert had been cleared away and it was time to prepare for the show. Rhona called it the "déshabillé." "Déshabillé" sounded to Leon like lounging around in your underwear.

As coffee, cheese and fruit were served to the guests, Rhona led the three performers out to the room that had been set aside as the dressing room. In every venue this was a different type of room rigged up for the night. It could be a maid's room or a storage cupboard or an anteroom off the lounge. Tonight they ended up in the swimming pool annex. The weather, as usual for Los Angeles, was warm and the annex roof had been opened so that the smoggy yellow stars could blink weakly down on them.

"Chlorine, ugh." Kathryn waved her hand in front of her face.

"Hurry up, then. The sooner we get ready the sooner we're out of here." Rhona ushered Kathryn to a bench where her makeup kit and a mirror were laid out.

Yuri wrestled with Christos's left wing in the corner of the room while Leon stripped off his cravat and shirt and undershirt.

Rhona offered to help Yuri with the wings. Christos refused. "He has to learn to do it alone."

"What about you, Leon? Can I do anything?"

He told her to help Kathryn, who had slipped off her cloak, and was twisting herself around trying to pick something off the seat of her sari and muttering about how the filthy rich were so filthy they couldn't keep their chairs clean. There was little for Leon to do in preparation for the show except pump his arms a few times to try to make the muscles stand out, and oil up.

In the early rehearsals, where they had performed for a few of Rhona's friends, he had paraded his clammy white chest around the room, flailing his skinny arms in an ungainly attempt at graceful movement. He could sense in the room a hum, if not of disgust, of distaste. He was a weakling, a puny survivor of an outrageous medical procedure that should have killed him, and that's how he looked. Rhona brought in fitness equipment, a personal trainer and a dance teacher, and she sent him off to get spray-tanned.

The transformation took months of daily workouts, but once he had built himself up he finally saw in the mirror a fit and erect man rather than a weak, flabby patient debilitated by major surgery. Instead of the quickly smothered gasp of dismay he used to hear when he walked into the room with his torso bare and his heart winking inside its cavern, now he heard the admiring grunts of an enraptured crowd. Rhona was right again.

The observers had become an audience—the specimen had become the performer. Leon wished his father could see this new Leon, who may not have become the sporty robust man his father hoped for but had built, at least, the muscles that would move that man.

Back in the room set aside for the performance, the tech dimmed the room lights and started Leon's signature music, "Dido's Lament." The first bars played in the darkness, the singing voice calling round and prayerful.

> *Thy hand, Belinda, darkness shades me,*
> *On thy bosom let me rest,*
> *More I would, but Death invades me;*
> *Death is now a welcome guest.*

At the moment the recitative ended, the tech snapped on a spotlight aimed at the door where Leon would enter. The voice swelled. As the singer launched into the lament, he pushed through the doorway. The only object clearly visible in the room was the gleaming polished brass of his heart seeming to float in the air inside its titanium cage.

> *When I am laid, am laid in earth, may my wrongs create*
> *No trouble, no trouble in thy breast;*
> *Remember me, remember me, but ah! forget my fate.*
> *Remember me, but ah! forget my fate.*

Tremulous sighs and groans from the crowd formed a sibilant bass accompaniment to the aria. Every time he heard this music of humanity, even though it may have happened three nights in a row, goose bumps erupted on his skin, and his own breath stuttered in his chest. Under the music was a deep man's voice that Rhona had recorded while they were setting up the show. It was almost inaudible, perhaps subliminal, but he could hear it because he knew it was there.

The spotlight shone into his heart. He raised his arms in a wide embrace of the room and turned slowly. He moved around the space, between the furniture, followed by the spotlight. In the last few moments of the performance, when the singer's voice had soared to the last line and he stood where he had entered, hands at his sides, head bowed, the man's voice spoke under the music, directly into the minds of the audience. "What a piece of work is a man," the voice said, and without knowing they had been prompted, the spectators burst into applause. The whole performance took four and a half minutes.

With his part of the show over, he backed out through the doorway to where Kathryn was preparing to go onstage. They always left three full minutes between each appearance for people to chat and for the anticipation to build.

"They're laying down their short-term memories," Rhona had told them. "Let them talk about what they've seen, turn it over in their minds. They'll remember you better. If you go out bang bang bang one after another, it's too much. They'll only remember one of you."

"More circus wisdom?" Kathryn asked.

"You might sneer, my girl, but 'circus wisdom,' as you call it, is making us all rich."

After Leon had come offstage, the music dropped to the low Muzak sound track that would enhance the buzz of the audience but not intrude into their excited chatter. Kathryn did some stretches to warm up. She moved with the litheness of a cat, although Leon would never dare say so.

Kathryn had originally wanted a rock-and-roll song as her tune, but Rhona overrode her choice. Pop music was too ephemeral, she said. The song would become unfashionable and Kathryn would seem outdated. Classical, she insisted, or jazz. "It's us who will determine what these rubes go away thinking, not some cheap ditty from a pop song that's lodged in their brains. And even though I hate most of that opera wailing, there are some songs that make the tingle start in your tailbone and rise up to your skull, and that's what we want."

"Are you ready, Kathryn?" Yuri pulled the door open a fraction. He managed the timing of the show as well as looking after Christos's wings. None of them wanted too many strangers running around. He signaled to the tech, who used the remote to start up Kathryn's tune, the aria from *La Wally* by Catalani. A tune that had graced a hundred television ads yet still made people close their eyes in a wash of pleasure.

During the dinner she had been wearing a scarf on her head that folded down into her cape so only her face showed. As she reached the doorway, the audience could see that the scarf went much further, that her body was wrapped from head to toe in a kind of sari arrangement. She stood silhouetted against a faint flickering candlelight as the orchestra introduced the music. The moment the pure voice of the singer floated into the room, Kathryn stepped through, and the sari began to unwind and fall in folds behind her as she moved, until by the end of the first verse, she stood naked, arms crossed over her breasts, eyes heavenward. There was no gasping from the audience during Kathryn's piece, only a stunned silence. Women sometimes reached out their hands, as if to take Kathryn, as if to hold her.

In these private shows, if Kathryn's woolly arm did brush a woman's outstretched hand, Kathryn smiled. Later, all touching was disallowed, but in these early exclusive shows, the worst anyone did was snicker behind their hands or rear away when one of the performers passed by too close. They were the innocent times. Tonight Leon watched as Kathryn crouched and whispered into Maria Eleven's ear.

Kathryn tripped offstage, skidding and clattering in her ridiculous high heels and laughing.

"Did you see that woman? That stunning woman, the goddess?"

"I was sitting next to her. Maria. She's nice."

"Leon, are you kidding? Nice? She's out of this world. She's"—Kathryn looked to the side, searching for one of her rehabilitated words—"utterly ravishing. I told her she was the fourth wonder in the room and she giggled."

Christos came to stand at the entrance with Yuri following, adjusting the wings as he walked. "She probably thinks the same about you, sexy lady. You're ravishing."

Kathryn pulled up as if she had been slapped. She looked down at her body, then up at Christos. She shook her head. "I still can't believe it. Skanky old me, turned into a sexy thing."

Yuri made a final adjustment to the wings, signaled the tech to start Christos's tune, and wiped Christos's oiled chest with a cloth before slipping into the shadows as the door opened. The wide-angle spotlight snapped on and burned a beam from heaven onto Christos's body. His signature tune was so clichéd Leon had doubted it would have any effect, but each time he raised his wings to the dramatic notes of "O Fortuna," the power of the image and the music combined to arouse extraordinary emotions. They had seen women begin to cry, men half stand before sinking into their seats with their mouths drooping open. The fingers on the metal wings spread and folded while people sobbed. Leon was not sure why it was so powerful for them. Perhaps the religion, all the angel mythology. Christos had obviously known exactly what he was doing when he started the wing project.

14

ONLY FIVE REMAINING circus animals were living at Over-ington with the Wonders. Two elephants, a chimpanzee, an old brown bear and a miniature pony. The elephants, the chimpanzee and the pony roamed the grounds, and the chimpanzee, Rosa, also had the run of the house. She never urinated inside, but sometimes Leon would notice a puckered turd in a corner of a room or a banana peel or fruit rind under a table. Still, she was good company, and her screeches sounded uncannily reminiscent of Rhona's laughter. Rosa had arrived after the chimpanzee kidnap and assault incidents. She had only known hard work in Hollywood and this new life of leisure.

August, the brown bear, had his own enclosure on the south side of the house, a large wilderness of trees, vines, bushes and artificial caves surrounded by a double fence. In winter, he slept long hours in a cave dug into the side of a slope in the enclosure. During the rest of the year, his food was thrown in at different points along the fence to simulate, according to Rhona, a life in the wild where he would have to hunt. Not that the food was alive—he was fed meat with shreds of fur and bone, whole fishes, buckets of fruit—but he did have to find it. Leon couldn't see the point since August had been trained to dance and walk on a rolling barrel, probably in captivity from when he was a cub. The keeper put his age between thirty and thirty-five years old. Six years earlier, he had attacked and mauled his trainer. He was destined for the needle before the animal rights group contacted Rhona to give him a home. "He's not dangerous, I'm sure," Rhona had told Leon. "But the keeper says he's happy in there alone. Bears are solitary animals."

Leon had ventured into August's enclosure a couple of times, wielding a Taser for safety. He glimpsed a gray snout poking from the shadows of the trees and that was enough of a thrill for him. Christos liked to enter the enclosure and spend time with the bear. He said that it was because he believed the bear must be lonely, having been brought up in the company of humans.

"In the wild they are alone, but he is no wild bear. Plus, we performers," he said to Leon once, and as usual Leon couldn't tell whether he was joking, "need to perform. I go in there and I let August perform for me. He shuffles a few steps, takes a bow, makes a fake roar. It is the only thing he knows how to do. For other bears, hunting is their work. For August it is performing. The same as us. We are made to hunt and gather, so now we create other work for ourselves."

Kathryn's familiar was the pony. When she went for a stroll in the fresh air, usually with her scarlet outdoor cloak draped across her shoulders, Agnes the pony cantered up and nuzzled her, trying to get under her cloak to the hidden pockets in its lining. She fed the stumpy pony apples and hay and carrots, and they ambled together through the different habitats that had originally been set up for the lions and tigers, the donkeys, the zebras, the camels.

Leon had not bonded with any of the animals in particular, but if he had free time, like today, he walked around the grounds. Walking alone, he found the empty enclosures eerie. Tall trees with lanky trunks that resembled the legs of the former giraffe occupants gave way to the arid sands of the old camel enclosure, which led to a vine-looped jungle area that once belonged to the chimps. The walls had been removed so that they were no longer technically enclosures, yet the contrast in vegetation and topography and even soil in the purpose-built sections made it seem as though in fifty paces he had crossed continents and oceans, strayed into the domain of creatures from other worlds. Invisible creatures also, for most of them had long since died, and all that remained of them were scraps of fur caught on twigs, gray patches of dirt worn into the grass or pasture where the animal used to sleep, the ripe odor of certain spots where it may have sprayed or rutted or simply rubbed its scent over a tree trunk or a boulder.

"One day the whole earth might be empty. No animals left."

He hadn't noticed Christos and Yuri behind him. It was Yuri who had spoken. From things he had said here and there, his veganism, his cotton clothes and hemp sandals, and the way he took care with everything he used, it was clear that Yuri, alone among the residents at Overington, believed this way of life could not last forever. He was afraid humans may have gone too far, that they had poisoned the planet beyond redemption, that they should be showing greater respect to the animals and plants of the earth.

"Do you really think so?" Leon was glad to hear Yuri speak. He wanted to have a long conversation with him one day, but so far Yuri had always found a reason to slip away after a few moments. At twenty-two, his unlined Russian face shone with boyish innocence. Leon had the peculiar impression it was a face recently released from having a great big hand pressed against it—the expression was consequently a mixture of surprise and relief looking out at the big world. Or perhaps that was his true expression, the expression of a young man unshackled from poverty and aimlessness in Russia by an accidental meeting outside a gallery.

Christos gestured around the dusty landscape they had entered. "This reminds me of our island in the hot summer." His need to dominate the conversation may have been one reason Yuri was so quiet. "Except for our land. We had a vegetable patch, always green." Christos smiled with the memory. "My mother sent me out to harvest olives from the trees that grew wild on the hills. She kept a couple of goats and fermented the milk to make cheese."

Yuri shook his head in wonder. "Paradise."

"Hard work."

Leon tried to imagine it. "Goats! In the country town where I grew up, we had bottlebrush and geraniums in our garden. You couldn't kill them if you tried. My parents preferred playing sport to gardening. Or to reading. Or to anything, really."

They reached the mound in the former lions' enclosure. It had been designed so the big cats could sleep high up, alert for intruders, which, during their lives as captives and performing animals, would have been human beings, the ultimate predators. The mound was a series of small hills undulating into occasional hollows filled with the seeds and dried grass of earlier generations of spring weeds. Together the three men climbed the rise and stood on the highest mound, about twenty feet above the terrain around it, admiring the grand vision of the house and its stately timber louvers.

"I want to see this place where you grew up, Leon." When Christos announced such desires in his sonorous voice they could have been commands. "I want to visit your hometown. And I want to see the council flat where Kathryn grew up in Dublin, the slum. And Yuri's family house in Kashin, and then you must all come to my village on Chios."

"What about Rhona? Should we visit her home as well?" Yuri, always the diplomat.

"We live in her home."

"But this is not where she was born."

"Then we should ask her. We are family now."

Even though Christos was prone to grandiloquent statements, sometimes he said things that Leon knew to be true. This was one of them. They were family now. Leon's blood relatives were distant in space and distant in consciousness. The year of silence, when Susan had forbidden him to contact anyone, even family, had only shown him how little he missed his family, and probably they him. There was no bad feeling, only an emptiness, and that had begun to be filled by the people he spent each day with at Overington.

The two elephants still living at Rhona's, Maisie and Maximus, were free to roam, but sections of the grounds were cordoned off so that the vegetation had time to recover from their grazing. Both Maisie and Maximus seemed docile enough. Rhona said they were probably in their forties or fifties. Older than the Wonders.

Yuri said he had seen Maisie standing on her two front legs, then her two back legs, a trick she must have been taught in the circus. If you wore a hat outside and didn't keep your eyes peeled, Maximus would lift it from your head and blow it to the top of a tree. You might have to wait for a windy day to recover your headgear. If the breeze blew from the south, something to do with the orientation of the trees, a bandanna or ladies' broad-brimmed hat or beret from Rhona's parties of old had been known to fly into the air and swoop incongruously onto the lawn or a flower bed.

"Oh, I used to love that hat!" Rhona exclaimed one time as she and Leon stood at the window watching a big creamy chiffon and straw concoction flip across the lawn. "I wore that to my cousin's second wedding in 2009."

It was because of these pitiful remnants of the elephants' working life that the residents of Overington forgot the elephants were wild animals. Even when Maximus trumpeted right behind them and they shrieked at being startled, they didn't consider, or at least Leon didn't consider, that Maximus was actually speaking to them, trying to tell them something.

So when Maisie trampled the groundskeeper's car, Leon presumed there had been some mistake, or that Maisie had stumbled and fallen on the car, or that it was a practical joke and Rhona would produce a new car for the groundskeeper, who sat on the outside stairs of the house shocked and speechless at the sight of the steering wheel protruding from the windshield.

By the time Kathryn discovered the car and the groundskeeper, Maisie and Maximus had wandered off again. Kathryn shouted for someone to come. Leon ran out first, followed by Yuri and Christos. Rhona was on a call. When she emerged, she gasped at the scene of destruction. She stood staring at it for some time, lips pressed together. The groundskeeper had left the scene by then. He'd crab-walked over to Leon and Kathryn while Rhona was still inside, and he'd dropped his voice and muttered to them that he didn't want to have to sue but, really, who could put up with this. He'd seen that female one, the lady elephant, look straight at him as she punched a hole in the hood with her foot. It was terrifying. It was traumatic and he'd need time off and he wasn't sure if he'd ever recover and . . .

Kathryn hadn't bothered listening any further. She'd

walked away to talk to Yuri while Leon had to endure the man complaining for another five minutes about his pay and the responsibilities and no one warning him it would be a fucking zoo in here, he was a gardener and handyman, not an animal lover. Glad that Kathryn had missed that comment, Leon watched the man's mean hunched back as he shouldered into his cottage and slammed the door behind him. Once he had gone, Kathryn and Yuri returned to Leon's side.

Maximus and Maisie were still somewhere out on the grounds. It was the one day of the week that the elephant keeper had off.

"I'm worried she might have cut her foot on the glass." Rhona peered at the ground, searching for traces of blood.

"Do we need an elephant therapist?" Christos took Rhona's hand and held it tight between his own hands. He knew, they all knew, how devoted she was to caring for the animals on the property. "What happened, do you think? Will she hurt us?"

Rhona sighed. "When I was a very small girl, one of the elephants at my father's circus went mad. Completely crazy. It trampled its trainer to death, tore down tents, pushed over vans and concession stands and afterward tried to throw itself repeatedly into a mass of barbed wire that the site occupier before us had left on the ground behind where we set up the big top. The elephant was trying to kill itself. The next day it did have to be put down because it had killed a man, so luckily those injuries from the barbed wire didn't cause it pain for too long." Rhona was speaking slowly. "The thing is, everyone knew that the trainer was one of the cruelest men in the circus. He used an electric prod and a sharp pointed hook to beat the beast into doing what he wanted. It had huge scabs under its forelegs that the audience never saw but that must have caused it agony. He never fed it anything but subsistence food because he wanted more money for himself. He wouldn't get another elephant, even though that one was nearly dying of loneliness. If you have ever heard a lonely elephant cry, you have heard the saddest sound in the world."

"Oh," Kathryn said. She turned and ran up the stairs into the main house. Rhona went on.

"Elephants are very like us, you know. The keeper tells a story about when there were only four hundred elephants left in Uganda. They were all young, their parents killed for their ivory. Teenage elephants had to become matriarchs. There were no bull elephants left, no male role models. So the young male elephants turned into juvenile delinquents, aggressive, attacking each other and other animals for no reason. Doesn't that remind you of human beings?"

"But Maisie, she is not a wild elephant," Yuri said.

"No, and she and Maximus came from a good trainer, a man who was the son of a friend of my father's. From a different type of circus, not the Enchanted Circus kind. More . . . contemporary." Rhona paused, but no one spoke. Leon knew what she meant—he'd read about the careless brutality of the Enchanted Circus.

Rhona continued. "Maisie's trainer, Frankie, adored his elephants, and he trained her and Maximus with rewards, not punishment. That's why they are such loving elephants. They grieved terribly when Frankie died. And they have a sense of humor because Frankie was a joker, and he made them laugh. Elephants can laugh, you know."

"So why would she do this?"

Rhona looked at the cottage into which the groundskeeper had vanished. "You know that saying, an elephant never forgets. It's true. They don't forget people and what they've done. I'd trust Maisie every time over a human. I guess she can't tell us why she hates this man enough to destroy his car, so we'll have to take this as her sign."

The shattered pieces of the windshield lay scattered in icy

blue chips at their feet. Leon picked up a thick fragment of glass. He held it up and angled it to catch the sunshine. When he first arrived at Overington and Rhona led him out to meet the animals she'd told him to hold his hand near Maximus's right ear. He was amazed to feel intense heat radiating from the great leathery muscular flap. For cooling, she'd explained. When he offered the elephants a handful of peanuts, Maisie's trunk reached to his palm and picked up the peanuts one by one with delicate precision, depositing a bubble of snot in the process. Her small eye framed by its stiff brush eyelashes gazed into him with the sympathy of an old wise woman. He couldn't imagine anyone but a sadist doing anything to hurt these animals.

The next day Rhona paid the groundskeeper for the car, gave him a substantial bonus and let him go. In the local tabloid the following week, the headline read FREAK FARM HAS ROGUE ELEPHANT TOO. WHAT NEXT?

"Good," Rhona said. "All the more mystique for us. We've got the permits, there's nothing anyone can do. Bring them on. And we'll find a good groundskeeper. I need staff we can love and who'll love us, all of us, human and animal. There's too much awfulness in the world without bringing it inside the house."

Days like that, when she was their protective tiger, Leon felt safer than he had ever felt in his life. He had never been a confident man, but with part of his body replaced by a mechanical device, with a hole bored through his chest and arteries of transparent tubing, he had become aware of his vulnerability, his proximity to death every minute of every day. He had hidden in his dark apartment during the year of recovery, cautious about everything from sudden heart-shaking movement to the off chance someone might glimpse his altered body through a window. But now, thanks to Rhona, thanks to Overington and its loopy circus, he had entered a world where difference was celebrated rather than scorned.

15

LEON WOKE TO shouts and door slams strafing the settled air of the main Overington building. It was five thirty in the afternoon. He had been napping before dinner. He crept toward the common room and peeked around the corner. Minh, the doctor, was doing the same at the doorway of the opposite corridor. Christos materialized from his apartment. He strode straight to the middle of the room to confront Rhona and Kathryn.

"What is going on? I am trying to concentrate."

"None of your fecking business!" Kathryn shouted. She started to walk toward her apartment but Rhona caught hold of her oversized overcoat and pulled her back to the fireplace.

"Don't you dare walk out on me like that, girl. I haven't finished. You are not slinking off until you apologize to him."

"Fine. I'll do it in the morning."

"No, you won't, because he won't be here. He's been fired."

The sudden silence was broken by Christos. "Who has been fired?"

Ignoring him, Rhona picked up the department store bag from the couch and thrust it at Kathryn. "Here you are. Take it. Was this worth a man's livelihood?"

"I didn't fire him—you did. It's your responsibility." Kathryn took the bag and bundled it under her arm.

"No, the security firm fired him because he called them in a panic when he lost you. When you slipped away and hid from him. Childish behavior!"

"I need some feckin' time on my own. I can't bear always being followed around by these guards. I don't even want this stupid hat." She lifted the bag and emptied its contents of mauve tissue paper and crimson wool and ribbon onto the floor.

"Then come to me and I'll set it up." Rhona stooped to gather the paper and hat and stuff them back into the bag. "Just don't run away. That man was terrified, and so was I when the security firm called me. Give me another heart attack and the whole circus will be over because I'll be in a goddamn coffin."

Later that night, unable to sleep, Leon wandered out to the common room, where he found Rhona and Christos and Yuri curled up on chairs around a tray with a bottle of whiskey and a barrel of ice. Rhona looked exhausted. She poured another finger of whiskey and rattled the ice cubes around the glass before taking a sip.

"She was silly, sneaking away from her bodyguard like that, but I have to forgive her. The life she's had . . ."

She told them stories she had heard from Kathryn of growing up on a council estate—a public housing project—in Dublin, running with the local gang that supplied speed to the schools of the area. She was the youngest in the gang, a scrawny girl with the knowledge of every vacant flat, every lane and getaway route, the plate numbers of every unmarked district police car. Her mother worked two jobs: one for the council cleaning flats for the elderly and disabled, the other serving drinks at the local pub. She was trying to get Kathryn and her brother out of there, to save the down payment for a flat or a house over on the other side of Dublin where they could start again without the influence of the gangs that ruled her children's lives.

It was already too late for Kathryn's brother. He was two years older than Kathryn, dealing speed and coke to the boys in a private school four suburbs away. He had three warrants out for his arrest by the time he was sixteen. When one of the private-school boys was caught snorting speed by his father, he ~~a~~pologized by informing on Kathryn's brother, setting up a buy. ~~T~~wo years in juvenile detention, the thinning of his body into ~~so~~mething hard and long-muscled, then out and dealing again. Another arrest. Two more years. The lawyer who had been his best customer for cocaine saw him waiting on a bench outside the court for his trial, gave him a pat on the back and hurried off, gown flapping, shiny five-hundred-quid shoes tapping on the stone floor.

The few times Leon had heard mention of Kathryn's brother from her own mouth, she was heaping scorn on one of his moneymaking schemes.

"Where is your big brother now? Why haven't we met him?" Christos demanded once. He had introduced nine of his family members as guests to Overington so far. Two bulky shopkeeper brothers and their wives during an uncomfortable week that had Leon hiding in his room reading books, three cousins, a teenage niece. The oldest, his grandmother Yiayia Nina, arrived with a bagful of dolmades that leaked oil from her suitcase in a trail down the driveway. She stayed for three weeks in Christos and Yuri's apartment, cooking every day, wandering the garden every morning at dawn rubbing rosary beads through her wrinkled fingers and muttering her prayers. When she left, Christos sobbed on the doorstep, waving at the blunt back of the limousine driving her away. He was always telling stories about himself and his family, everything down to the uncle who used to fondle Christos's penis when he was a boy. "I liked it," Christos said. "It felt good, no one was hurt. He paid me in chocolate."

Kathryn shrugged. "I don't see my brother anymore. He was a friend of my husband."

Silence. Another of the topics that would never bloom into conversation, at least while Kathryn was around. The crew had discussed the husband when Kathryn wasn't there. Rhona had dealings with him because he was trying to sue her for a percentage of Kathryn's income, which Kathryn didn't know and had no need to know. But the husband's actions before she escaped him had all been recorded online in media reports and interviews, and the words of friends who wrote about him.

Kathryn's husband took photos of her skin as the wool emerged. He posed her naked on the floor to document every new growth of wool with a cheap camera and a blinding flash. He filed a lawsuit against the hospital where she had her treatment. They settled out of court for a sum that was never published. Yet when Kathryn arrived at Overington she was penniless. He had taken all the money and lost it in bad investments and partnerships with con men who recognized him for the fool he was. After Kathryn had gone he sold the remaining photos and his story, complete with invented details of her raging sexual appetites and bizarre antics, which he claimed were brought on by the change.

"I didn't know whether we could rescue her from that humiliation," Rhona told Leon and Christos and Yuri. The staff had gone to bed, and a soft powder of sadness had fallen in the room, sadness for their old lives and for their new ones. "Everyone had seen everything. Her body was public property. She was shrunken and crushed and barely able to speak. It's an odd word to use, but she was dishonored. Others had dishonored her and she had no honor left for herself. She made me cry. I decided that even if she could not recover enough to perform, I would have her here with whatever she needed. It took months of quiet and rest, and she'd already worn out two shrinks at the sanatorium before she even got here."

The Kathryn who shared their life was unrecognizable as that cowed woman in the obscene photos smeared across the media when her change first began. Her husband had snapped her stretched out, curled up, bent over in positions a porn star might use. In some he posed her like a fashion model, for reasons Leon couldn't fathom. Or perhaps those two extremes were the only images of women the husband understood. The early photos showed the wool as a shadow, a dirty smudge appearing on her legs and back. Later it covered most of her body, but angry pink bald patches still shone through on her belly and her shoulders. In the last photos, the wool had grown long and was matted, greasy and ropy. She wore no makeup or shoes. She could have been an escapee from an ancient alien swamp. Leon hated to think about her life with her husband, how it could have turned Kathryn, blindsided by the treatment that caused the wool to grow, into the cringing, dirty, ugly creature who had been exposed to the world in those parodies of glamour portraits.

"But she did recover," Leon said. "She's incredible now, so gutsy and beautiful. And a bit scary when she starts with that smart mouth." Two nights before, she had called him Tin Man and threatened to leave a magnet in his bed. On a bad day she could wither him with a glance.

Rhona patted Leon's arm, partly to reassure him, partly to

correct him. "Underneath, Leon, she is still as flimsy as tissue. Outside—spunky and tough. Inside—still terribly scarred."

That night as he lay in bed he imagined, as he had in the first days of arriving at Overington, how it would feel to have wool under his fingers. To sense the swell of a breast under soft curly fleece. To reach between warm woolly thighs to find moisture. To rub his cheek along the shorn black ripples of wool and push his tongue into the hollow of her throat where the wool ended and silky skin emerged. But it was a fantasy, not something he wanted to become real. He could imagine her afterward in a rage, unsatisfied, battering him with words, her possibility for pleasure bound tight by the punishing past written into her body. His fantasies were for late at night, for a quick uncomplicated release before sleep.

In the six months he had known her, Kathryn had not been with a man or a woman, had not shown any interest in romance or sex. While Rhona and Christos teased Leon about getting a girlfriend, they never pressed Kathryn. Despite being named as the sexiest woman who had ever lived by a salacious men's magazine that couldn't let a week go by without a mention of her, it was as if she had turned her own sexuality off.

Only once did Christos bring up the idea of her meeting someone. "When are you going to find yourself a playboy?" he asked.

Kathryn smiled even as she kept her gaze focused on the book in her lap. "Didn't you guess? I'm waiting for Pan."

16

TODAY MINH LAY on a chaise longue in a finger of afternoon sun beside the elephant house, ankles crossed, face tipped back to catch the sun. She was talking on a phone, and from her lighthearted laugh, Leon guessed she was on the line with Kathryn, who was in Los Angeles talking to producers about a biopic.

The arrival of Minh at Overington had soothed its small fraught world. Leon found it difficult to define exactly what her presence had done, but for one thing he felt healthier, even though she had done nothing but represcribe his medications and run tests and assays. Even Kathryn had relaxed since Minh's appearance. She and Minh could often be found chatting with their heads bent together, Minh's black hair glossy and smooth beside Kathryn's tight woolen curls, or lying on opposite couches reading quietly, or teasing Christos while Yuri fussed around cleaning the wings or working on specifications for the design of Christos's next project.

Sometimes Leon caught sight of Minh sitting on her camp

stool in the grounds, concentrating on a sketch or staring dreamily at something in the distance. In the short time she had been here, her skin had become tawny and fresh as she rambled and sketched the artificial wildernesses of the Overington grounds. Much as Leon wished he could pass by and comment casually on her artwork or on the scenery or even the weather, he had never been comfortable about approaching women, even for an innocent chat. He was sure they would be polite while wishing he'd leave them alone, or talk with him out of pity, or worse, give him a brusque response that left no doubt about their wish to be rid of this annoying bug. "Sad Leon" he used to be called in high school. With his forlorn face, he looked older than his physical age. Sad old Leon. He was brimming with the same wishes and hopes as everyone else, but all that was hidden behind his mournful visage. The women who took the initiative with him were often disappointed too. They had made their move presuming that face reflected a melancholy soul, a tortured poet, but what they discovered was a man of longing, eager to please yet unable to find the right tone or note or pitch to satisfy their expectations.

So, at Overington, Leon skirted around the luminous presence of Minh. He would wave from a distance, bowing with a Prussian gentleman's dip of the head, then stroll off, hands clasped behind his back, a socially inept idiot.

Seeing Minh today, he performed his stupid nod and pivoted on his heel, ready to head off in the other direction and silently berate himself for his gracelessness, but she called to him.

"That was Kathryn on the phone. She says she's never going to be a star. They want her to play herself in the early scene of when the wool starts to grow. They can't understand why she won't do it."

Leon stood stiffly to attention on the spot where he had

begun to turn away. Should he walk toward Minh? Should he reply and continue on his way? Should he be frank—say that Kathryn deserved more than a hammy biopic? He thrust his fists into his pockets and clenched them for courage before he spoke.

"I think she's doing the right thing. She shouldn't have to live through that again."

"That's what I said, Leon. I don't know why she's even considering this Hollywood film. It must be Rhona's idea."

"Or Kyle's." Kyle had accompanied Kathryn to Los Angeles. Leon wondered if the whole thing was a ploy for Kyle to spend time alone with her.

Minh cleared her throat. "Would you like to sit down?"

He hadn't noticed the second chaise longue on the other side of Minh. Of course, she and Kathryn sometimes lay here in the early morning. Soaking up their weekly dose of vitamin D, they said. He walked around behind Minh and eased himself onto the low cedar chaise with its padded cushions. His thighs were tense, a sure sign he was feeling anxious.

He adjusted his buttocks further onto the cushion pad. "It's comfortable."

"You sound surprised." Minh picked up a pair of sunglasses from a basket beside her and handed them to Leon. "You could put these on and lie down. I promise you'll be relaxed in no time. It works for Kathryn and me. This sheer autumn sunshine—it's therapy without the talking."

Thirty minutes later Leon woke with a start. The strip of sun had moved down his body and now lit a stripe across his calves. Minh was sitting up, sketching Maisie and Maximus grazing in a copse of trees to the south, her long legs braced either side of the chaise longue, the sketchbook balanced on the flat of the seat.

"Feel better?" she asked without shifting her gaze from the elephants. Her hand made rapid strokes on the paper as if it were working alone, without her conscious mind.

"Mm."

"I watched your breathing while you were asleep. I could see you've lost some lung capacity."

Leon yawned and stretched, feeling the shift of tendon and muscle along bone. He was looser than he had been in months.

"Leon, I know you're not supposed to talk about how you got the heart implanted, but I have to ask. It's so incredible. Could you maybe tell me about where it was done? I know it wasn't a hospital. No hospital could have kept you a secret."

Although Leon had lived in the basement under the university engineering department for a year while Susan and Howard operated on him, the memory of his physical pain had begun to fade as soon as he emerged into the sunlight and caught the train to his hometown. Susan and Howard often appeared in his dreams—after all, theirs were the faces he had watched the way a baby watches its mother's face, trying to read and understand the language they used and what it might mean for him. But he pushed the images away. He would never encounter that kind of pain again and he wanted to numb himself against the memory of it. As he became famous and the questions became more persistent about who had made his heart, who had implanted it, where the operation had been performed, he practiced the tricks of detachment he had used early on to avoid reminders of what he had been through. Rhona had told him not to speak to anyone about it, and in truth, he hadn't wanted to.

But now that Minh had asked, Leon was bursting to tell her how it had been. Something had changed in him. He wanted Minh to know. He wanted her to know how he had changed, even though she had never met Leon before his heart failed, the man who spent his time reading books about how to live and barely doing the living. Minh, with her different way of being in the world, would understand that everything had changed not only for him but in him. He wanted to be known by her.

Still lying on his back on the cushions, with his arm bent across his face, he started to speak and the words rolled out as if they had been prepared for this moment.

"We were in a basement under a university building. A secret basement that had been blocked off, that people had forgotten was there. No natural light, no view, no other people. Just the three of us underground. It was madness. The intensity, the paranoia, the claustrophobia turned us reckless. We were children trapped inside on a rainy day. We played made-up games with rules that changed as we went along. We repeated phrases thousands of times to make each other laugh. The phrase or word had struck us as funny once, so why not stretch that out, spin it fine, twist it, repeat it, upend it. I put together twenty-four elaborate jigsaw puzzles. I learned to do cryptic crosswords. Susan brought me games and toys as if I was a child in hospital."

"Susan?"

"My surgeon. And my friend. And my nurse and my shrink and my teacher. I remember once, when I asked her to tell me more about how my new heart would work, she handed me a rubber heart, a royal-blue-and-crimson-colored thing, and instead of waiting for her to explain, I started to juggle it in both hands and poke my finger into the cut-off stem of the aorta. I shook it until the vibrating rubber made a sound like wet gums flapping together. I couldn't stop laughing. Susan caught the laughter. We became a little hysterical. Later I became totally obsessed with anatomy, surgery techniques, biochemistry—I've always loved research anyway—but early on, everything was a plaything for me. I'd regressed, I suppose." Leon smiled, remembering the boredom of the first months as he was being prepared for surgery, left alone in the basement for long periods each day. How quickly he had turned to the pursuits of his childhood. "All the games and puzzles and quizzes. Anyway, I asked her if that rubber toy was how my new heart would look. I thought the artificial heart Howard was creating in the screened-off section of the basement would be a flexible, malleable thing like a real heart."

"Howard?"

"The engineer who made it. Designed it, built it himself. She told me that my heart would be nothing like that piece of rubber. That was what she used in her teaching at the university. I asked if I could go to a lecture, but she refused. 'I don't want you to be seen with me, Leon. We mustn't be associated. If this works and you get to go out and live a life, no one can know that Howard and I were the ones who did it.' I begged her to tell me why. I'd asked her a million times already but I couldn't believe her reasons were as simple as she made out. If it worked, surely they'd win the Nobel Prize. Surely no one would care how it had happened."

Minh finally dropped her pencil and pad to the side of the chair and swung her legs over so she sat facing him. "That's what everyone has been saying. What kind of crazy person would bring someone back to life the way they did with you and not want to boast about it? You'd already had an organic heart transplant that failed, right? And you were going to die. Who wouldn't claim you as their very own miracle?"

"Susan said it was illegal. She'd contacted me after somehow getting hold of the transplant waiting list. She'd started from the bottom. She explained that they weren't working in a registered hospital. It was an experimental procedure that hadn't been authorized. Howard had been refused funding and trials of his artificial heart time and time again. He'd go to jail if they were caught. They were married, did I tell you that? Susan and Howard were husband and wife."

Minh drummed her fingers on her knees. "But, Leon, why couldn't they wait until he got the heart approved? I understand that for you it was urgent. But, no offense, there are plenty of people on the last-chance transplant list. They could have held off and found another patient. Because what did they get out of it? If they weren't ever going to tell anyone it was them?"

"It was more complicated than I first realized. Susan threatened once to let me die. She was tired of my questions. I'd hinted that I wanted to call my family and let them know what was going on. Susan said, 'Fine, call them. We'll shut down the operation, clean up, move. But much worse, Leon, you will die. I am a doctor. I am distressed when my patients die. But people do die all the time and we both know you will die very soon if we do nothing. Legally, we are supposed to do nothing.'"

He had already come close to dying in that basement several times. Susan went part-time at the hospital and cut her teaching down to one lecture a week. She nursed him night after night when infections tore through his bloodstream, she carried his pans of vomit and piss and shit to the basement toilet and changed his sheets twice a week, or twice a night when he was feverish. He had been in preparation for sixteen weeks, swallowing a cupful of colored pills each day, doing exercises to strengthen his abdominal and back musculature, lying under the sunlamp for vitamin D and to keep his sanity, growing weaker and more breathless as the weeks passed. Dying. In pain. Without hope.

Susan and Howard argued about Leon in angry whispers

behind the screen. One night, he'd heard Howard say to let him go. The heart Howard had built was malfunctioning. It would kill Leon. They had moved too early. Howard needed another couple of months.

Susan made a sound of derision, a high disbelieving squeak. "Let him go? And he leaves and tells everyone where we are, what we're doing, and we end up front-page news and on trial? My god, Howard, how did I agree to this? How can I love you so much I would do this for you? I used to think I was a rational woman." She exhaled loudly and from his cot Leon could picture how she would be rubbing her cheeks with both hands, the way she did when she was exhausted.

"No, I mean let him go," Howard said quietly. "It might be kinder anyway. What if I die before he does? It will all have been for nothing. He could have a gentle passage, palliative care."

Whenever the basement was quiet, as it was at that moment with the machines turned off and no one speaking, Leon could feel the rumble of the world beneath the university. Sewage and wastewater gushing through pipes, the thump of generators, underground passages from building to building shifting and their stone walls cracking and sighing.

Finally he spoke. "I can hear, you know."

Susan poked her small head with its neat gray hair around the screen. "Oh god. He didn't mean it, Leon. It was—"

"I don't care." He was sick and tired and lonely. Hope was a small rainbow-sheened bubble hovering near the ceiling, out of his reach. "I don't care. Let me die."

He had no will to die, merely the absence of a will to live. Even the lowest animal has a will to live. Perhaps he was dead already. Perhaps, like Dr. Frankenstein, Howard and Susan truly were attempting to bring a corpse to life.

"No." Susan pushed aside the screen behind which

Howard, the small, hunched, greasy-haired mad scientist Leon knew she adored more than anything, more than her career, more than her whole life, was manipulating a 3-D model of the heart on a computer screen. Leon watched her align herself so that both men were in her eye line before she spoke. "You will not die yet, Leon. If you're going to die, it's going to be us who will have killed you through trying to save you."

Howard raised his gaunt yellow head from staring at the computer screen and nodded. He pushed himself up from the bench with stick arms and a shirt that hung on him in folds of useless excess material. Only two days before, Leon had learned that he was not the only one dying in the room. Susan's devotion, her willingness to take the risk of losing her license to practice medicine, Howard's doggedness that kept him working even when he was so tired his speech became burbling and incomprehensible were all because he had no time. Howard had only a few months left, and he was determined to get his artificial heart into a body and keep the body alive, to make all his years of research worthwhile. While he would die of cancer that had metastasized to his liver, Leon might live. Perhaps Howard lay in bed at night wishing it was an artificial liver he had designed.

In the following days, Leon's withered second heart, which was killing him, was replaced with two temporary mechanical pumps to keep him alive, with luck, until Howard's heart was ready. From that day forward, Leon carried an automaton instead of a heart.

"Wow." Minh slumped onto the chaise longue and sighed. "No wonder Rhona wants you to keep that story quiet. That'll be a movie one day."

"We'll all be in a movie one day." Leon gestured around,

indicating Overington and everyone inside. "I just hope they make us out to be better people than we actually are."

"I guess poor Howard died. He was a hero, really, wasn't he? And what happened to Susan?"

"She disappeared." Leon had felt for a while as though he had lost a mother. A mother who had told him to forget her. He grieved her absence even as he hoped she was all right, living somewhere quietly, celebrating Howard's triumph in her own way. "I hope she's seen us on the news. Maybe she'll turn up one day."

"Will you search for her?"

Susan had forbidden him to search for her. It was the last thing she'd said to him as she dropped him at the station.

"Leave me and Howard with this time together," she said. "I want to nurse him now. I want us to enjoy some peace. He's achieved his dream. We haven't much time left and I couldn't bear it to be wrecked by charges and courts and the threat of prison."

He had obeyed her. He had sent the updates she requested, heard the electronic whoosh as they zapped into the ether, and never attempted to see her. When he discovered she was gone from the university where she had worked it was as though she had died without his having the opportunity to say good-bye.

"She said not to. And I haven't. It's hard to explain how things were. I'd been taken apart and put back together. I hardly knew who I was by the end of that time. For the year afterward when I was recovering I had searing flashbacks, nights when I couldn't move for fear I would break apart, and others when I walked around my apartment for hour after hour to keep from sleeping and dreaming. In the end, all I wanted was to drive the memories out of my mind."

"Oh, Leon, that's a response to severe trauma. It must have been hell."

"I don't feel that way now though. I want to talk about it. It's such a relief speaking to you like this."

"I'm happy to listen anytime. Anytime at all."

He had felt no desire to contact Susan before. It was too much to even think about. But that was before his third life. Of course he should search for her. He was famous. Everything had changed. He was famous and he could do things normal people could not. It had taken no time at all for him to realize that people with true fame have no limits on their behavior. Violence, rape, murder—celebrities never had to pay anything but a fine, or a few hours working at a community center. So what did it mean to break a few medical rules if the result was a lifesaving breakthrough?

Susan couldn't have known that the power of the world he would join overrode medical rules and regulations, overrode the courts and the state, overrode everything.

He must find her and thank her. Give her some of the money that Rhona said was rolling in faster than even she had anticipated. Fund whatever project Susan wanted. She probably still had all the specifications for the heart. He could pay for Howard's heart design to be analyzed, manufactured, massproduced for all those other people on the waiting lists who had little hope of receiving a live heart in time.

He turned to Minh. "I should. I will. Yes, I will."

Minh wriggled to the edge of her seat and placed a hand on his forearm. "I can help if you want. I mean, I don't want to intrude. But I think she deserves to see you, to see the heart in a healthy man."

He wouldn't tell Rhona. She might object in case finding

Susan stole the limelight from the Wonders. But it was the right thing to do.

"Thank you," he said. Their gaze snagged briefly before Minh swung around to adjust the back of her chaise. He felt a tremor, a tic, as if that moment of their trapped gaze had slipped under his skin.

17

RHONA HAD CALLED them all to the projection room, even the house and garden staff, who stood in a row at the back. Christos grumbled his way to his seat, and Kathryn brought a book, as she always did in case she was bored. Minh sat beside her flicking through a collection of images by a contemporary watercolorist on her tablet. Leon hoped it wasn't another series of footage the Wonders were supposed to watch while Rhona and Kyle pointed out faults in their performances and harangued them on technique, although he couldn't imagine why the animal keeper would need to hear that.

"I want you all to see this from me before you run into it somewhere else." Rhona looked off to the side for a moment before continuing, as if someone over there was forcing her into this action. "And we might as well see it in its full glory because it went online an hour ago and half the world is looking at it right now. It's not pretty."

She switched on the projector. The screen wall opposite filled with an image of Leon's body. As he watched, the air around him metamorphosed to unbreathable lead. He felt his sphincter clench and the shit inside him turn to liquid. Yuri leaned over from the seat behind to pat his back. The warm hand soothed Leon into blinking and bracing himself for more.

"Like I said, not pretty." Rhona switched to another image, even worse.

Everyone in the room was silent as she flipped through three more grotesque images. In the three months since the launch, Leon had become accustomed to the flattering photos, the airbrushed stills and the strictly managed video appearances. He'd half-convinced himself his long mournful countenance was not too bad looking. He'd worked hard on his body, exercising and eating well. His teeth had been straightened and capped, and he'd even had a small operation to pin his ears back. All that work was moot when he was confronted with these images.

Leon bending over behind the changing screen at the pool pulling off his swimming trunks. Skinny buttocks pocked and scarred from the massive injections Susan used to give him in the basement. A pathetic wrinkled hairy crack, and the shadow of the sad sac between his thighs. Four similar shots as he stepped out of the trunks and pulled on dry shorts, then a fifth of him poolside in a chair. Puffy, red-faced, mouth as wide as a laughing clown. Obviously blind drunk.

The photos were from Kathryn's birthday celebration, back in the late summer. Christos and Yuri had been in New York at an exhibition opening. Leon, Kathryn, Rhona, Kyle and Minh drank daiquiris after lunch and Leon floated in the pool until his skin wrinkled. Minh suggested they give the daiquiris a rest before she headed to her room. Kyle lasted another half hour before retiring. Later Leon and Kathryn fell asleep in the deck chairs. Staff came while they were dozing and moved big striped umbrellas around with the sun to protect them from burning.

Kathryn slammed her fist onto the arm of the couch. "For fuck's sake, they're in our garden, our pool. It must be one of our staff." She turned to glare at the people lined up at the back of the projection room. They had gasped as loudly as the Wonders when the images filled the screen.

"No, miss! Not us," Vidonia said in her loud chef's voice. "You know who to trust. You know that."

"It's okay, Vee. I trust you, of course I do." Kathryn sank back into her seat.

"Darling, prepare yourself. They have you too." Rhona switched to the next shot and three more of Kathryn beside the pool. The angle made her look huge in the hips and buttocks, as if she was stuffed with great wads of cotton under the wool. In the fourth photo she was bent over, massive bottom half out of the shot, face looming between her arm and torso as though she could see the camera. Her upside-down face jowly and mis-shapen, eyes bloodshot. Looking half human.

"I've had much worse than that courtesy of my delightful husband. They'll have to do a lot better to humiliate me. But poor Leon here is gobsmacked. He looks as if he's been hit with a hammer."

Leon did feel like he'd been hit with a hammer. The others were staring at him, perhaps seeing something new. Minh tsked behind him, reached over and held his shoulder for a moment.

"Don't take any notice of this," Minh said. "It's important you don't get upset. Everyone's been working very hard. You're all overtaxed and I don't want you stressed as well."

At the back of the room the staff were protesting their in-nocence.

Rhona promised to track down the person responsible. "Welcome to celebrity, Leon," she said. "It's only when people despise you that you know you've really made it."

18

SOON AFTER HE had moved into Overington, Leon ordered books that referenced Rhona's father, the infamous Penny King. From the first time they had met, Rhona had been conjuring up her dead father to explain why Leon would grow rich, why she could summon forty media reporters and they would arrive within an hour, why her logo had a hint of a striped awning, why she sometimes called herself a barker. "He taught me what I need to know to survive in this business. In any business, really."

The books and websites told a much more complex story of Samuel Burke, the man who built the greatest circus in the United States after the war, and whose fame peaked when a purposely lit fire burned down the circus as it was playing Denver. Forty-two patrons and staff died, trapped in tents of canvas that wrapped around their bodies in flaming sheets when they tried to break through to the outside. Witness accounts told of people running with their bodies burning, how the torn canvas that had caught on their clothes gave them fiery wings and tails like devils straight from hell. Animals burned to death shrieking and howling in their cages. The circus went bankrupt, and a month later the Penny King disappeared.

His show was called the Enchanted Circus, a perverse name for a circus known for its brutal mistreatment of animals, punishing working conditions and mysterious connections with the criminal underworld.

"Some men would come around," Rhona said once, offhandedly, "collecting money. I don't know. Probably it was the games. Cards. A cockfight every now and then."

She spoke this way as though she knew little and cared less, but that had never been true of Rhona so Leon didn't believe a word of it. Rhona knew everything that went on. He could imagine her as a child, the way she had described it to him, following her father around, watching, listening, learning everything about how the circus ran.

"There were some protests," he had heard her say another time, a casual remark when Kathryn was asking about the circus.

He hadn't finished with the research into Rhona's background, but he had also turned his attention to the new project: finding Susan. He couldn't help this drive to dig out information. He had learned to be solitary and yet it was his nature to want to know, to hunt in books and online until he had ferreted out answers. He and Minh were working their way through lists in their search for his old surgeon, not hurrying, covering ground carefully and thoroughly. The last time they compared their findings, Minh had said he should be either a private detective or a therapist.

"I know you'll find her. You have that quiet persistent determination. It's a rare quality. I'd better be careful or I'll spill all my secrets to you."

"You can do that if you like." Leon barely believed the words had come out of his mouth. Was he flirting? Was this how you flirted?

She laughed her infectious laugh. "I might not be able to help myself." They were bent together over the screen, talking at it instead of facing each other. He couldn't bear to turn and look at her face in case she was toying with him and he would see her lip lifted in a sneer or her burned-toffee eyes rolling in disbelief. He could smell her skin, sweetish with a hint of cardamom. A teardrop crystal dangling on the end of a chain at her throat caught the light from the screen and gave it back as a rainbow. It was too much. He stood up.

Minh stayed leaning into the screen. She closed the Susan file. When she turned to face him, he noticed fingers of pink on her throat.

"I read about Rhona's father's circus too. An incredible story," he said.

"So tell me. We all want to know. She never gives much away."

He told her what he'd learned. In 1949, when the circus was performing in Idaho, the safety tie-rope of a young trapeze artist snapped as he flew beyond the top of his usual arc and somersaulted too late in a practice session. He fell forty feet to the sawdust-covered floor. The rope was frayed and untwisted, fifteen years old, gray and tired and worn. The Penny King had laughed when the trapeze boy asked for a loan against his salary to buy a new rope. The report on the incident quoted the trapeze artist's father, a strongman in the circus:

He laughed at my boy and sneered and told him not to be a
sissy. Well, my boy was no sissy but now he's dead and that
man has the blame right there on his shoulders. Only he won't

take it. He won't take the blame and to my mind that makes him a coward. A real sniveling coward.

All of the performers had attended the funeral in their costumes as a mark of respect. After the funeral they returned to the camp, had a few drinks in the big top under the trapeze wires, and fueled their resentment at their treatment by the Penny King.

Later that evening they gathered at the circus gate where crowds were queuing for the night's show. The Penny King had refused to close the circus, even for one night, even though the performers had offered to give up their night's wages.

The dead boy's father spoke to the crowd first. He had a fellow performer bring him a crate to stand on. He was weeping as only a strongman can weep, with his whole body. He asked the audience to go home, to respect the memory of a young man who had died. Some of the people looked away as if not seeing him might make him vanish. The ticket seller was counting out change as slowly as she could, placing the coins one by one on the lip of the wooden counter that jutted out from the window of the booth.

About half the people in the queue drifted away. The dwarf clown walked along the line of the people who remained and spoke to them individually. "You think about how you'd like someone turning up to your house when your son has just died. Asking to come in and play a game of cards or listen to your radio. How'd you like that?" More people left. As the demonstrators passed around the whiskey and the remaining small crowd shuffled uncertainly around the ticket booth, the Penny King appeared at the gate. He wore his ringmaster costume, red and gold with brass buttons and shiny black knee boots. He carried, as always, his whip.

"Ladies and gentlemen," he shouted in the voice that never failed to thrill children and convince their parents that the ticket price was money well spent. "There *will* be a show tonight. You will see performing elephants, wild tigers, a strongman"—here he focused his attention momentarily on the father of the dead boy—"and everything you ever expected from the greatest circus in the United States of America. This will be a show to commemorate the life of one of our special performers who died in a tragic accident yesterday as we rehearsed to bring the show to you here in Boise. So tonight will be a tribute show in honor of our terrible loss and in honor of all the great circus performers who have lost their lives bringing joy to audiences around the world. Our people"—he gestured at his disgruntled employees—"want to show their respect. And because of that, all tickets will be half price."

The people waiting to get in sent their children to let everyone know about the cheap tickets, and the crowd swelled to its largest-ever size for that town. The strongman retired to his van, but the other performers, except the high-wire acts who were too drunk to take the risk, came out for the spontaneous "tribute" show, which was reported around the country and gave the Enchanted Circus more publicity than it had seen in years.

The next day the strongman left the circus and applied to the US Postal Service for a job.

That was the first demonstration, and the smallest. The big ones came a couple of years later. The two strikes by unpaid workers, followed by the humane society rally in 1953 that brought animal lovers from across the country. Nine hundred people protesting the beating and starvation of circus animals that had been documented by an undercover reporter and published with graphic photographs and eyewitness accounts in a major daily newspaper.

The Penny King managed to ride that out too. He was a masterful manipulator of people and of the truth. Whether he cleaned up the circus or not isn't clear, but he managed to keep out of the press for the next couple of years. Then came the fire, and his disappearance.

The most curious thing about Leon's research into the Enchanted Circus was that every source said the Penny King was single and had no known children.

19

IT SEEMED TO Leon that two cracks had opened in the world. Out of one poured the human longing for mystery, bringing love letters and exaltation. From the other spewed the ghosts of human discontent and envy. The leaked ugly photos. Hate letters. Threats boxed like gifts, nestled in tissue paper and ribbon. Religious groups had been muttering online that the "freaks" were devils or messengers from hell. The complaints came from fundamentalists of all different denominations: Christian, Muslim, Jewish, even Satanists. The worst of them took everything literally. In their rantings, Leon was a demonic machine, Kathryn was a talking animal and Christos was an evil angel. Security had to be tightened, Hap said. He could provide the staff, but the Wonders needed to be more alert themselves. "Do not relax in public," he told them.

It was not easy to be alert to danger on a clear, crisp, beautiful night in New York City. On the way into dinner at Rockefeller Center, the Wonders paused on a walkway to look down through the glass at handsome couples spinning on the small ice rink. The skaters held hands and glided around with the precision of elegant figures in a brass automaton. Groups of onlookers hung over the rails above, their breath mingling in steamy clouds of conversation. Kathryn watched the skaters for a few moments before turning to Christos.

"Be my escort? I used to hate skating, but I feel more confident now I have extra padding. I was always a bony thing. Falling down used to hurt."

Christos told Kathryn he would sit by the side of the rink and watch her. Risky sports put him in danger. "If I fall on my back . . ."

Kathryn sniffed. "Precious fecking princess," she said so softly that only Leon heard.

She turned to Yuri. "Yuri? Will you?"

"So sorry, Kathryn. I cannot skate. My mother was afraid to let me on the ice."

"How about you, Leon? Will you take me skating?"

"You know the way my heart works—I'd have to spend twenty minutes warming up to get my blood flow in sync with the pace of exercise. By the time I was ready you'd be chewing your own foot off."

"Leon, keep making that kind of animal reference and I will smack your prissy face."

"Stop it. I can't stand this childish behavior." Rhona may not have enjoyed the role of exasperated mother, but she played it perfectly.

They had come to New York to perform an exclusive show-and-tell dinner in a private room in the Maison Française building of Rockefeller Center. The day had started badly with Kathryn and Christos bickering on the trip down about the use of the gym equipment. Everyone was drained by too many shows, too many nights of being paraded and gawped at.

They'd been at it for six months, at least a show a week, with only a two-week break for Christmas. When the private show finished, they raced to change and escape through the service corridors. Leon was in a hurry to get home and follow up on more leads on Susan.

He and Minh were working their way through the list he had compiled on search engines and networking sites, sending e-mails and messages with a carefully worded inquiry that only "his" Susan would recognize. They each spent an hour whenever they could on the project and came together every couple of weeks to compare responses. That time spent together, poring over lists of names and following leads, was deliriously fun for no obvious reason except that they were two serious people who surprisingly could make each other laugh.

At the Rockefeller event one of the staff had leaked that the Wonders were appearing. Two paparazzi had already tried to sneak into the room dressed as waiters, cameras bulging in unsightly swellings under their uniforms. Rhona had no idea how many more were waiting for them outside, but the management had assured her that they could slip out a hidden way. Security would come around to meet them at the exit.

They filed out through a back door on the second floor of the building, wrapped in enough coats and scarves and mittens and hats to survive a hockey game. The door opened onto fire-escape stairs leading down to a cul-de-sac alley behind the building. At the bottom of the fire escape, silver spokes and eyeglasses winked in the striped light from barred kitchen windows. Steam surged from an exhaust grille in the building opposite.

A small crowd was fermenting below.

A voice shrieked, "You aren't freaks. You're too fucking beautiful. I bet your shit doesn't even stink. You're fucking movie stars. You're fakes, not freaks."

"Oh shit." Rhona backed up against Leon, and he stumbled into Kathryn. Rhona's hands were trembling. "Demonstrators."

As Rhona and the others tripped and staggered backward in a Keystone Cops parade, Christos's bag caught in the door, wedging it open. A young man clanged up the stairs in an arm-windmilling whirl, grabbed the door and held it wide so that they were exposed at the top of the stairs, framed and staged by the lights in the corridor behind them.

"Assholes! This is fucking exploitation!" Again from down below.

Kathryn swore and started talking. "And who are we exploiting? Ourselves? Or maybe I'm exploiting you two. Christos, do you feel exploited? Leon?"

"We'll go out the other way. Where the hell is security?" Rhona pushed them backward into the passageway. Leon tightened his scarf around his neck. He didn't like being pushed. He didn't like any sudden pressure against his body. No matter how solid and securely his heart was anchored in his chest, he still feared that a knock would jolt it from its moorings, leave him spurting blood from a severed join, dying after his miracle because of some ridiculous accident.

"No." Kathryn elbowed Leon aside and stepped onto the metal walkway that led to the stairs. "What do you want us to do, huh?" she shouted down at the group of demonstrators.

A woman and a man were in wheelchairs, one man had a seeing-eye dog and another was missing an arm below the elbow. Even in the dim alley light Leon could see the pin holding his empty right sleeve. The others seemed able-bodied. But then, so did the Wonders.

"Stop your show. You are shaming us all. You're whores in a peep show."

"Right. We should give up performing and go home and

live on social security the way you do? You think that's something worth fighting for? We're making money, you fuckwits. We're working for a living." Kathryn's voice was bouncing off the alley walls, a fighting punchy voice. Probably none of the people below remembered what she had been through before the Wonders.

"I work for a living," the blind man bellowed. "I work at a real job. I do something for the world. I don't trade on being a freak. I don't run around posing like a slut and trying to be a celebrity."

Rhona tugged at Leon's sleeve and pulled him further into the passage. The gesture made Leon think about how no one would dare touch the empty sleeve or the hard gnarly stub of the man who waited below. If the man was not married, he probably felt the same loneliness Leon had been experiencing since he was implanted with his brass heart. It was more than sexual frustration. It was a deep ache of physical loneliness. A hunger. Wanting to be gripped by the wrist when a friend was making a point or to have a hand pressed against his back as he was guided through a doorway. Leon was nervous about being touched and yet he craved it. And he knew from experience how disfigurement caused such discomfort and, at the same time, such fascination in most people that they were afraid to touch you even though it was the one thing they longed to do.

"Kathryn," Rhona hissed out through the doorway. "Stop it. Don't provoke them. We're going to leave the other way."

"Not me." Kathryn slung her handbag over her shoulder and started down the staircase, her heels ringing on the pimpled metal.

Rhona turned to Leon and Christos. "Hell, we'll have to go with her. Are you two okay to do this?"

Leon was afraid but too embarrassed to say so. Christos

drew his overcoat around him before striding onto the metal platform and down the stairs. Yuri was still in the dining room, packing up the gear.

"Go on, have a good look," Leon heard Kathryn say down below. "Here. This is what people pay a fortune to see. Count yourselves lucky."

She tossed her hat behind her, unwound her scarf and threw it to the ground, and flung open her long cloak. The activists fell silent. They stared. The rest of the group arrived at the bottom of the staircase, its metal scaffolding clanging and bouncing under their weight as they each came off the last step. Rhona hurried to Kathryn's side and nudged her to close her cloak.

"My name is Rhona Burke. I'm the manager of the Wonders and if you have anything to say you should address it to me."

"They can't." Kathryn laughed derisively. "They're gob-smacked. Hey, Leon, open your shirt. Let's give them a really good show."

"I can't believe that as a differently abled person yourself, you're calling us *them*." The wheelchair woman who had been shrieking before was speaking at a lower volume now, but her voice still had the tight timbre of fury.

"I'm not differently abled. I'm super-abled."

"Sure, me too. I've got wheels and gears. Most people only have working legs."

Kathryn's spine straightened. Leon hoped it was a straightening of interest at the smart mouth of her opponent and not a straightening of anger at someone challenging her. Christos had plumped himself down on the bottom of the staircase, exhausted from the show, while Rhona rushed around with her arm out, an odd long-necked bird trying to shake hands with people.

"Lady, I don't have a hand. It's a bit hard to shake." The man with the pinned-up sleeve thrust his shoulder in her direction. "You wanna bump?" He snickered and turned to his companion. "I've always wanted to say that to someone."

"What do you want from us?" Leon asked. Down among them he wasn't afraid anymore. These people were angry. Maybe they had a point. It was only fair to hear them out.

"We want you to stop this freak show. You're dragging the disability rights movement into the dark ages." One of the women who appeared to be fully abled spoke. She was the same height as Leon and she moved toward him, focusing on his face like a predator who thinks her prey will bolt if she loses eye contact.

His eyes had adjusted to the darkness of the alley. The man in the wheelchair rolled his head. His mouth hung open with drool glistening on his gray lips. His neck, folded back, protruded thick and muscular from a T-shirt that said in luminous pink lettering: STEPHEN HAWKING ON MARS. His thin arms and legs embraced the mechanical angles of the chair. Mediated through an electronic device, his words rang out in the night. "Not all disabled people can be celebrities. We have to struggle every day to have our most basic needs met."

Kathryn jerked around to face him. "So what? Not all normal people can be celebrities either. Most people have to work at boring jobs and struggle to make ends meet."

Leon had learned early not to go crying to Kathryn. The only pity she'd ever shown was for mistreated animals.

"You're disabled but you can't be famous, you can't get noticed, so you attack us. Is that it?" She advanced on the wheelchair-bound man, who tried to twist away from her. "Are we supposed to go and hide?"

"No," said one of the women, who had a face tinged a bilious green by the light of the exit sign on the side of the building. "We're not attacking you. We're asking you to stop parading around in the media and inviting people to stare at you."

"I want them to stare. Their parents have taught them not to stare. You should encourage people to stare. To ask questions. Then you wouldn't be freaks yourselves, with everyone trying not to look at you."

"Kathryn, stop it! Leave them alone. I'm sorry, everyone." Rhona spread her hands in a conciliatory gesture.

"Leave them alone? They're demonstrating against us! Rhona, don't ask me to be polite to someone who has told me I think my shit doesn't stink."

"Hey, Lady Sheep, or whatever you're called. Can't you see that what you're doing is an insult to these people here?" This was the seemingly able-bodied man muttering from behind the other two.

"And you're their spokesman? Can't they talk for themselves? What's wrong with you anyway? Or are you hanging around these disabled people for some other reason?"

"I'm here with my wife," the man said. "And it's not just us. There's a big group around the front."

"Is that a fur coat your wife's wearing?"

In the cold everyone was bundled up. It was dark except for the exit lights of the building and a few bars of light from narrow windows. But Leon could see she was right: the woman was wearing an expensive fur coat. When she moved, the fine hairs on the coat shimmered like rippling water in sunlight.

"Don't change the subject. We're talking about humans, not animals."

The man saw the hole he had dug for himself only after the words came out. The last word he spoke was clipped, its tail cut off. Kathryn rocked backward and forward on her heels.

"I see." That's all she needed to say.

Rhona was looking around nervously. "Can we go into the light and talk about this?"

A couple of security guards arrived at the end of the alley. Their marching boots sent cans and bottles skittering across the concrete. They headed toward the small crowd with the forward lean and wide-shouldered gait of bulldogs.

"We're not going anywhere with you." This time it was another woman. She wore a hood that shaded her face and a scarf wound tightly against the cold. Her breath jetted in white puffs through the wool of her scarf. "You don't want to listen. You think because you're beautiful that being a freak is a glamorous job."

Rhona circled Leon and Kathryn and Christos, a wolf herding her cubs, before she turned to the demonstrators. "I'm sorry but we have to go. Here's my card. You can contact me if you have something to say. But stay away from my clients."

She led the three out of the alley, threading her way in small steps past the blind man and his dog and between the two wheelchairs. She told the security guards that everything was fine, and they swiveled on their combat boots to escort them out. With Rhona ahead talking on the phone to Yuri, the others followed silently in file, Kathryn, Leon, then Christos, his teeth chattering with the cold. The heating units and exhaust fans venting into the alley gave it a moist and complicated odor in the freezing night.

As they passed the woman with her head covered and her face wrapped in the scarf, Leon heard the hissed words under the hum and clatter of the machinery. So did Kathryn; he could see from the way she stopped dead, then broke into a jog to catch up with Rhona.

You'd understand what it is to be a real freak if someone threw acid in your face.

They never mentioned what they had heard to Rhona, but from that day on Kathryn stopped shouting at people who abused them.

Was it a threat? Or had one of them, perhaps that woman, perhaps another of the bundled-up demonstrators they couldn't see properly in the darkness, been the victim of an acid attack?

Leon imagined being scarred by acid, trying not to flinch when a child pointed out the shiny scarified lumpy mass that was his face. He would hate the Wonders too.

Back home, listening to the recounting of the night's events, Kyle twitched the knot of his tie with his forefinger and thumb as he paced around the room. Rhona's theory was that the leaked photos had sparked the demonstration, that they had broken the spell of the magical Wonders and let loose the envy.

"It couldn't be the *Bared* photos. They're normal tabloid fodder, there was nothing in them that made you out to be superior. They were the opposite of superior. If that's what they were worried about, those disabled people should have applauded."

"Well, it's your job to shut that garbage down anyway. You're the PR guy. Make it stop."

Kyle went back to his pacing. "Don't get this mixed up, Rhona. One thing is publicity, the other is security. I do publicity, period. Being caught up in a protest is a failure of security."

As the man behind the scenes, Kyle rarely traveled with the Wonders. He worked ahead of them, either physically, checking out venues and meeting potential sponsors, or digitally, sowing the seeds of the next story. Even his body language, constantly leaning forward and on the move, read like someone peering into the future, sniffing opportunity. That youthful eager face. When they were all together at Overington, he spent more time talking on the phone than with the people lying on the couches in the room near him. His world, his life, seemed to be one story after another.

Leon had once heard Rhona asking Kyle to spend more time with them.

"Get to know us better. Be part of the family," she said.

"You've got to understand," Kyle had replied, "I do know you, and them, but I can't be their friend. In this job, I have to do things that upset people. One gets a big boost in promotion, the others are jealous. I have to tell them when their performances are crap. A friend can't do that. I have friends. You're my clients. For sure, the strangest clients I'll ever have."

Later that night, Leon thought about what Rhona had told him of her father and the Enchanted Circus. People see glitter and fairy wings, she'd said, but up close the performers have corns and bad teeth. It was the same with him and the other Wonders. Their bodies on the stage were beautiful, extraordinary, dumbfounding, demanding of important philosophical and moral attention. At home, their bodies were painful, constipated, itchy, flaky, brittle, liable to exude pus or blood, weak and easily worn out. The most amazing humans were also the most feeble and vulnerable. Philosophical inquiry meant nothing to a man straining on the toilet.

He supposed he was an exaggerated version of every human. Keeping up appearances in public and collapsing into pathetic debility at home.

20

YOU'RE ADDICTED, ADMIT it. You're in love with it." Kathryn sneered as she tossed insults Leon's way. Christos was out of the country, visiting his grandmother, and Kathryn had no one to joust with, so she had turned on Leon. Minh was working in her office, supervising the installation of a new monitoring unit. If she were here, Kathryn would be kinder to Leon. Minh made everyone around her kinder by paying no attention to meanness until it dissipated into the atmosphere. What appeared to be an attitude of common sense and practicality belied Minh's understanding of what made other people behave the way they did. Leon was sure she knew more about him than he knew himself.

But she was not in the room now, and Kathryn was lashing and sparking like a shorn electricity wire. This temper must have been the result of last night's phone call. Someone had tracked down the private number at Overington, asked for Kathryn, then spilled a savage discharge of venom into her ear. She wouldn't tell anyone what the caller had said.

"I've got used to the attention, that's all." Leon ran his

finger down the ribbed velvet of his chair. "Being stared at doesn't frighten me anymore."

The living room at Overington could have passed as a furniture showroom. Everyone had chosen different styles of furniture to suit their modified body shapes. Rhona, Kyle, Yuri and Minh sat on the original couches and chairs. Leon had ordered a big padded sofa and armchair with cushions that he often found himself absentmindedly clutching over the hole in his chest, whereas Christos had commissioned purpose-built chairs with apertures that supported his lumbar region without touching the ceramic lilies on either side of his spine. Today Kathryn sat on the other side of the room on her favorite chair, a designer vinyl and steel piece, flat and pocked with red cloth upholstery buttons. A frosted glass lamp shade in the shape of a tulip arched over the chair for her reading. But now she wasn't reading, she was tap-tapping the heel of her pink sling-backs against the flat metal support of the chair. The pillar of books on the table beside the chair swayed with each tap.

"I was right about those disabled people, you know. They should invite the idiots to stare. Then the staring would become boring. If everyone was allowed to stare, they wouldn't. They'd have one good look, then forget about it."

Leon wasn't sure. Were he and Kathryn and Christos, the beautiful monsters, making everything worse for the different ones who were not beautiful? The image he had seen once in a news bulletin of an acid-scarred Afghani woman had come to him after the demonstration, and it flashed into his mind now and then, causing him to shudder. Could she bear to be stared at, even glimpsed, by a stranger?

"Stop it!" That's what his mother would say when he was a child. A stern hiss. "Don't stare." "Stop looking." Her hot hand would grab Leon's and ball it into her fist and she would wrench him away. Because staring was the most satisfying pleasure but one of the most taboo. Anything odd, different. Anything too big or too small. Anything broken or too neat. Anything. Lips apart, jaw loose, a fold of frown. His favorite object of intense scrutiny for years was the lady who worked in the local fish and chip shop. He could get away with it when the neighbors were there buying their own fish and chips and his mother was distracted, chatting with them.

Mrs. Mac from the fish-and-chippery on Main Road had a mole below her lip from which sprouted three magnificent thick hairs, two black and one white. One of her bottom front teeth was missing. She swiveled her body around behind the deep counter as if her left side was useless, swinging huge baskets of cooked chips out of the bubbling oil onto the fryer drain and slamming fish around in flour before dipping it into the stainless steel batter bowl crusted with drips of dried batter and flinging it into the fish section of the oil vats. Best of all was her voice, so deep it was deeper than a man's. All wrapped in a big greasy floral apron. To make the experience perfect, at the end of it Leon was handed salty hot chips to eat on the way home.

With his first transplant, surgeons and doctors and nurses never stared at him. He could remember so clearly the day he heard his failing heart would be replaced. In Rosebud, a beach suburb where the sea smell washed through the tea tree and banksia and the long flat highway drove straight through town without an invitation to stop, a young woman, nineteen years old, assistant in a pharmacy and student of hairdressing, tripped on an uneven slab of pavement. She teetered for a moment, arms full of boxes, then fell backward, the cardboard flying up and bouncing lightly off her body. Her buttocks hit the ground first, and she must have shouted or cried out with the pain. Then her head cracked against a jutting curb that pierced the skull. The boxes came to rest around her in a soft sculpture. An artery in her head was damaged. Blood began seeping through the tissue of her brain. By the time the ambulance arrived she was beyond saving. Leon was called. He had a bag already packed, like a woman waiting to give birth, and he raced to the hospital to receive the brawny gift of a dead teenager.

The doctors at the hospital examined him, a different procedure altogether from staring. An examination is an attempt to interrogate the body. It is detached from the person who is being examined. "Look at this," the surgeon would say, pointing out the puckered skin around Leon's stitched-up incision to his interns. "See the ooze here? You may think it indicates a rupture of the . . ." And the interns would gather in close and peer at the point of interest, nodding, making notes, offering interpretations. Behind them hovered the overworked nurses, impatient to do their jobs and move on to the next patient.

The stare is a different thing altogether. Leon had come to think of the stare as admiration. Maybe Kathryn was right. A child uses the stare as a tool of curiosity and wonder. The grotesque is wonderful. The malformed is wonderful, the unexpected is wonderful and so is the beautiful. There is far less judgment in the unguarded stare of a child than the hush-ups of their adult companions.

He told Kathryn how, at a private dinner, a child who was waiting in the corridor for her waitress mother to finish work had asked him if he was a robot. That made him laugh. "Is your brain made of metal too?" she asked. She was five, the age when the questions pour out of a child like milk out of a jug. "Do you eat nails? Why did they put it in that way? Do you have feelings?"

"Oh yes," Leon answered her. "I have so many feelings that sometimes I think I'll burst."

"Me too," she replied gravely. She touched his hand and

looked up at his face with serious eyes. Eyes that didn't waver. Eyes that never flickered once to the hole in his chest.

When Susan and Howard were working on him in that machine-packed laboratory theater, preparing him to receive the third heart, he felt comforted by their stares. They observed him constantly—examining him, scrutinizing him, checking with a glance whenever he coughed or groaned. His body was made solid by the way they created him with their gaze. Exhausted and feverish and weak and sometimes wishing he was dead, he could be buoyed by an appraisal from Susan, an inspection by Howard. He did sometimes call himself Frankensteins' monster—they were the Doctors Frankenstein who were stitching him together. But at the same time, they loved his body. They looked into him, reached into him, broke him and cut parts out of him, mended him as best they could. And all the time they kept their eyes on him and at the end, he was the wondrous monster they had hoped to create. Then finally they could look again at each other.

Eight months before, when Leon had his first sessions of standing onstage, whether the stage was someone's art-deco-inspired living room or the private meeting room of an international hotel decked out in modular red armless chairs and smoky glass-topped tables, the experience was agony. He twisted under the pinning gaze of the paying audience. He squirmed. He was wrong for the celebrity life; he would be better off hiding himself inside a normal life. He could put on an undershirt and a shirt and no one would know. He could be the same as everyone else.

But he had learned. Over time, a part of him had eased into the role as the object of fascination, even though he was reluctant to admit that to Kathryn. He had come to understand that if he stayed silent and let his body speak for him, he remained calm. Before too long it was only when he failed to cause the shock, when someone's gaze slid away too fast, that he became apprehensive, concerned he was doing something wrong. To appear as the exhibit was not difficult: he could stand still while people peered at his heart, sighed, murmured their consternation. He revealed nothing of his real self to these strangers. But being himself in a crowd of strangers was harder than it had ever been. He wasn't even sure what "himself" might be.

Did he really enjoy being the spectacle, as Kathryn accused? Did it matter anymore? He was something new again, and not only in his body. Onstage he wasn't Leon, a man living his life. He was Clockwork Man, living a superlife to give other people the satisfaction of encountering a wonder of the world.

They gazed at his body, at the horror of it. They were silenced too, by its glory. Sometimes it seemed they were about to fall to their knees.

21

"I THINK THIS IS it." Minh held out the screen for Leon to see. He placed his hand on her arm to steady it so that he could read the message.

"I don't know why I'm so nervous," she said with a laugh. "She's your surgeon, not mine."

All the messages and e-mails had been sent under Minh's name. The contact note gave the dates Leon had been under the care of a Dr. Susan Nowinski whom Dr. Minh Trang was attempting to find. Leon would know it was the real Susan if she could explain where his surgery had taken place. Apologies and sympathy notes and attacks from people who believed they were being scammed had flowed in.

It's not me, but wishing you luck in your search.

Hope you find her.

Keep at it. She's out there somewhere.

I know this is an attempt to steal my identity. Rot in hell, you scumbag.

They had finished with Australia and moved on to America,

first mapping out regions, tracing the state and county lines in thick black pen on a large map stuck to the wall, turning the USA into a jigsaw of possibility. The washed-out greens and yellows of the map, the resistance of the wall behind when Leon pressed a finger to a city gave the task a materiality missing from their electronic work.

The reply on Minh's screen said, *Dr. Trang, please pass along this message. Dear Leon, how lovely it would be to see you. I treated you at a university in Melbourne, Australia. I have information to give you. Please send me your contact details.*

Leon dropped his hands between his knees and let his head fall forward. "It's not specific enough and Susan would never say *how lovely*. It's another phishing reply. I hate that there are so many people who want to rip you off." His hair had been styled in a 1920s cut with a part on the side and the hair slicked up and across. The cut might have looked good for the fans but whenever he bent over as he just had, hair fell down in a thick greasy flop over his eyes. He groaned, pushed it back into place and wiped his gelled hand on his trousers. "I'll never find her. The Americas will take years and years to work through."

Minh used her feet to push her office chair away from the desk. It rolled backward and sideways until she was facing Leon.

"I think it's worth going on. We'll find her eventually." She ran her fingers through her hair and stretched her hands to the ceiling as she yawned.

"If I last that long," he said.

Again she used her feet to steer the chair, this time a little closer so that her knees lined up opposite Leon's. "Sometimes you talk about yourself as if you are a machine, Leon. *If I last that long.* Washing machines last. Phones last. Part of staying healthy is believing that you are."

PADDY O'REILLY

In her warm spicy presence, aware of her feet poised on the toes ready to push her off into another direction, Leon felt insubstantial, a mantle of inconsequential flesh grown around the clockwork heart.

"I am a machine." He shrugged. "There's no use pretending."

"We are all machines in a way. But we are all more too. Especially you, Leon. You take care to know people. Every day, I see you listen when someone talks to you, really listen, and then think and then, only then, do you speak. You allow people to be." She pushed off again, rolling to the desk, where she caught the edge with her fingers and steadied herself. She was blushing. "Sorry. I didn't mean to . . ."

This was the Leon she saw? His breath was coming fast. No one had ever said such a thing to him. It seemed that no one had ever cared enough until that moment to want to know him.

"Anyway, none of us know how long we will live. We doctors are more sure of that than anyone. You'd think we'd make more of our lives, take more chances."

"Aha, I suspected I'd find you two squirrelled away in here." Rhona pushed open the door to the study and maneuvered her hips through the opening. The study was a repurposed dressing room fitted with a desk, two chairs and a small bookcase. The room was so compact that Rhona's round presence joining Leon and Minh filled it to capacity. "What are you up to anyway, hmm? I've seen you slipping away to this cubbyhole."

Minh waved her hand as if to brush away any possibility of impropriety. "Research, Rhona. You know how Leon loves his research."

"Research about?" She put her hands on her hips and raised her eyebrows.

"About metal hearts," Leon lied quickly.

In the small room Rhona lifted her head as if she had caught

— 142 —

the moment of surprise, the imperceptible shift in understanding between Leon and Minh.

"Really? Is that right, Leon? And what have you found out?"

He was silent. He could have been at school, suffering the accusing glare of the teacher, crushing the offending note in a closed fist under the desk.

"Well?"

Beside him, Minh glowed pink, a flushing rose in the bland beige cupboard room.

"All right. I'm trying to track down Susan, the surgeon who, you know, put in my heart." He had never been able to face down a direct question.

"And you've roped this poor girl into it too?" Rhona grasped the back of Minh's chair and tugged it toward her. The rolling chair jerked along the carpeted floor until Minh staggered to her feet. "Minh, go back to your apartment. Leon, you should be ashamed. You shouldn't have asked her to do this."

"He didn't. I offered!"

"I don't care. Please leave. I need to have a few words with Leon."

Once Minh had left the room, Rhona sat heavily in the chair she had vacated.

"Why would you do this, Leon? When you told me Susan expressly asked you not to look for her?"

"But, Rhona, things have changed. How could she know I would end up like this, a Wonder?"

"I see the celebrity bubble has already blanked you out, hon. That didn't take long. Sure, when she last saw you this doctor might not have known what would happen, but you'd have to be completely off the grid not to have heard about the Wonders these days. She could contact you in a second, Leon. Ever considered why she hasn't?"

"Because she doesn't understand, that's what I think. She was afraid she and Howard would be prosecuted. She still might be afraid of being prosecuted herself. But it won't happen. The Wonders are too public, too visible. You said to me once, way back, Rhona, that you reach a point in fame where the only things that can really hurt you are yourself and the people you love. That fame is power and it takes care of the rest. Remember?"

"Did you hear me, Leon? She knows where you are. If she wanted to contact you she would. Contacting you doesn't mean the police would come knocking at her door. If she wanted a simple meeting she would have called. Now let it go. Leave the poor woman alone."

Rhona scanned the screen before switching the tablet off and dropping it on the desk. Leon didn't care. Everything was backed up. He would delete the database from this device and install it on his private computer in his apartment.

"Are we agreed?" She stood and faced him, looking down, hands on hips, cowgirl shirt fringe swinging from her bustline. In this nondescript office cum wardrobe she looked even more anachronistic than usual.

"Okay."

"Good. You may well be the only one in this damn troupe who listens to me, Leon. I'm telling you now, I appreciate it, honey. I only do things for your own good."

"Yes, I know."

"So you're done with it?"

"Yes, I'm done with it."

He was a poor liar, but Rhona had already started reading a message on her phone.

"I'll tell Minh," she said over her shoulder on her way out of the study. "She should get back to her art."

— 144 —

He wouldn't bring Minh into it again. It would be unfair to ask her to lie to Rhona. But it was an affront to his nature to give up. During these last months he had taken pleasure in the soothing repetition of the search tasks, the slow accretion of data, the expansion of his reach across continents in his search for one woman. Locating Susan did not mean he had to contact her. He would change his methodology, see how he felt once he had tracked her down. The work would still be satisfying, even if the surprise exhilaration of working with Minh had been taken away.

22

TWO WEEKS LATER, the night after a show at the New Mexico ranch of a man who had made his fortune from removable car bumper stickers, Rhona suggested they book a floor of the local Holiday Inn and pass a day or two in the clean dry air.

"We've been spending too much time in planes and hotels and stuffy rooms. Tomorrow we could go out. A guided tour, or a hike."

Christos folded his arms and stared out through the window. "I do not hike. I spent my youth traipsing over the hills of a Greek island fetching this and that, taking messages, doing chores. Now I prefer to take my exercise in the gymnasium."

"You especially, Christos, need some air. When you saw those trash media shots of yourself, I thought you were going to faint. You don't need a gym. You need to get out there and stride through nature. Get some perspective."

"Those filthy photographs made me sick, that is why I almost fainted. What kind of animal hides in a changing room? Spies on another human being like that? I'm not going outside where the perverts can photograph whatever they want of me!"

The footage of Christos had shown him trying on clothes in the spacious changing booth of an upmarket store in LA. Against a backdrop of silk hangings and mirrors on three walls, he preened in front of each mirror, trying different stances, looking over his shoulder and patting his own buttocks, running his fingers down the ridged muscles on his belly and obviously admiring himself. Leon and the others had laughed uncontrollably. Christos was mortified.

"Fine, a tour, then. In a car. You never have to leave the vehicle if you don't want to. Who wants to go?"

Kathryn tapped the side of her chair. "As long as we don't have fifteen photographers chasing us. I swear to you, Rhona, if one of those filthy paparazzi gets near me again I'll deck him."

"Darling, I won't tell the tour company who we are. You dress up in your long shirt and pants and hat. We'll be fine. It'll be fun."

Rhona booked the tour under the name of one of her many mysterious businesses, but the next day Christos and Kathryn both changed their minds. Kathryn was exhausted and Minh had told her to rest. Kyle had to fly to Japan to prepare for the next show. Yuri wouldn't come if Christos didn't come, and so it was Rhona, Leon and Minh waiting in the hotel lobby for the guide. Minh carried the bag with sketchbook and pencils and crayons and charcoal sticks that she hauled around whenever she took a trip. She had wanted to come on this trip especially so she could do some drawing, and she'd already been out on her own the day before.

When the guide turned up, tall and tanned in shorts and a short-sleeved shirt, Minh took on a special glow. From that moment on the guide addressed all his conversation in her direction.

"I think Minh's behaving a bit . . ." Leon fell in next to Rhona, behind Minh and the guide who was leading them to the minibus. "You know, a bit . . ."

"Yes, Leon?" Rhona was using her patient voice.

"Well, do you think my doctor should be flirting with some tourist guide?"

"So she's only your doctor now. Didn't I hire her as the doctor for all the Wonders?"

Minh slid into the passenger seat beside the tour guide. Since she had stopped working on the Susan search, Leon had only encountered her at meals and for his weekly checkup. He had relapsed into his usual strained formality.

Leon ignored Rhona and climbed into the rear of the van. He felt the muscles around his heart twinge and tighten as they did sometimes when he was overtired or anxious.

"I'm feeling a bit odd. I might need Minh to examine me before we start."

"Leon, will you take a good look at yourself? No wonder you're thirty-two and never married. Sheesh."

He wanted to put on a haughty offended tone and ask Rhona what she meant by that, but his dignity prevented him.

Following Rhona's instructions, the guide took a gentle route along the road of the mesa plain. Leon's chest muscles were performing an orchestral overture, but it had no relation to the movement of the car. He couldn't call out to Minh—that would attract the scorn of Rhona. When he placed his hand on the unbroken part of the chest, as Minh had taught him to do, he could feel very faintly the reassuring thrum of the mechanisms engaging and shunting inside the heart.

"I think I'm stressed. Last night's gig went on a long time."

"It went exactly as long as it was supposed to, Leon. You really don't know what's going on, do you, hon?"

"I don't think it's anything to do with my heart. Maybe some kind of indigestion."

A laugh streamed out of her. She shook her head and looked away and kept laughing. Her cowgirl-shirt fringe danced with her laughter. Outside the window the plain stretched away in a flat blanket hooked with sprays of grass and a few bushes.

"If it was my heart, I think I'd know." Leon was trying to reassure her, but Rhona laughed even louder. In fact, she couldn't stop. She cackled away, bent over in her seat, gasping and simmering down to "oh, oh" noises before setting herself off again.

"We'll be reaching the edge of the mesa plain soon," the tour guide called back. "You okay, lady?"

Rhona lifted her head. Her eyes were red from laughter, and she was sniffling. She pulled a tissue from her handbag and blew into it. "Oh yes. Oh hell, this is a funny, funny day."

She was making Leon cross. He didn't think it was funny that he felt physically ill.

"Rhona? Is something wrong?"

So now Minh was paying some attention. Rhona has a laughing fit and that's worth a doctor's attention, but not Leon, one of the people she was hired to look after.

"Don't start me up again." Rhona sighed. Wiped her eyes with her damp tissue. "Let's just get to this sightseeing place."

"Yep, we're there already." The guide eased the car to a stop, then sprang out of his seat to race around to Minh's door and open it for her.

Rhona and Leon managed to battle their own way out of the rear section of the van. Rhona passed Leon a bottle of water, and together they walked to the edge of the mesa, a wide plain sitting thirty feet above the surrounding land. Minh and the guide stood gazing into the distance.

"So this is what 'mesa' means." Minh lifted her hand to shade her eyes. The lower plain stretched out in a tufted sweep of grass and scrub. An occasional scraggly tree broke the monotony.

"Nothing much could survive out there, right?" the guide said.

Rhona and Leon might as well have not been there. The guide pointed across Minh to the west. Leon watched in horror. It seemed to him that the guide's elbow might be brushing against Minh's breast. He couldn't understand why she didn't flinch.

"Snakes, lizards, even jackrabbits live here. Plenty of bugs too, so watch out for the little stingers."

"Leon." Rhona took his elbow in her hand. "Leon, would you like to walk a little with me?"

"No thanks, Rhona. I think we should stay with the guide." And with Minh, who, after all, was his doctor and should, as an employee, be keeping an eye on him. Under the disconcerting heat of the sun, sweat began to squeeze through his pores. The capillaries near the surface of his skin would be dilating to pull the blood away from his core to cool.

Mapping the mechanics of physical and osmotic exchanges always calmed him. When he was in the basement with Susan and Howard he used to study their texts. The orderliness of the chemical processes, the gaseous exchanges, the Newtonian motion of the levers that were his limbs and the mechanical advantage of multiplied effort, settled hysteria into reason for him. When his mind was beginning to race and trip and stumble with panic, as it had so many times during the ordeal of having his body remodeled for the heart, he had trained it to focus on analyzing the body's response until everything slowed—knowledge as a ballast.

"Leon, please escort me." Rhona sometimes put on the

Southern-belle lady thing. It didn't suit her cowgirl outfits and brash manner at all, but somehow she pulled it off. Her hand hung in the air waiting for an arm, which Leon was obliged to provide.

"Where do you want to walk?" he asked. He glanced over his shoulder. It seemed that the guide, even taller from a distance and with quite the movie-star rugged looks, was leading Minh in the other direction. "What about we head for that sticking-up rock over there?" Leon indicated the rock that could be seen in the distance beyond Minh.

"No, Leon. We need to walk away from there."

"Why?" he asked, still craning his neck to see where Minh and guide man were going. Why wasn't Minh sitting on her heels and sketching as she usually did when she saw something striking or unusual?

"Leon!"

"What, Rhona?"

Her hand, which was supposed to be resting on Leon's arm as he led her in a constitutional ramble, clenched his forearm until he winced in pain.

"Come with me and listen for a minute."

They walked in the opposite direction from Minh and the guide, striking out across the plain. He could feel burrs catching in his socks. The top of his head began to sting where only a few days ago he had noticed in the mirror a lighter patch, as if his hair might be thinning there. He'd rushed to the common room, where Christos and Yuri were playing a board game while the news droned in the background. "Can you see my head?" he'd demanded, bending from the waist to give them the best possible view of his crown. "Yes, I can see your head," Christos had answered. "Is this some kind of riddle?"

"Leon, look at the horizon." Rhona released his arm.

He immediately reached up to finger his burning crown. His finger almost sizzled. He lifted his cool water bottle and rolled it across the top of his head.

"I think I need to go to the van and get a hat, Rhona."

"You will not get cancer in five minutes. Stop and smell the mesa for a moment, Leon."

Leon did understand what she was saying. Good health involves a sound and collected mind, and today something was throwing him off balance. He passed her the water. He closed his eyes, folded his hands across the thinning spot on his head to protect it and took a long slow breath of the clear dry air. He pictured the hemoglobin picking up oxygen molecules in the lungs the way a train picks up passengers from a crowded station, distributing them around the body to fuel the work.

He envisioned miles and miles of scrubby bush. A dead flat horizon, which the guide had said dropped away at the edge of the mesa. Blue distant sky. Two planes intersecting at a line where white-blue met pale washed-out yellow. No animals, no color, no life. Not even the vibrant red sand of the Australian desert. Gripping his burning head, he wished he hadn't come.

"Listen to this." Rhona pulled a brochure from her handbag. "'The vegetation of this plain is dominated by sand sagebrush, Mormon tea, squawbush and yuccas.' Aren't they beautiful names, Leon? Mormon tea. I wonder if the Mormons really made tea from it. Squawbush."

"Mm."

Rhona jabbed him in the thigh. "Look, Leon."

He opened his eyes. The landscape bloomed before him. Lavender streaks and purple tufts and even violet hues in the shade of sage green.

"Is that an animal down there?"

"Yes, darling, I think it is. Good boy. Keep looking."

Above the vast plain a brown-and-white kite wheeled with the air currents, silent, watching, while a flicker at Leon's feet was a tiny lizard slipping between stones. In the distance a few large-bottomed gray birds waddled through the sparse vegetation.

"It's beautiful, Rhona. You're right."

To his amazement she took his hand and held it between her two dry palms.

"When you stop and allow yourself to see, Leon . . ."

"Yes?"

"I'm starting to sound like a greeting card but, Leon, you have to look quite hard to see what's in front of you."

"I see what you mean, Rhona." He didn't, exactly.

"You always seemed so self-aware, Leon. Always examining yourself, your thoughts. I guess we all have our blind spots."

He was still standing beside Rhona and staring in a trance at the tableau of muted color laid out before them when Minh and the guide came up behind.

"Hey, isn't this stunning?" Minh's voice was more animated than Leon had ever heard it. "I need one of Kathryn's rehabilitated words to describe it. Sumptuous. Sumptuous and rich and so colorful. If you stand here long enough, you get new eyes. I wish I'd brought my camera. I need to paint this."

He wasn't sure what was happening. Minh's voice, a stream of liquid gold, slid inside him. The hole in his chest closed over and his heart heaved as if it was a flesh-and-blood organ newly steeped in life-giving fluid.

Rhona seemed to know. She rubbed her hand in the small of his back. She applied enough pressure to make him turn around. Minh looked at his face and she knew too. She flushed and blinked and laughed all at once. And then Leon understood.

The next night Leon and Minh were standing on the hotel balcony overlooking the plain. They watched as a last flare of light fingered the sky. The sun sank below the horizon, and after a few moments of deep darkness, silver stars began to bloom.

Leon was thick with panic, his whole body a twisted tongue. Would she refuse him? Did she see him as the useless disabled man without a heart that she was hired to nursemaid? When he tipped the champagne glass to his mouth, a spill dribbled down his chin and onto his gray shirt. It was dark. He pretended nothing had happened.

"I haven't been . . . you know, with a woman, since I first became ill . . ." He couldn't say it.

"Are you talking about sex? It won't hurt you, Leon. A little challenging to the heart, but nothing you can't handle." Brusque, clear, efficient. So she wasn't interested. He was certain now. She was his doctor, simple as that. Answering him as if he'd asked her advice on a routine medical matter.

He balanced his champagne glass on the balcony rail, then watched with alarm as it tipped and fell. For a while there was no sound.

"Oh god."

The glass broke into a faint tinkle below. Minh stretched over the balcony rail to look. They were on the twenty-seventh floor. Afraid she would fall, Leon clutched at her. He grasped a fold of her silky dress, feeling the ripple of her warm skin underneath. When she pulled back from the edge, she stumbled against him.

Her hair lay along his throat. Her bare shoulder blade pressed into his chest. He only had to move his hand inches to reach around her waist and press his palm and splayed fingers across her flat belly. She was firm and warm and solid and whole.

If it were possible, his clunky metal heart would have been

hammering around the walls of his cavity in terror and passion. Instead, his fingers and nose prickled with the adrenaline surge. His stomach hollowed into a skin drum. Knees clenched, jaw clenched, buttocks clenched.

He whispered into the screen of her hair, behind her ear, "I love you," and she pressed into him and turned her face to be kissed.

23

THEY'D HARDLY BEEN back at Overington from New Mexico twenty-four hours before Rhona called a meeting to discuss security.

The Wonders Incorporated was the global sensation Rhona had planned. A Russian engineering society was dedicated to replicating Leon's heart. Christos had inspired a school of techno-body art. Artists around the world were transplanting circuits, wheels, levers, switches and other assorted mechanical devices onto and into different parts of their bodies. The Wonders were besieged by messages from fans across the globe.

Kathryn received so much mail and so many electronic communications that a woman came twice a week to assist in sorting through them. The old saying could have been made for her. Men wanted Kathryn; women wanted to be her. Or hated her. If Leon and Christos were wonders of the body, Kathryn was a wonder of the consciousness. She was awesome, mythic, fantastical.

Her correspondence assistant sent out signed black-and-white photographs in reply to many of the messages. These retro souvenirs had regained popularity after the fashion of digital photos and electronic frames flickering relentlessly on people's mantelpieces. The fans liked to hold something original in their hands, something that couldn't be downloaded off any old website or printed at home, something with the imprint of a handwritten signature that could be passed around and discussed and held up close to the face to examine. Once a young woman in jeans and a grubby tracksuit top waved one of the publicity shots as the Wonders walked the red carpet to a film premiere.

"I sleep with this, Lady," she called out. "I love you." She thrust out the battered photograph, which had creased and wrinkled like old skin.

"Lady" was what everyone called Kathryn by now. Sometimes "Lady Kathryn," as if she had become royalty. The "Lamb" part of the moniker had been dropped. Leon's new nickname, originally used in an ad for heart-shaped chocolate with a printed pattern imitating the mechanical workings of his own heart, wrapped in silver foil and promoted heavily before Valentine's Day, was Valentino. The name pleased him. It was the opposite of Clockwork Man—alive and passionate. And Christos had become Angel. They were each familiar enough to the world to be known by a single name.

If a message to Kathryn seemed threatening or contained obscene material, and many were and did, the assistant forwarded two copies: one to Hap, the security chief, who ran it through his own threat-assessment program, and the second copy to the police.

"I've dealt with thousands of these letters in my time," Hap said, taking the latest wad of printouts from Rhona. "We analyze them, sort them into threat levels. I'm not saying it doesn't happen, but statistically it's rare for the ones who keep sending letters or trying to get in contact to actually attempt anything violent. We call them the howlers. The other ones, the hunters, they're the types we have to be wary of, because you don't see them until they're on you."

Hap caught sight of the look on Leon's face. "It seems frightening at first, but you'll get used to it. Celebrity attracts stalkers. You learn to get on with it and not even notice them."

"I remember the days when film stars lived on normal streets," Rhona said, sighing. She fingered the fringe of her shirt, then smoothed the leather strips into a neat row as she pondered. "Where the hell do all these lunatics come from?"

"I think you're remembering days that never happened, ma'am. Fame has always paid a high price." Hap folded the sheaf of papers into a satchel on the table beside him.

Some of the paper letters were handwritten in thick black jagged pen on pieces of writing paper covered in flowers and curly lime tendrils, as if the writer had stolen the precious notepaper of a young teenage girl or found it in a wardrobe in the family home under layers of old tennis rackets and cracked leather belts and shoe boxes of children's treasures. There were pages from printed books with tiny spiky handwriting filling the margins. There were crude animations made on free software, videos with the Wonders' faces clumsily superimposed on the actors, music tributes recorded in fans' bedrooms, photos of guns and other weapons.

Some missives were simply the ravings of mad people and their purpose could not be ascertained. Some were warm and funny. Proposals of marriage abounded, especially for Kathryn and often from men whose skills in charm and romance demonstrated why they were single themselves. Leon had received plenty of proposals himself, several of which, he remarked as he sorted through the pile one night in the common room, were quite tempting. To which Rhona pointed out that the photos more often than not belonged to someone other than the person writing the letter.

Kathryn caused the greatest upwelling of anger. Early on, one obscure Christian sect had spent considerable amounts of money promoting the idea that she was an incarnation of Baphomet, a half goat who would appear on earth to herald the imminent arrival of Satan. The barrage of ads and billboards and media interviews with church officials was eventually silenced by a lawsuit.

From the most recent surge of threats, the police had expressed serious concern about a particular letter addressed to Kathryn. They had classed it as a top-level alert. They recommended extreme measures. They had already issued an arrest warrant for the letter writer, whom they believed, from similarities in the cases, to have been involved in another episode of celebrity stalking that had escalated to a violent attack. Hap stood at the side of the room, shaking his head.

"I'll say it again, ma'am, I do not think this particular letter is cause for alarm. This guy has been on my radar for months already. He's crazy, sure, he's obsessed, sure, but is he violent? I don't think so. I'm convinced this is not the guy who attacked the actress. I've been doing this work for twelve years. They have the wrong guy."

"I know you say that, Hap, but can we take the chance?" Rhona crossed her short legs and the star-shaped spurs she was wearing that day jingled with inappropriate cheeriness. "It might be time for us to finish. Today the police say there is another credible threat against Kathryn. Tomorrow it could be Christos or Leon. Your safety is worth far more than money. Should we shut up shop?"

Leon didn't know what to think. Surely Hap knew what he was doing? Minh, sitting beside Kathryn on the wine-colored vinyl couch, stared at her hands in her lap. She had kissed him for an hour the night before, at the hotel in the desert. He could still taste her warm mouth, tart and sweet at the same time, and feel the heat of her bare skin under his hand. They had planned dinner for two in her cottage tomorrow night. Vidonia promised something succulent and light and irresistible delivered on a tray with roses and champagne. It could be the night that he dared make love to her. If this was all about to end, she might pull away.

As he relived the sensation of her lips moving across his cheek, his throat and then back to his mouth, Minh spoke. "I know it isn't up to me, but shouldn't safety come first? The shows are only about money. Safety versus money, really? Isn't it obvious?"

"But Hap looks after us! He says we're okay." Leon had to convince everyone to stay, if only to have his arms around Minh again.

Christos shrugged. "No matter what you all decide, I will continue my work anyway," he said. "Although I suppose I would have to perform on my own. I haven't acquired enough capital to finance my next project."

"No," Kathryn said. She rose from the low couch, pulling her cape tightly around her body. "I won't be bullied by some nutter with a Sharpie pen and bad spelling." She stamped her foot so the slipper with its fluffy purple pompom and kitten heel rapped like a silver hammer on the parquet floor. "No, no, no. I'm not afraid of some pathetic dickless wonder who scurries around in the dark writing grubby letters." She laughed before flapping her cape like bat wings and putting on a breathy movie-trailer voice. "The Wonders meet the Dickless Wonder— our archenemy, the Moriarty to our Holmes, the Riddler to our Batman."

Rhona smiled, looking away to hide it from Kathryn. "We do need to take this seriously, darling."

Leon went back to his apartment after the decision and celebrated with a small glass of Scotch. His relief wasn't only because he had a date the next night with Minh. He had always wondered why wealthy rock musicians kept playing the same old tunes to audiences around the world year after year, why elderly revered actors made more bad films, why businessmen started up new enterprises when their other companies were already spectacularly successful. Now he was starting to experience the real effect of fame. It was a drug. It made you want more. When the clapping and the cheering had faded, you began to look forward to the next time people stared or screamed in awe. Soon you longed for it. It made you feel alive, wanted, charged with power. Without the screaming fans, the overawed juniors, you had to center yourself, and that was much harder. Celebrity and success, he was discovering, were ferociously addictive.

A week later the lunatic letter writer was in custody and charged with stalking. The Wonders were unstoppable. They would go on: with more security, with more restrictions, with more frequent looks over their shoulders. Each performer had a similar goal—enough money to build a new life, either to disappear into or, in Christos's case, to burst out of. They would continue to expose themselves in order to be able to hide away.

24

FASHIONED BY RHONA as the male heartthrob of the Wonders, Christos posed for photographs with jeans pulled low and his thick hair flopping sexily across one eye. One shoot, which he had complained about for weeks afterward, involved him kneeling above a prostrate woman in a scanty lingerie arrangement, with his wings extended and his head dropped as if he was about to kiss her throat. "Or rip it out," he said when he saw the shot. That was an ad for one of the first major merchandise launches, the Seraphiel scent for men. Since then Kathryn had released a range of lanolin skin creams, Leon was the poster boy for a Swiss watch company and they were all models for the Wonders action figures. Leon's doll had a windup ticking heart. Kathryn's was clothed in real wool. Christos's figure had two extra moving limbs. Plus electronic games, posters, storybooks, clothing, trading cards, photos, key rings, coffee mugs.

The catalog of merchandise was twelve pages long. A collectable set of figures hand-produced in a limited edition of ten thousand could be had for a mere thousand dollars each.

A range of tiny designer stilettos gave Kathryn's action figure "a whole new look" as she rode in a Lady Convertible or sat in the Lady Suite with the Lady Cocktail Set. Children could construct an oversized working metal heart to learn about cogs, wheels, valves and pumps using the Valentino Mechanics Kit. Naturally it was not a replica of Leon's heart, whose inner workings were still unexplored, but a clockwork machine that ticked and pumped. Christos's pages in the catalog included a soldering iron and metal rods to make facsimile wings.

Kathryn had said they should market a toy art gallery for Christos. "All the kiddies can learn to curate."

Even Christos laughed.

They were easier with each other these days. Their family-style petty spats and fireworks flared and faded, and Leon had gained enough confidence to ask Christos why he used his body for art.

"Kathryn and I had no choice. We would have died without medical intervention. But sometimes the agony of what I went through during my recovery was so dreadful that I wished I could die. It must have felt the same for you. Why would you choose pain like that?"

"Leon," Christos said in a voice that belonged in a theater, "the body as our beast of burden is over. The body is an outdated piece of flesh that in its original form inhibits our true expression as human beings, as artists. All human beings can be artists. Every child is an artist. The trouble is that we lose the ability to imagine and create when we are schooled and when we are punished for being children.

"But the body. The body should be the vehicle for the creativity. The mind-body-mind is a canvas for our tattoos, our ornaments, our piercings, our scars, our implants, our replants, our transplants. What is the point of paper and canvas when we have skin, when we have flesh, when we have a form of self-expression that we carry around as a part of our identity, wedded mindbody, the slippery blood and tissue that holds our consciousness intact? You yourself must understand, Leon, with that heart of yours, that the flow of blood to the extremities of the body must not be taken for granted. The flow of blood to the outer reaches of the body is the only art that has meaning."

He told Leon how his first work out of art school used the body as a surface for the application of art. An experiment in the body as a palimpsest of the artist's work. Miniature replicas of famous European and Asian paintings were stenciled on his skin in semipermanent ink that would fade as his body aged.

"So the works gained a mortality that is usually denied art," he explained, "which museums and collectors love to preserve and restore and hide away in grand buildings so that it will not be lost to us. But, Leon, mortality is what makes humans great. Knowing that we will come to an end gives passion, urgency, horror to our desires and drives. So I made mortal art on my mortal body, and we mapped the disintegration, the degradation of the art together with the physical aging of my body over one year. The shedding of skin, nails and hair growing and coarsening, wiry wrinkles etching themselves into the body's contours. With each documentation, the stenciled art had faded and drifted in minute measures across the skin like a tectonic plate. Until one day the images could no longer be identified. And further, further down the track, all that remained were faint blooms of color. That piece, I called *Palliative Art Care*."

After Leon's first heart transplant failed, his mother's idea of palliative care had been to serve up the dishes he had loved as a child. One morning, she even surprised him with a bowl of crackling Coco Pops in chocolate milk.

What Christos was doing with the wings he still called art,

but when sales of his Seraphiel scent passed five million units, he stopped complaining about being exploited for money and started asking whether it was fair that profits from his scent should be shared among everyone. Was it not his image that sold the product? And his trade name? His sex appeal?

"And didn't I make up your name? And didn't I commission the perfume company and didn't I set up the marketing campaign and, actually, Mr. Seraphiel, didn't I have the goddamn idea in the first place?"

Leon settled back into the couch to enjoy Rhona sending off sparks.

"So if you want me to deduct my fees for all of that, plus the massive penalties for breaking your contract, and then hand over the remaining profits to you, sure. And the others and I will share our ninety-two percent of the great fat trunk of money we're making and you can go fuck yourself. Sound okay, Christos?"

He sniffed and wobbled his head as if he couldn't decide whether to walk off in a huff or stand up to her. After a few seconds he stalked, head held high, out of the room.

That evening he claimed to be too exhausted to perform at the Board of Plastic Surgeons' dinner. Yuri carried out his stage-managing duties with his head bowed, as though he was to blame for Christos's absence. Rhona breathed through her nose all night, short sharp out-breaths punctuated by long loud intakes.

Back at Overington the day after the show Leon and Minh felt the shouting through the walls. Christos's deep voice vibrated through the plaster and timber, followed by Rhona's nasal delivery cutting a track through the air. The following morning, Christos was back on the team, back sharing the income, back doing exactly the same job as before, feigning nonchalance but snapping at Yuri for any tiny misstep.

Minh lay in bed the next night and rested her hand on Leon's arm. She told him that listening to Christos, a man she had respected for his difficult art and his dedication to it, try to justify why he deserved more money than the others had made her ashamed. She had been aware of the maid waiting behind the doorway to clear the plates, Vidonia the cook sweating over the massive stove, after which she would drive home to kiss her kids good night before turning up again at lunchtime the next day. Minh's parents still kept their calls to her short—habit after a lifetime of economy on phone bills and heating and food and everything else so that their children could go to college and enter the adult world buttressed by financial and social capital.

Suddenly Minh sat up. "Can I do something peculiar?" she said softly in the darkness of the bedroom.

A multitude of possibilities occurred to him in a second. "What?"

"Maybe it's silly," she said, "but I've wanted to do it since I first met you."

"Okay." Leon found himself holding his breath. Since they had gotten together it had all seemed so perfect, too perfect perhaps. Was she going to turn out to have some kinky sexual peccadillo?

"Take off your vest."

He pushed himself up in bed with his elbows, unzipped the tight vinyl-ribbed sleeping vest that kept his heart contained in the night and slipped it off. Felt the familiar trace of cool air passing through his cavity.

Leon reached across and let his hand rest on Minh's back as she lowered her face to his chest. The vertebrae in her spine rose like an arching cat under his fingers. He felt her hair brush his shoulder, then her cheek, warm, pressing against the center of his chest beside the cavity inside which his heart whirred, faint but audible in the quiet of the dark bedroom. His cock stirred, and he moved his hand to cup her breast.

"I love you, Leon." Minh's whisper entered the cavity where Leon's heart rested. Her warm breath tickled the edges of the cavity, and he shivered with pleasure.

"I love you, Leon, your mind and your body and even this metal heart inside you, but I don't love your money. When we're done with this, if we're still together, I'd like to give some of it away. And I want to work for the rest of my life, and make art. I don't ever want to behave as if money gives us value."

She straightened up, and her mouth found his in the darkness. Their lips held together for a moment before pulling apart.

"Whatever you want." He clasped her closer and she swung her leg over until she was astride him. He bent his head to her breasts, but Minh took his chin in her hand and lifted his face. In the darkness her pale face hovered glowing above him.

25

THROUGH THE TALL windows of Overington, Leon had watched the passage of a year's seasons: trees shimmering with budding leaves in the raw air of spring, flowers splashed across summer beds, the whole garden bowing to autumn winds, and the bare white limbs of winter. Now, in his second summer on the estate, he walked with Minh through the gardens instead of alone. He never wanted to be alone again. He had considered dropping to one knee to propose when they reached the fir tree forest where they had once made love in the twilight, but he couldn't wait. As soon as they had passed out of view of the house he took her hand.

"Marry me, Minh?"

"Oh, Leon, I had no idea you were going to . . . You know I love you. But we're just getting to know each other. And anyway, I've never understood the whole marriage thing. Isn't it enough that we've chosen each other?"

"Please, Minh. A wedding and a ring. It's a pledge for life. I want you for life."

"I thought Rhona said you can't wear a ring. That it's bad for your image in the show."

"I'll have it though. I'll have that symbol. From you."

He asked again and again until she relented, because she did love him. She had one condition for the wedding: no one from outside would be invited. "Make it a simple party and I'll do it. I have never had a party in my honor, ever. Not even a birthday party." Her parents were migrants working in their cousin's dry-cleaning business in the heat of Orange County. They spent all day in the pungent perchloroethylene mist of the spot-cleaning bench. Minh said she was lucky she hadn't been born with two heads. She had been a runner for the shop before and after school, delivering freshly pressed suits and coats and dresses around the neighborhood, wheeling a clothing stand along the footpath and heaving it over the lip of the road at crossings, pushing receipts into the bag around her waist. Neighborhood kids followed her, teasing. "Stinky bin. Stinky Minh, stinky bin."

"Now all those white kids are working in shops and driving cabs, while we stinkies are lawyers and accountants and doctors. Doesn't take away the sting when I remember it though. Stinky Minh. I'll never forget."

"No wonder Maisie and Maximus love you. You have the memory of an elephant."

"It's hard to forget being the freak of the school. You don't have to have a hole in your chest to feel like a monster. I'm sure that's part of the reason you Wonders have been such a sensation. You're tapping into the way we all feel sometimes—as if we're different, wrong, imperfect. And yet you're doing fine. You make being weird seem okay."

On the day of the wedding the summer wind blew streamers everywhere and the firecrackers were soaked in a surprise morning shower and wouldn't light. With the wind making the trees sway and the furniture for the wedding feast having to be moved indoors after the tablecloths began to flap wildly, it seemed as if the whole event might up and fly away, and Leon's dream of happiness with it.

"Probably a good thing those firecrackers got wet," Rhona remarked. "I'm not sure Maisie and Maximus have ever heard firecrackers. Stampeding elephants would make for an eventful wedding."

The celebrant waited with Leon at the rose bower Rhona had bought for the occasion. He clutched his papers to his breast against the gusts of wind, and Leon stared at the grass crushed by his polished black shoes, half afraid that Minh had changed her mind. He was the see-through man, and Minh had seen that he was a pathetic, weak, unwell man and she could do much better. She was probably on a plane to Orange County to marry some employee of her cousin's business or the son of a family friend who had made a name for himself in orthodontics.

As he pushed the flattened grass around with the toe of his shoe, imagining the gleeful pity that would be showered on him by the media when they found out he had been stood up at the altar, Kathryn clicked along the path toward them. Minh would be out in a minute, she said.

On the lawn, bracing themselves against the wind, the household members stood beside their chairs in their best fripperies. Wandering around the ceremony, and once through it, were Maisie and Maximus, decked out in flower garlands and painted with the symbols for health, happiness and longevity. Rosa the chimp rode Yuri's shoulders, pulling at his ears and hair to tease him as he batted at her with both hands like a man trying to swat away a fly. To the side of the garden the pony nibbled on her special wedding-day nose bag of mash. The garden was the domain of the animals, and everyone had agreed that they should be a part of whatever happened there.

Earlier in the day Kathryn and Rhona had prepared a special surprise for Maximus. When the participants first came out into the warm windy garden, after the staff had set up the white plastic chairs wrapped in ribbon for the ceremony, they each wore a hat and walked nonchalantly past Maximus. He never tired of the hat trick. One by one, their hats were lifted gently off their heads and tossed into the trees. Maisie trumpeted her delight and reared up on her hind legs.

The only outsiders were a friend of Christos and her three children who happened to be visiting Overington. Now the children were racing after the hats as the wind made them cartwheel across the grass. The little girl, eight years old and full of so much energy she seemed to radiate electricity, kept running after she caught up a bowler hat in her left hand. She ran with her left arm outstretched and the black bowler clamped to her head with her right hand. On and on she ran, joy embodied, her thin legs pumping and her dress flying out behind her.

"She can't run onto the road?" Her mother put her hand on Christos's arm.

"No, no, she is safe, there is a very high fence."

"Hello." A gentle voice behind Leon. The voice of his soon-to-be wife.

He spun around and grasped her to him.

"You'll ruin the dress." Her muffled voice into his shoulder.

He held her at arm's length, taking in the oyster satin dress, the pale high heels. Pulled her close again. "I was afraid you'd chickened out."

Minh laughed. "Come on. Let's do it."

It was only after they had made their vows and run into the

house under a shower of rice that the little girl raced back from the fence. The bowler hat was gone.

"The wind blew the hat over the fence and a lady on the road called out that she couldn't throw it back because she was in a wheelchair."

Rhona heard and hurried over. "Did she say anything else to you?" she asked the girl.

"I told her there was a wedding and she said to tell you congratulations."

They came at random times to camp outside the fence. The vigil of the disabled. The early groups of demonstrators had been moved away from the gate by security, but one or two people appeared every now and then, somewhere along the perimeter of the grounds. The press wouldn't come anymore so they were only performing for the Wonders. A woman in a wheelchair, a man with stubby arms and half-formed hands, the acid-attack victim they saw sometimes on TV current affairs shows after another reconstruction attempt on her face. They left messages in the mail or painted on the footpath or sprayed onto the hedge. The latest message, painted in blue on the timber struts of the first gate, said:

YOU ARE CANNIBALS, FEEDING OFF OUR DISABILITY. WITHOUT US, YOUR SHADOW FREAKS, YOU WOULD ONLY BE HALF THE HUMANS YOU ARE.

26

AFTER THE WEDDING the Wonders took a three-week break from performances so Leon and Minh could hide away on an island in the Pacific for their honeymoon. They swam at the private beach and rinsed the sand off each other at the outdoor shower on the side of the cabin facing the sea. They lay on the bed with the sea rushing outside and traveled the continents of each other's bodies, limb by limb, expanse by expanse. When they returned to Overington, skin caramel from the sun, a new looseness in their walk, Christos took one look at Leon and declared him a new man.

"In fact, I would say that at last you have become a man." He turned to Yuri. "You see? I told you all he needed was a woman."

The performance work resumed at an even greater pace. Dinners, media interviews, private showings. In January the Wonders flew into Dubai for a commissioned exhibition. They drove through Dubai streets as wide as rivers. White cars slipped along soundlessly in sedate tides of traffic heading from one skyscraper to another. The limousine driver wore an arrangement of a peaked cap over a cloth ghutra that seemed to straddle the two worlds with equal discomfort.

Their latest employer, a dealer in finance, owned hundreds of thousands of square miles of desert in the region. His schedule for the performance, as laid out in the contract, took the Wonders on a short flight out of the city and a desert drive to a camp that would be the stage for the performance. The site had been set up with tents, carpets and cushions, cooking and serving equipment, and a chef to prepare a feast for the guests. There would be music and dancers, and as a finale, the Wonders would perform.

When the booking had come in, Rhona had showed the Wonders pictures of Dubai's bizarre program of construction. Snow slopes in a climate of hundred-degree heat. Artificial islands in the shape of palm trees large enough to be seen from the moon. Seven-star hotels with empty seven-star rooms. And Dubailand, the most immense leisure complex on the planet, abandoned half-built, its debt almost crippling lender nations, a monument to greed and hubris. "I think their freakish country might even out-freak the Wonders," she'd said.

Their tiny plane out of the city touched down on a strip of concrete flanked on either side by a small army of men shoveling sand out of the path of the wheels. Leon and the others hopped down from the wobbly aircraft steps and looked around. The desert was searingly bright. Yellow sand burned under the soles of their shoes. Dunes with no distinguishing features swelled and sank to the billowing horizon.

While they struggled through deep sand to the luxury four-wheel-drive van parked at the edge of the runway, behind them the plane slewed around on the sandy strip until it faced the way they had come, then took off in a sandstorm of yellow grit. There was no building in sight. Nothing but the undulating dunes, bleached sky, gassy sun. Leon's eyes were already watering from the glare. He pulled his sunglasses from his shirt pocket and hooked them on, took off his hat and perched it on Minh's head.

When they climbed into the van, Christos and Yuri took the seats with their backs to the driver while Leon and Minh sat on the bench seat facing the sliding door. Kathryn took the single seat at the back. The driver called back that they should help themselves to drinks from the cabinet, but no one took up the offer.

"Just get us there," Rhona said.

In a dip in the dunes to the west, four more four-wheel drives were parked in a line. Men in white thobe and headdress with gold jewelry glinting in the morning sunlight and others in colored robes stood around smoking cigarettes and talking. Two westerners in jeans and shirts moved around the vehicles, shifting boxes from one car to another, passing out drinks.

Finally, the convoy took off. As the cars wound in their ungainly serpent through the dunes, Leon experienced the first symptoms of panic. Each jolt of the vehicle jarred his bones. Fear was forcing his respiration into fast shallow breaths that left him even more breathless. His hand clutched at his chest, over the hole covered by his vest and shirt. The vehicle was soon thumping violently over the sand and tossing the passengers into the air above their seats.

Leon was too shocked and afraid to speak. He could imagine his blood pouring into his unguarded heart, swelling the artificial tubes fit to bursting. Each jolt sent him witheringly cold followed by flashes of burning heat as he waited with dread for blood to come spurting from a broken vessel. He wanted to scream, but his voice was gone, as if his full energy was concentrated on keeping his heart intact. Minh gripped the safety handle on the ceiling and swung herself around to face him. She began to unbutton his shirt. As she reached the fourth button down, the van jerked forward and her hand accidentally pushed against Leon's chest.

"That's it," she shouted. "Stop the car." Her hand stayed steady on his chest, warm and reassuring.

Rhona twisted around, gripping the shoulder of her seat. "You okay?"

"Leon can't tolerate this kind of lurching and bumping. As his accountable physician I will not take responsibility for his health if we continue to bounce around. It's extremely dangerous."

When the van had slid to a halt at the base of a dune, Minh eased Leon's shirt off his shoulders and unzipped his protective vest. She pulled a tiny flashlight from her medical bag and peered into his chest. He grasped her knee and held it as he stared at the roof of the vehicle.

"It's okay. Nothing's moved." She snapped off the flashlight and fitted it into its pocket in the medical bag. "Leave your shirt off. I want to keep my eye on you."

They set off again, this time traveling at a reasonable pace along the ridge of a single dune, rather than rolling over one dune after another like a boat cresting heavy seas. Kathryn had withdrawn inside her veil. Yuri and Christos leaned against each other and stared out the window at the endless waves of sand. Minh pulled her head scarf across her shoulders and gazed through the opposite window. She was holding Leon's hand. She had told him to squeeze if he felt anything was wrong.

"Don't worry, Leon." Rhona swiveled to talk over the headrest of her seat. "We can stop anytime. Let us know what's happening. Any pain, anything."

"I wish we hadn't come. How much further?" Kathryn's voice was muffled by her veil, which was now wrapped three times around her face, as if she could erase herself by concealment.

"Only another mile, honey, to a camp that's already set up. Don't worry. Everything is under control. We do our show and then we leave. Immediately."

What Kathryn meant to people who saw her for the first time and how they reacted was never predictable but was always from the gut, beyond reason. As many people became wrathful as entranced. Some spectators surprised themselves by hissing. Minh had told Leon that when they discussed such practical matters—yes, we will perform here; no, there will be no mood lighting; yes, Kathryn will appear but for only three minutes— she longed to hold Kathryn, to pull her close and protect her, even though Kathryn could only bear the lightest of touches.

The van was skimming smoothly along the lip of a low dune when the left-hand side of the vehicle punched up like a rickety toy spring and Kathryn shot out of her seat and slammed into Christos. The next few moments were a storm of noise and light and rolling and tumbling and connecting with metal and flesh and boxes and glass. And pain.

Nothing more. No sound except the hiss of the desert sand against the windows. The driver hung by his seat belt and dripped blood onto the gearshift. Hiss, hiss, and the pat, pat of drips of blood. Was Leon the only one awake and listening? The roar of an engine accelerating over a dune. Car doors opening. Still the ominous hiss of that relentless sand.

Near Leon's window, guttural voices arguing.

Inside the vehicle, Rhona's voice, a weak whistle. "Is everyone okay?"

The hot smell of urine filled the van before dissipating into the other acrid fumes.

"Kathryn? Leon? Please, everyone, say something to me." Rhona's voice sounded like it had sand in it.

Murmurs answered her. Leon was reaching to touch Minh's

face. Behind Yuri's head, sand slid up against the window like water, as if the van was sinking into a parched lake.

Shouting outside. The driver's door opened upward. Now that Leon had oriented himself he could see that the van had fallen on its side and he lay supine along the side bench seat. Heaped into a pile at the end of the seat like tossed-out clothes were Yuri, Christos and Kathryn, all awake and staring at him. Beside him lay Minh.

"Are you all right, Minh?" He stretched out a hand and stroked her cheek. There was a heavy weight on his leg, warm and suddenly wet, and he jerked spontaneously trying to shake it off.

A white-clad body reached into the vehicle and unclipped the driver's seat belt, causing the driver to collapse onto Rhona below him. Rhona sobbed.

Minh lifted her head.

"I'm okay," she said, struggling to extricate herself. "Nothing broken. You, darling? Everyone else?"

In the front, the men were lifting the driver out. His legs cracked against the door and his scruffy leather moccasin flipped off his left foot and tumbled to rest beside Leon's head. He gagged at the stink of it.

It felt like hours but it had only been minutes since they rolled. Minh finally wrestled aside the bag that was pinning her down. She looked first into Leon's heart, then into his face. When Leon nodded that he felt okay, she picked her way gingerly across him to reach the tangle of bodies that was Kathryn, Christos and Yuri.

The driver was gone. Now the white-clad men with their beards and brown faces pushed in through the driver's door and took hold of Rhona.

"Get the others out first," she said.

Men's grunts and shouts accompanied a heaving as they tried to open the door above Leon. Finally it gave with a metal scream and slid open. The inside of the car was doused with light and heat. Christos moaned.

The smallest man used his arms to swing into the cavity of the van. He lowered his feet carefully and ended up straddling the edge of a seat and some baggage. His robe brushed Leon's leg.

"Pass me that case." Minh pointed to her medical case at the other end of the van.

The man shook his head, unable to follow.

"Case! Case!" She made an oblong shape in the air with her hands and pointed again, and he understood and picked his way over to pass the case to her.

Behind her Kathryn and Christos and Yuri were slowly unknotting as the toffee-smelling heat from outside oozed into the van.

Another two faces appeared above in the gap of the door. "We get doctor. Doctor come soon."

Minh didn't answer. She tapped Yuri on the cheek with three fingers. "Can you hear me?"

"But it's my birthday tomorrow." He was whispering, his lavender eyes with their blunt black lashes focused on the rising line of sand at the window.

Minh's hands traveled across Kathryn's body, pressing and tugging to make sure all parts were moving. Kathryn pushed her away.

"Look." Kathryn reached under Christos. Her fingers came back smeared with blood.

Christos let out a weak cry.

"Stay still." Minh lifted her face to the four heads now peering in through the open door above. "Ambulance. Helicopter. Helicopter ambulance now."

27

CHRISTOS HAD BEEN airlifted to Los Angeles. Leon, Minh, Kathryn and Rhona flew home in a private jet. Their limousine was waiting for them at the airport.

As the gates to Overington swung open, Rhona wound down the window to speak to the guards. "Make sure the fence is secure, okay?"

"Anything you want, ma'am." A square-faced man in boots, tight pants and a black T-shirt squatted so he was at eye level with Rhona's window while they waited for the metal gates to open fully. "We're here for you."

As Rhona, then the others, stepped gingerly from the car, Kyle ran from the front door to greet them. He stopped short, unable to look away from Kathryn. "Thank god you're all right."

The next morning Leon and Minh joined the others in the common room. The morning light cast their tired faces in an ivory pallor. All of them were bruised and tender. Minh's arm hung in a sling: the doctors had only discovered the cracked bone when the anesthesia of the shock wore off.

Rhona spoke first. "No one can explain exactly how we managed to run over an antipersonnel mine in a place where no mines have ever been laid. They say it could have been one that drifted over from Kuwait or the Saudi desert. I don't believe a word of it. Something bad was already going down with that desert trip. I felt it. Was it deliberate?"

"I felt it too," Kathryn said. "But I always feel it."

Behind Rhona stood Hap, head of security, in his usual stance. You could pick out the ex-military men around the property by that stance—legs so thick at the thighs that the knees didn't meet, arms hooped around to the back to keep the emphasis on the puffed-out chest, chin tucked in and neck missing.

Hap shook his head. It rotated like a mechanical device, no wobbling flab or floppy hair. "I don't know what they intended, ma'am, but that's a lesson learned. From now on, I travel everywhere with you."

"They won't admit the bomb was for us. A drifting mine, my ass. I knew we should have had security with us."

Hap shifted his weight, then settled again into the stance. "Actually, it most likely was an accident. I honestly do not think it was a bomb intended for you. There have been other incidents in that region due to abandoned munitions. Maybe meeting the Arabs, the desert, you know, since 9/11 a lot of people are uneasy . . ."

"I'm not like that," Rhona protested. "I felt something was wrong, that's all. I'm not a racist!"

"I know from my other clients, ma'am, that fear seeps into you. You don't even know it's happening. People saying things, movies, the way they report stuff on the news. Then someone's wearing different clothes, sounding different, looking different. I'm just saying, that's all. Sometimes you don't realize what you're afraid of until you meet right up with it."

That caused them all to pause. How many people out there were afraid of the Wonders? The religious fanatics' revulsion masked a terror of Kathryn, a woman whose only dangerous weapon was her tongue.

"But it's done and over, ma'am. We need to look ahead. Plan your security with new vigilance. The main thing is that you were out of our protection, and we can't allow that to happen again. If I had been on that trip, I would have traveled the route beforehand and checked out the location of the show."

"Exactly. We have to be more careful. And that means"— Rhona pointed at Kathryn—"no more sneaky shopping trips, no slipping out to the movies with the staff. I know you've been good about keeping me in the loop, but they have to stop. You have to be protected, darling. There's nothing more to it."

Kathryn frowned. She looked as if she was about to stamp her foot.

"Don't argue. I'm trying to look after you."

Kyle joined in from the sofa where he was sitting and observing. "It would be dumb to be injured for the sake of a pretty pair of shoes. We can have the pretty shoes brought to you."

"Oh, Kyle. It's not about the shoes." Minh rolled her eyes. "I thought you were a people expert!"

"Thank you, Minh." Kathryn lifted her head and sniffed. "You're right. It's about freedom. About not being trapped. Penned in, so to speak." She laughed, lifted one foot and flexed her toes so that the slip-on snapped against her sole. "The shoes are a side benefit."

Kyle shrugged. He was integral to the Wonders yet he was apart from them. When they performed, whether it was a show or an interview or a walk-through, he watched, often on a screen from thousands of miles away. He made notes. He goaded and seduced the media, he corrected the Wonders' answers, he gave advice on their walks and their carriage, he wrote speeches. All the while, his surreptitious glance alighted on Kathryn whenever he thought no one could see, flitting off when anyone drew his attention.

Outside the common-room window, Maisie lifted her trunk and trumpeted. The glass in the windows vibrated with the sound. She and Maximus had been mooning around the house, two gray swaying monoliths in the snow, since the hour when the keeper had let them out of the winter shelter for their morning exercise.

"For god's sake, Minh," Rhona said, "will you please go out and reassure the elephants before Maisie makes us all go deaf?"

"I don't want to miss anything."

"Minh, go out there. They can sense something is wrong and they need to get back into the warmth of their pen. In fact all of you can leave except Kyle and Hap. I need to talk about our new security arrangements at Overington and none of you need to be here. Afterward, I think we'll talk again about the possibility of closing down."

"Come with me, Leon. A walk will settle us both down." Minh took Leon's hand to lead him out through the garden doors.

"Actually, one quick word before you go, Kathryn," Rhona said.

As Minh pulled him through the doorway, Leon turned and saw Rhona grasp Kathryn's fingers as she spoke to her. It was as much physical contact as Kathryn would allow. He gripped Minh's hand tighter.

Kyle had let their families know they were all right immediately after the accident, aware that the news would headline across the globe. That night Leon called his mother. She asked if he and Minh wanted to come to Australia and recuperate there with her. "It has to be safer," she said. "Nothing happens here."

When Leon was a teenager, he and his mother would sometimes find themselves standing awkwardly together on the verandah of their weatherboard house. It was the place where she would try to talk to him as if he was a young man, to treat him as a young adult, and he would sigh and roll his eyes like the lumpen adolescent he was. As the conversation stammered hopelessly between them, they both gazed beyond the wooden fence at the bottom of the unkempt garden to the patch of bush behind the house. Leon used to wonder what kind of fool would call that patch of degraded bush outside an Australian country town Canadian Forest, as if it was a magnificent forest on a rugged mountain instead of a series of thin-treed lumpy hills marred by mounds of dumped rubbish and burned-out cars.

With a small portion of his mounting Wonders income, he had bought his mother a new house on the other side of town, next to the lake where the people with money lived, and when the Wonders flew to Australia to dine with a media mogul and his young wife, Leon traveled up to visit his mother in her new place. From her back door, instead of the scrubby wasteland of the Canadian Forest, the view was of a landscaped garden with a sunken arena and a pond full of carp. In the moonlight, the star-jasmine flowers glowed against the russet brick fence. His mother had looped her arm around his waist.

"Thank you, Leon. Your sister and the kids have been to visit. They think you're so kind to have bought this for me."

"Very sweet. But I hardly need thanking." He adjusted his weight from one foot to the other.

"Oh god." She snatched her hand away from his body. "Oh god, did I hurt you?" And she stumbled away, crashing into the bench behind her. "I'm so sorry, darling. I didn't mean to . . . Did I hurt you?"

"No, Mum. You can touch me." Leon picked up her hand from her side and guided it to where she had laid it above his left hip.

She'd left her hand resting there for a short time, obviously embarrassed to move it, yet so uncomfortable that her hand was a wooden block pressing against Leon's body. Physical affection had never been their language. He supposed that their physical relationship was written into their bodies and would never change. Their own kind of cellular memory.

In the garden at Overington, Leon pulled Minh to him, careful not to jolt her arm in the sling. "Are you afraid?"

"Of course I am. I'm afraid for Christos, and I'm afraid for all of us."

"Do you want to go to Australia? We could stay with my mother."

Minh hugged him with her good arm. "That would be as much fun as moving in with my parents. Anyway, we can't leave Rhona now."

"Let's go to bed." He wanted to be inside her, to have the shuddering release of orgasm and the peace that came after. The oneness of his body with its metal heart that he only truly felt in the stillness after sex.

"Later. Maisie needs me more than you right now." Minh produced a pawpaw from her coat pocket. Maisie's small eyes widened. She snaked her trunk to Minh's hand and lifted the fruit with prehensile agility.

28

ACH DAY RHONA spoke with staff at the hospital where Christos lay in intensive care. Splinters from his implant had pierced one of his kidneys. Jittery and in pain with her own bruising, she joked uneasily about how Christos was the one who always wanted the attention, how pleased he would be to feature on the front page again.

On the fourth day, Christos's surgeon from the wing project flew in carrying a replacement ceramic join. The original manufacturers had created six of the lilies, three for each side, in case the wet joins failed and the lilies needed replacing. A team came together to work on Christos. They took seven hours to extract the splinters and stop the bleeding from the old join and thought it too dangerous to continue. His heart had stopped twice and his blood pressure had dropped to critically low levels. They sent him back to the ICU.

Leon could imagine the pain receptors in Christos's body electrified at the moment of impact and again, afterward, with each movement Christos made. The sharp, pricking pain of the

A-delta fibers and the burning, throbbing pain of the C fibers shooting through the nerve pathway, up the spinal cord, slamming into the thalamus and, he was certain, causing Christos to cry out.

In the university basement, Leon's ribs had been sawn apart and sections replaced with titanium and hinges and tensile joining fiber. He had become obsessed with understanding pain. The main object of his feverish reverie was his pain homunculus, a collection of nerve cells nestled in the brain that experiences all the body's pain. Leon imagined his own pain homunculus as a small angry monster with huge hands and face. Its skin was hard, thick and dense, its bones and muscles limp and puny in comparison—the places where the nerve cells clustered more densely in the body shaped the sensation of pain felt by the homunculus.

On day ten, the surgeons woke Christos and told him that replacing the join was too risky. The best option was to extract the other join and close Christos up to allow him to recover. He would lose the wings and the damaged kidney, but he would have a much better chance of survival.

He refused. He wanted the broken join replaced even though he would still lose the kidney. Art was everything and his project was unfinished. When Leon heard Christos was willing to take that risk, he pictured Christos's pain homunculus: it was completely different from the one Leon had imagined for himself. Christos's homunculus was a miniature superman, a hero, a devourer of pain who would grow stronger with each jolt, who would grimace and bear it and flex his tiny muscles until he was oblivious and riding the pain waves. If anyone could survive such a surgery, it was Christos.

In the Overington house fear dampened the air, made it chilly and difficult to breathe. Christos's and Yuri's empty chairs in the common room drove the others away. They congregated in the dining room or walked in pairs or threes through rooms that seemed too large.

One morning Kathryn came inside from the garden with leaves and twigs caught in her coat.

"Where have you been?" Leon asked. "Minh was expecting you for coffee."

"I went to find August, the bear. When I found him, he led me to a clearing. He had a baton buried in there and he dug it up while I watched, then twirled it in his claws. His head was bobbing as if he could hear some music that I couldn't hear. At the end, he curtsied. A great big bear curtsying like a ballerina. Christos was right, it is his life's work. He needs to perform. They both do."

29

THEY WAITED TEN weeks for Christos to come home from the hospital. By the third week he had been out of danger but the healing and rehabilitation of the muscles around his replacement implant were taking longer than expected: his forty-three-year-old body had lost its youthful resilience. Rhona wondered aloud whether he was foolish for trying to continue with a career in body-techno art.

"What else could he do? Imagine Christos as a waiter!" Kathryn cackled like an old crone at the thought. "Christos as a clerk! A clown!"

That idea was so unimaginable that Minh laughed until she spilled her tea and squealed as the hot liquid soaked through her skirt.

"They'll be home next week." Rhona pulled her phone from her pocket. "That reminds me, I'd better get the apartment cleaned. And let Vidonia and security know."

While the others recovered from their bruises and cracked bones and waited for Christos to recuperate, Rhona fretted around the house, refitting the rehearsal room, decking out the library with more books for Kathryn, planning new performance pieces for the three Wonders.

"Rhona, for the love of Mary, sit down and relax for a minute," Kathryn said after Rhona had brought in three fitness consultants to be interviewed about creating new individual programs. "Can't you learn how to be still? I am tired and sore. I want this time off, not to have a full-body makeover. Leave us alone for one fecking minute, will you?"

It was Rhona who didn't want to be alone. In the years between evicting her greedy friends and when the Wonders moved in, she told Leon, she had kept an eye on her shows that were still touring, even though she had sold them off to other producers. "I'd fly in, make a few suggestions to freshen up the show, catch up with old buddies and maybe invest in a new production. Semiretired, you might call it. But it didn't suit me," she'd said. "I need people around, a bit of noise and life."

These days friends from the trade came to visit every so often. They stayed a few nights, told stories of the old days, left Rhona buoyant with laughter and nostalgia when they had gone. Leon had met a couple of retired promoters and a multimillionaire who had made his fortune from bingo. No family ever visited.

"You never talk about your mother," Leon dared to say to Rhona as they sat on the verandah watching Agnes, the mare, canter in a circle on the end of Kathryn's lunge rope as if she was a feisty untamed Thoroughbred rather than a solid placid pony.

"No, I don't."

He had mothers on his mind. Real mothers, that is—the one he had left behind in Australia, who had seemed old, so old when he spoke to her after the Dubai accident, and his surrogate mother during the year of pain, Susan. After Minh had stopped helping with the project, Leon kept making his methodical way through the databases and phone listings until one day he calculated it would take him another three years simply to cover the USA and Canada. He hired an agency, gave them a budget and told them to hurry. And they had found her. Yesterday the agent had called with the news. Now Leon had to decide whether to contact her. The question twisted around every moment of the day.

Rhona had no brothers or sisters. If her mother had any other family, they had never been in contact. When Leon had gone looking for information about Rhona's mother, it took him months to find anything. He had to hire a student over the Internet to do the last part of the work because the training schedule was too tight for him to take the trip to see newspaper records in Denver, where the circus had caught fire in 1955.

Rhona's mother had died in her van. She perished in bed. After the fire Rhona had been taken in by the local girls' boarding school. What had initially mystified Leon was how Rhona had escaped from the van while her mother burned in her bed. Rhona was ten at the time. Old enough to find someone to help. Old enough to drag her mother out. Or so he had presumed.

The story Rhona had told him of following her father around the circus may have been true, but her real name was not Rhona Burke. She took Samuel Burke's name in her twenties, after she started her career as a promoter. Before that, when she was a child in the circus and later the despised orphan at the boarding school, she had been Rhona Overington, sole offspring of Alisha Overington, the fat lady of the circus, sideshow exhibit, four hundred pounds in weight, able to move only with great effort from her bed in the specially designed and reinforced trailer to the sideshow tent for her show once a day. Too fat to run in a fire. Too fat even to get off the bed in time to escape. Impregnated by the ringmaster who came to her trailer in the dark and buried himself in the forgiving pillows of her flesh. Never acknowledging her or his child until he disappeared and became Rhona's mysterious benefactor, paying for her upbringing in the boarding school and leaving her a fortune in untouched tax-haven accounts on his death.

Each of the residents of Overington had come to this mismatched family from a family of their own that had failed in some way. Even Christos, to whom family meant everything, had only once mentioned his dead father, and that was to say that the old peasant had disowned Christos for refusing to live in the mud and eat shit. With this group of misfits as examples, it seemed there were no successful families, only ones whose members didn't manage to destroy each other. The question of whether Leon and Minh could make something different together bit into his dreams some nights.

After Leon left Rhona he went to Minh's studio. She was busy sorting sketches. Intoxicating fumes from recently sprayed fixative drifted through the room. Minh was tossing white cartridge sheets, some scored with thick charcoal strokes, others crosshatched in pencil, into a tin rubbish bin beside the bench. Her paintings were stacked on the floor, leaning against the wall, only the bones of their frames and the ragged edge of the tacked canvas visible. Leon peered over Minh's shoulder at the sketches on the bench.

"When I came here," she said without pausing in her task, "I had no idea that what you do would be dangerous. I thought you three had overcome the danger of your illnesses and surgeries, and my job would be routine. You're performers. Performers don't die doing their jobs."

He threaded his hand under her hair to experience that intensely intimate frisson of it spilling through his fingers. "Minh . . ." He hesitated.

"Christos nearly died. What if something had happened to you?"

"Minh, I've found Susan."

She pulled away. Leon's hand was left caressing cool air. "Why didn't you tell me you'd gone on with the search?"

"I didn't want to make you lie to Rhona."

"My decision, I would have thought, Leon. A decision I would make after we'd talked, because couples are supposed to talk about these things. And now? You'll contact Susan?"

"I don't know."

Minh picked up another sketch and tore it into four pieces before dropping it into the bin.

"Why are you throwing these drawings away?" Leon bent to pull out a few sheets.

"Leave them," she said. "I can't believe you went on looking for her without telling me."

Leon let the paper in his hands slide back into the bin and settle on top of the other work.

"Minh, I—"

"I'm throwing them out because they're just pretty pictures. Here you all are around me and yet I've been drawing you the same way I've always drawn people. I have to rethink the human body. I don't know what it is anymore." She folded another sheet into a small square before speaking again. "Of course you'll contact Susan. How could you not?"

He waited in case Minh had more to say but she returned to her task, ripping and discarding, ripping and discarding, tearing more work off the walls until the studio had been stripped of months of drawing and painting, and the bare walls were left with splotches and smudges, pinholes and staples and penciled notes and adhesive hooks and the yellowed outlines of work now gone.

30

I N THE MONTH since Christos had returned to performance, his ascendancy in the tabloids via the constant reports on his courageous recovery had fallen away. Kathryn was back in the spotlight. Following a live interview where she claimed that there could not be a god because no god would allow what had happened to her, her hate mail had come close to overwhelming the threat-assessment system. One lunatic had painted in huge lettering on the Flatiron Building in New York that Kathryn, the Lamb of God, had betrayed her father and she must die.

They had already discussed many times how long they would continue to work, and to Leon's relief they had set their retirement date at three months in the future. Only three more months of displaying their bodies to people whose rapturous attention no longer meant anything, three more months of cities dissolving and forming between cushioned rides in planes and limousines, of seeing their own faces everywhere as though the world was a mirror maze, only three more months before he and Minh could retire to a proper life, a normal married life with squabbles about who should do the cleaning and what movie to see.

Kathryn had already found a small Caribbean island she wanted to buy. Christos had hired staff and set up a lab in Malaysia that was working on preproduction for his mysterious new art project. After the final show in three months, there would be no more Wonders. Leon and Minh would withdraw into a private world. All they had to do was stay safe till then.

Now Hap was proposing they stop their small shows and move to large auditoriums.

"I don't understand. There will be way more people than we've ever had. Crowds of crazies. Big open spaces. How on earth can that be secure?" Kathryn sat on the couch with her legs crossed and a cape wound in a tight bandage around her. She rocked backward and forward. "It's sending the lamb to the slaughter."

"I know it sounds counterintuitive." Hap rolled his shoulders as if he wished he was outside punching boxing bags or whatever he did to build the steely physique, the pillar of muscle that was his body. "But think bulletproof glass, metal detectors, cameras. No actual contact with the public. Think moving you three in and out of a protected greenroom under armed guard. I need to be able to contain you."

That phrase threw Leon back to the laboratory with Susan and Howard, the day they had made the decision to cut away the necrotic tissue in his chest.

Susan had told him it was a radical surgery that had never been attempted before. "It's wildly risky, but the damage to your tissue is spreading fast. We need to be able to contain the risk of infection and rejection. Containment is the key. There will be no return, Leon. Once this is done, you can never have an organic heart. And this heart will be your last. If it fails, you die."

Two mechanical pumps in his chest were pushing his depleted blood through his veins and lungs. He could hear the pumps, gurgling with the sound of a swimming pool filter, day and night. The sound made him nauseous. But the pumps were keeping him alive until the final operation, the one where Howard's specially constructed heart would be implanted in his body. Meanwhile Howard was tinkering late into the night in the computer room next to the cubicle where Leon slept fitfully on his hospital bed, blanketed by hot pain and uncertainty.

"Or I die anyway. Without the new heart I die anyway."

"Yes, you die anyway. And some of your tissue is already dead."

"It will be painful?"

"It will be excruciating."

"But I'd die without it."

"You may die because of it."

"But I'd die anyway."

The next day they began work on the possibilities for his replacement ribs. They would be smoother, shinier and stronger than his original ribs. They would have hinges. They would enclose a space that no other human body had ever contained. A hollow for his brass heart and the secrets that his body would harbor from now on.

"I can make it work." Rhona's voice brought Leon back to the present. She was thinking fast, playing on her screen. "I can make us even bigger, even better this way. And it solves the problem of those stupid commentators who are always trying to discredit us. We'll be out and available and yet more protected than we've ever been."

"That's right. It's the only way." Hap nodded vigorously. His T-shirt bulged with enthusiasm. "The only way."

"Oh my god!" Rhona lurched to her feet, dropping the tablet, which bounced a few times and emitted a few jumbled sounds. "Of course, of course! We'll bring in the rubes to a show in a huge space. Aerialists, strongmen, acrobats, jugglers, whatever we can find. Wandering through the space, barking at the crowd, performing their incredible feats. It'll be—"

"Rhona, really?" Kyle interrupted. "Aren't we going backward here?"

"It's vintage, darling. Everyone loves vintage. And we'll have cotton-candy stalls and toffee apples and magicians dressed in tails and top hats doing three-cup shuffles and the egg-and-coin trick. A few fortune-tellers and sideshow stands. Maybe even sawdust on the floor. Everywhere you look there'll be performers and music and magic and fun, old-fashioned fun. Then, wait for it, slowly, slowly the performers will melt away, the noise will recede, the lights will dim, until the audience is standing in a dark silent room. They'll stop talking. They always do when they don't know what's happening. And you, one by one, rise into the space, under glass, lit like gods." Rhona had been conducting the whole imaginary show with her arms and now she lifted pillows of air in her hands and held them above her head. "Lit like gods."

"Won't that cost a fortune?" Kathryn asked.

"We'll make a fortune, my love. It's a premium event, premium price. People will pay."

Kyle was nodding. "And a sound-and-light show to go with the Wonders. The past to the future."

Kathryn raised her teacup and held it out in a toast. "So at last you get your circus back, Rhona. Congratulations. I haven't seen you this happy in a long time."

Rhona spread her arms and took a long low bow. She rose scarlet and shiny. "There is nothing, nothing in the world like a circus, my darlings. My Enchanted Circus for my Enchanted Wonders."

That night Leon completed his message to Susan. He had been working on drafts for weeks to get the tone right. Grateful, warm, friendly, eager but not pushy. He wrote about his heart, his rejuvenated robust body. He described the world he lived in, the travel, the people who paid to see him. He told her he was married now, and happy. He tried to explain how he was within this world and without at the same time, a part of it yet a wonderstruck observer. *Come and see*, he wrote. *If you don't want to speak to me, soon we'll be performing in big venues where you can observe anonymously if you prefer. Come and see what you've made.*

When Minh read what Leon had written she frowned and said, "You've never told me anything like this."

Susan's answer came almost immediately.

Dear Leon,

    I have been keeping up with your exploits and the incredible world you live in. I'm so proud that you are well and happy. Congratulations on your marriage, by the way.

    I do appreciate that you want to thank me in person, but as I said when we parted, I am finished with the project of your heart. I lost Howard not long after you left and I still grieve for him. We should have had more time together.

    I have a different life now, with no wish to go back. So

THE WONDERS

I won't be coming to see you, and I hope you will respect my privacy.

Please enjoy the life you have been given. That's all anyone can do.

With love,
Susan Nowinski

31

A MONTH LATER LEON, Kathryn and Christos were shown the three booths that would be transported from venue to venue. Each booth was constructed of thick aluminum beams and a reinforced transparent material stronger than glass. The booths were wired for sound and lighting effects. One wall of the booth functioned as an invisible door that swung open for equipment to be taken in and out. The performers would enter on a platform that raised them from underneath the floor of the venue. Even the air would be pumped in. Once inside, they would be performers in bulletproof domes.

"Or popes!" Kathryn laughed. "I'll be the female pope in her very own popemobile. At last an Irish pope. Dublin will celebrate itself into a coma."

Rhona brought in a writer and a director to create short monologue shows for each of the Wonders.

"The general public has seen you on-screen and they know who you are. Seeing you in the flesh is going to blow their minds. But they have to have something to talk about later. Not just, 'Wow, did you see the hole?' We have to make you into a narrative. Each of you a different narrative, something memorable, something exotic. A stage personality. You have to have a story. Without a story, you're as good as a statue."

Over the next couple of weeks the Wonders each sat down separately with Jade, the young writer who had made her name penning plotlines for a science-fiction show on cable, and tossed around scenarios that might make a good bio story. She sat opposite Leon at the long rosewood table, sucking on the straw of an energy drink and rapping out ideas.

"Do you feel a connection with this one?"

"Flesh-eating microbes of the jungle invaded my chest? Jade, take a look at me. I'm not exactly Tarzan."

"The shark that took a piece out of your chest? A hole punched by an anaconda? No, wait, the heart was created first, and you, Leon, man of flesh, were grown around it in some crazy scientific laboratory!" Her glossy pink mouth dropped open as if she was tickled by her own brilliance. "Hothouse man. Test-tube man. No, that's been done. A man made for a heart. That's it. That's it, Leon. I love it."

Leon asked her what would happen when they made up some guff and the people he'd grown up with heard it. "And who would believe this rubbish anyway?"

"Come on, Leon, it is all bullshit and everyone knows it. You can say whatever you want. If someone pops up to contradict you, all the better. More coverage for you. Think about all those autobiography fakers. They must have had plenty of family, neighbors, friends who knew their real story, but they made millions and so no one said a thing. It was reporters who sniffed them out. Your fans don't care. What's a bit of creative license?"

Not long after the Wonders had gone global, Leon had seen photographs of the woman from the office who resuscitated him after his first heart attack. She was made up by a stylist and featured in a two-page spread in a women's magazine. Her skin was so pink it made him think of a pig's ass. Her eyes were a touched-up luminous blue instead of the faded denim of her real eyes, and they had airbrushed out the conspicuous mole on her neck. "I only did what I was trained to do as first-aid officer," she was quoted as saying. "But yes, I guess without me Leon would have died. He never did come to say thank you."

He had said thank you. He'd returned to work, fiddled around adjusting the height of his office chair, switched on his computer and tried to behave as if he was fine. He'd bought that filthy liar a bunch of flowers and apologized for the fuss.

All right, Leon decided, *I can do better than her.*

32

MEN IN THEIR best navy jackets cupped their arms around their wives' shoulders, craning their necks to see where the next part of the show might begin. Young women had come in pairs and small groups. They held sticks of spun cotton candy and gripped their handbags tight to their sides in the crowd. Older couples stood side by side, heads nodding unconsciously, waiting. These were the rubes, the public who had bought the magazines and the toys and played the online games and built avatars of the Wonders and written the obscene letters. The first part of the show, the circus performance, was complete. The performers had dispersed, the stalls had slid on rollers back to the walls, the music had faded away. The auditorium was eerily quiet.

To the roar of their signature themes, the Wonders rose one by one, starting with Christos, then Leon, then Kathryn, into the dazzlingly lit glass booths, spaced in an equilateral triangle around the room. The audience members shuffled around in formation as each of the performers appeared.

When Kathryn spoke the first few words of her monologue, Leon watched the audience run from the center of the hall in a tumbling cascade of bodies constrained by clothes and bags and the elbows and backs and feet of others. Once Kathryn was done, Leon began. People veered and thundered across the empty space of the floor toward him. His amplified voice skipped as if there had been a break in an electronic signal. He was half afraid they would crash into his booth and smash it open in their eagerness. Children under fifteen were not allowed into the booth shows, but the adults, with their hands splayed on the glass and their mouths open and pink and wet, were as enraptured as their offspring would have been.

The booths taught Leon what it was to be a rock star. The screaming. The voracious looks from women. He was already accustomed to the income. He and the other Wonders could buy anything they wanted. But this, the adulation, the saliva glistening on the lips of people who were so hysterically besotted they seemed to want to absorb him, the fainting and the shrieking, the throwing of handmade gifts and the weeping, the weeping as if these fans were undergoing a religious conversion—this made Leon feel invincible.

Only Christos was unimpressed.

"You've made us a proper circus now, Rhona. Entertainment, nothing else. Once I was an artist. Now I am a whore."

Kathryn tapped Leon on the knee and mimed at him, "*I'm an a-a-artist.*" He tried to hide his smile from Christos, who was ticking off the things he despised about the booth shows.

"Stupid costumes, an audience that wants to eat hot dogs and chatter to each other more than look at what they have paid to see, fake stories, the way I am supposed to smile all the time. Smile, smile, smile, you say. I have nothing to smile about in that glass prison with those monstrous people staring at me."

"It's just a job, Christos. And it won't go on much longer," Leon said.

"You know I nearly died after the accident, Leon, but I took the chance of destroying my health to continue with my wing project. My *art* project. We're more than circus clowns! You, Leon, Kathryn, of all people, should understand. We are the posthumans. What we do should have meaning."

Kathryn was silent, staring at the floor. Christos cuffed Leon's head as he left the room in the way of a parent with an errant child.

"He always forgets," Kathryn said after Christos had slammed the door behind him, "that he is the only one of us who chose to be this way."

Soon after their conversation, Christos began turning up late or pretending to have technical difficulties with his wings to delay going onstage. It wasn't long before he missed a complete performance. Two weeks later Yuri crept backstage three nights in a row to explain that Christos was unwell and would have to pull out again. "I'm so sorry," he said. "I'm sure he will be better soon." Christos declined to be examined by Minh. It was exhaustion rather than illness, he claimed. He needed rest.

"He's perfectly fine," Rhona said on day four. "Tell him he'd better get back onstage even if he is far too important to be performing with us. He can shove his art up his ass. This is business, and he's under contract."

At the end of a month of Christos's snide comments about the show and failures to perform, Rhona burst into the private room of the hotel where the Wonders were staying in Berlin. Everyone leaped from their chairs, terrified they were under attack, save Christos, who did nothing but raise his eyes to Rhona.

"So you say you can't perform tonight because you're exhausted? Enough of your bullshit, Christos. You fail to go onstage one more time, you're out, and I take my percentage of your fees plus the penalties that are written into your contract and good-bye. You'll have"—she pulled out her screen—"about four hundred and thirty-seven thousand dollars left in your account." She glared at him.

He ignored her. The armchair where he sat balancing a plate of cheese and crackers on his knees creaked as he recrossed his legs. He was getting fat. No exercise, eating all day. Stubble bristled on his softening jaw.

"I'm ordering you to perform tonight. It's only a couple more months, then you're free to fuck over whoever you like. Don't do it to me." Rhona didn't take her eyes off him. She had a glare honed by growing up in a van beside the lion cage. No animal or human could outstare her. Christos closed his eyes.

When the hour came for his performance he refused to go on. Rhona ordered again that a third of the ticket price be refunded to every audience member.

"What the hell will I say to the press this time?" Kyle asked as the group, minus Christos, crammed into the elevator to their floor in the hotel. He was seething. He had knocked on Christos's door and tried opening it, but Christos had locked it from the inside. Even Yuri was shut out and pacing the corridor.

"Say he's dead, for all I care." Rhona mashed her finger into the elevator button and the elevator, as if in protest, jerked to a start. "We are so close, so fucking close to the finale. I'm not going to let him ruin it. That was my last warning. He's out, he's finished."

She was up late on the phone to her lawyers instructing them to draw up the termination-of-contract documents.

"I'll say it to you too, Leon. Fuck him," she told Leon first thing the next morning when he found her bleary-eyed in the room adjoining their suites, still dressed in the clothes of the night before. She lifted her cup and drained the last of the coffee. "I'm going to strip Christos of every fucking cent. I made that man. I took him from obscure art galleries and measly grants and shady doctors to this. He's too old to compete in the art world now. He's fucked himself over and I'm not rescuing him this time."

"But, Rhona, he's not well." Minh had come in behind Leon. She rested her elbows on the mantelpiece, yawning and stretching her toes to the front, ballerina-style. Leon could smell the minty shampoo in her damp hair. "He's still recovering from the surgery after the accident. Something like that affects your mind as well as your body. And he's Christos!"

"I couldn't give a shit, Minh. He's pushed me too far. I'm tired. I knew I was taking on a lot with this project, but . . ." Rhona tapered off and rubbed her bloodshot eyes. "I'm tired, that's all. We're nearly at the climax and he pulls this. I've invested millions already in our final performance. Kyle and I have been planning it for months and Christos wants to ruin it. Well, he can fuck off right now. If he's been out for a while his absence at the gala won't be so obvious."

Minh straightened up.

"We can't let this happen," she said.

Leon wanted to offer a suggestion but this kind of thing, dealing directly with people, was his weakness. Minh had been so crotchety with him lately that he'd locked the door of his study and started haunting marriage-counseling websites. "If he's made up his mind, what can we do?" he asked.

"Let me fix it. Rhona, you know I'm right," Minh said as if she hadn't heard Leon speak. He reached for her but she pushed his hand away.

Kathryn appeared in the doorway, a cup of tea cradled in her hands. "What's going on?"

"Rhona's actually fired Christos this time."

Rhona stood up and shook her head. "I can't take his tantrums anymore. He's ruining our reputation. The three Wonders are two Wonders half the time anyway, and I refuse to pay him for nothing."

Leon saw the look that passed between Minh and Kathryn. For all the complaining Kathryn did about Christos, she was the one who defended him when others attacked. She was the one who would defend any of them.

"One more chance, Rhona," Kathryn said. "We'll talk to him."

After a minute of staring out through the window at the blooming roses in the beds at the side of the hotel driveway, Rhona sighed so hard and with such a shudder it could have been mistaken for a sob. "One chance. One only. I simply cannot take his shit any longer. So much for my Enchanted Circus."

"We tried every argument and all Christos did was stare at the floor," Minh told Rhona and Leon later. "We said, what about the transformative power of art? You are changing people's lives. 'It's not art,' he says. What about the money he'd need for his next project? 'I'll find it another way,' he says. On and on until finally Kathryn blurted out, 'Don't leave me.' He lifted his head then. She said, 'You told us we were family. Don't abandon us.' I think that's what did it. And we said we would all have turns helping with his wings. To show him that we respect what he does for his art. Yuri's told me about it and I think it's much harder than we've realized. Plus Yuri can't take much more of Christos swearing and shouting."

The next night Leon and Kathryn had the job of inserting a wing each on condition that Christos not emit a single word of complaint. It was a strange and strangely moving activity, taking the wire wings, those large fragile insects, into their arms, holding the posts above the bulbs of the joins between their gloved thumbs and forefingers and easing the bulbs into the ceramic lilies. Leon closed his eyes, as you do when your fingers try to read surface marks invisible to the eye. He held his breath as he concentrated on feeling, knowing, the moment when the bulb had clicked into the join. "Not yet, not yet," Christos cried as he heard Leon release his breath in a sigh of relief. The muscles in Christos's back convulsed. "It's not in properly. We have to try again," he said, and he heaved in a lungful of air and let it out in a gust. "Again, when I have relaxed my muscles enough to make the connection." Leon had never realized before how every stage of inserting and manipulating Christos's wings depended on an almost superhuman level of muscle control.

Rhona softened her stance as Christos, despite his moods and outbursts, worked hard for the next month. Kathryn held her tongue, and Yuri dodged the worst of Christos's temper. All they had to do till the end was keep the peace.

33

AFTER THEY RETURNED to Overington and the storm had settled, Kathryn had Leon and Minh to her apartment. She poured them a gin, lime and soda, and they toasted Yuri, the buffer who saved them so often from the wrath and rants of Christos.

"We have to make Christos be kinder to Yuri though. Imagine spending twenty-four hours a day with Mr. Pomposity. Mr. I'm-an-artist-and-you-are-a-peasant. Sometimes I worry Yuri will leave. I think I'd be more devastated than Christos."

"You'd be crabby too if you'd had the kind of surgery he's undergone, Kathryn."

"Sweet as always, Minh. But let's face it, he was an arsehole well before we met him."

"Maybe. But one who loves Yuri, even though he doesn't always show it that well." Minh reached around Leon's waist and into his jacket pocket, feeling around for the tissues she had put there before they left the apartment. Leon couldn't help placing his own hand on the outside of his pocket to experience the sensation of her slender fingers moving around inside in a gesture of such intimacy and ease. "And Yuri's found his own work, the photography. He disappears to do that when he needs to. He's so talented."

"I know," Kathryn said. "Still, Christos is a fool—no, a dunderhead, the way he treats Yuri like a slave. Yuri's our baby brother. He's the real angel here."

Kyle appeared in the doorway. He stood there, smiling at the three and smoothing his hair on the left side with the heel of his hand in an unconscious gesture Leon had seen a million times. Pressing the hair flat against the head again and again as if he could contain some unruly thoughts that threatened to escape.

"Do you want a drink, Kyle, or are you just going to stand there staring at us?" Kathryn said.

Kyle pushed himself away from the doorjamb and strolled over to the couch. "Thanks for asking." He sat down beside Kathryn and sank back into a plump scarlet cushion while she mixed him a drink on the tray on the coffee table. The housekeeper brought a fresh bucket of ice and was gone before anyone had a chance to thank her.

Leon could see that Kyle was making an effort not to accidentally brush against Kathryn as he caterpillared forward on the couch to receive his drink. Was this confident PR man actually nervous around Kathryn?

They lifted their glasses. The filtered light caught curls of lime peel in luminous movement as if they were live creatures swimming between the bubbles in the glasses. The four drank in silence, gazing out through the windows of Kathryn's apartment at the clouds shifting shape in the milky pink sky of sunset. In the distance one of the elephants trumpeted. The other answered with a muted call. The understory vegetation Leon had seen being planted when he first arrived at Overington had now formed a dense hedge. Ashy green blueberries swelled beneath the dappled shade of a stand of red spruce and maple trees. The four-pointed stars of partridgeberry flowers in their distinctive pairs glowed against the glossy leaves trailing the ground.

They drank another glass while the light faded in the garden. When Kathryn stifled a yawn, Minh stood and stretched and said she was going to her studio to finish some work. She was gone before Leon had time to stand up. He said his good-bye to Kathryn and Kyle and was halfway across the common room before he realized he had left his phone beside his chair.

Kyle was talking in a low voice as Leon walked back up the carpet runner of the hall to the doorway. Leon hesitated. He was reluctant to interrupt, but he needed his phone, and so he stood swaying in his indecision, trying not to listen. Kyle's voice stopped, then started, stopped, then started, a dogged drilling tool. In the third pause, as Leon was turning to leave, thinking he would call Kathryn and ask her to bring the phone to the apartment, Kathryn spoke.

"Kyle—"

Kyle's interruption was inaudible, a low buzz. Leon heard the swish of Kathryn's cape and a hollow tap as one of her heeled slippers clacked on the parquetry floor.

"I like you, Kyle—"

Again the buzz. Two quick clacks, as if Kathryn was edging backward. Or perhaps she was moving toward him. Perhaps it was the mating dance of to and fro, attraction and fear of rejection. How could Leon know, and why was he even pondering this when all he had wanted was to pick up his phone? It was time for him to stop hanging around behind the doorway.

"No, really, Kyle, you're a pal, but . . . Anyway, we have to work together. Let's keep it—"

Clack, clack. Now Leon was sure she was stepping away. He decided to go into the room, help break up the awkward moment. He rounded the doorway, hand on the architrave, and caught sight of Kyle standing close to Kathryn, closer than Leon had seen anyone to her, face-to-face. She must have been able to feel his breath on her lips. Shockingly, Kyle reached up and placed his hands around the back of Kathryn's neck, as if to pull her face toward his. She reared away, almost unbalancing as her slipper heel caught the edge of the rug, then righting herself.

"I've asked you not to touch me. I don't like being touched. I do like you, but not in that way. I'm sorry."

Leon had to speak, to make his presence known before they saw him standing there. "Hello? Um, I left my phone."

When they both turned to him, at such a speed he barely saw their heads move, Kyle's face was so full of emotion Leon felt as though he was seeing three or four faces struggling to take control. What a terrible mistake. Why hadn't he waited, or gone to the apartment and called? For a second he watched the turbulent performance of Kyle's features. By the time Kathryn had squeezed behind the couch and begun to poke around the chairs for Leon's phone, Kyle's face was composed again, but his arms had dropped as if broken at the shoulders.

"Have to keep moving." He smiled at Leon, the super-sincere toothy smile he could produce no matter what the occasion. "I'm out of here. Catch you later, Kathryn."

"Yeah, okay, sure."

Kyle pulled out his phone and began scrolling through screens as he sauntered past Leon and out the door.

"Found it." Kathryn held up Leon's phone.

"Great, thanks." He would pretend he'd seen nothing. He took the phone from her.

"So, Leon, shall we forget about that . . . little scene?"

"Of course," he said.

But he would never forget Kyle's face in that moment, the wretched expression caught between grinning and grimacing.

34

FOR THE LAST couple of weeks, Leon had been working with a ghostwriter on a book commissioned by Kyle, who had heard about Leon's library of self-help titles.

"Mate, do you think you could knock one of them out?" Kyle had asked. He often called Leon "mate," and occasionally tried out "no worries" or "she'll be right" with an upward inflection as if he was practicing a foreign language. "We'd get you a writer, of course."

Leon supposed it was worth a try. He must have read hundreds of them. And it would pass the time.

"We'll get a presale, market the hell out of it. This can be an ongoing income stream when we've shut down."

The ghostwriter's appearance was suitably spectral. He was in his fifties, with long thin blond hair. When he dipped his head to read or write, the hair closed in a lank curtain around his face. "What I do," he told Leon, "is listen to you talk and channel you into lively accessible prose."

The trouble was subject matter.

"Hearts would be logical. Broken hearts? Mending hearts?" the ghost asked. "Tell me your story. There has to be plenty of material in that. How did this all start?"

They worked on the book in the tiny study Leon and Minh had used when they were looking for Susan, a recorder on the desk between them, the ghost's pen poised over his pad. As yet, the book was a collection of chapter titles with almost no content: "Three Keys to a New Heart," "Broken Is a Way to Mend," "Unblock Your Emotional Artery," "Healthy Habits for a Healthy Heart."

"So, Leon," the ghost said, "all this physical stuff you've told me is great, but maybe you could give me a bit more about your emotional journey. You know, so we can take the physical and make it a metaphor. How about you think about it and we try again tomorrow."

Minh caught Leon on his way to the gym. He was wearing his rank old shorts, monster running shoes that seemed to be made to walk in space, and the chest brace that had been de-signed by Howard for him to wear whenever he exercised.

"You're wearing the brace," she said dully. "I always hated that brace."

The first night Leon had spent in Minh's cottage, when he was still anxious about his first sexual encounter after the surgery, he'd pulled away like a shy bride from Minh. They had been lying on the couch, kissing and stroking each other.

"Back in a moment," he said.

He'd hurried to his apartment, fitted himself out and slipped through the dark hallways and the garden to Minh's cottage. She had turned off the lights and opened her curtains onto the garden. The moon was a silver curl above the lions' hill. Maisie and Maximus were asleep, two black mounds leaning together under the grassy fringe of their open-walled summer shelter.

Inside the room Minh lay on the couch. She too had changed clothes while Leon was away. Her silky nightdress parted in a split to the top of her thighs. He walked to the couch and kissed her brow. She dropped her head backward to kiss his lips, but when she caught sight of what he was wearing she sat up straight, knocking against his head.

"You're not wearing that? How am I supposed to hold you?"

The brace was snug around his chest and had pads to protect the front and back of the cavity.

"It won't get in the way."

"You want me to hug a medical brace? You think we can be intimate with that between us?"

"But my heart . . ." He trailed off and watched as her fingers began to undo the side straps.

"I am a doctor. I look after you. I want to make love with you, not with some piece of S-and-M equipment."

With Minh in her nightgown before him, he raised his arms as she undid the brace and lifted it away. She dropped the brace on the floor and led him toward the window.

"Here." Minh spread her hand and pressed it against the hole in his chest, where the moonlight had been shining through. "I will not let anything happen to the gizmo. But I need you to pay attention to me, not to what your heart is doing. It is a machine, Leon. It is not you."

He had put his arms around her and absorbed the warmth of her body, the transfer of her energy into his own flesh.

Now he stood strapped into his leather brace before her on his way to the gym. Minh picked at her nails as she spoke.

"It's hard for me to say this, Leon, but I can't see the point in being together."

Leon shook his head, confused. What was she saying? "We love each other. We're together because we love each other."

"That's what I used to think was enough. But you know what? It's been almost a year and I don't know you any better than when we married. I shouldn't have said yes to such a quick wedding."

"You do," he said without thinking. "You know me better than anyone."

"No, I understood for sure when I read what you wrote to Susan. I don't know you, and you don't know me. We're not getting closer, we're running on a parallel track. I am your wife. You sleep with me every night. We spend most days together. How is it that a letter to a stranger reveals more about you than I have learned in a year? I think the only way you can know someone is through a screen or a speaker. You mediate your whole life so that you will never actually have to reveal yourself. I thought you were coming into the world more, Leon. So wrong. And you know what else? I wonder if you only married me because I'm a doctor. Your very own live-in doctor."

"Not true, not true." The light shining from her, that's what made him love her.

"And I don't understand why you aren't thinking about the future. You can't be a Wonder forever. Your only role right now is to be seen and to carry a metal heart around, and that can't sustain anyone."

"But I'm . . . we're writing a book. That's for the future."

"A self-help book, right? A self-help book that you don't even believe in. All that pain and suffering and the redemption of your bodies, and you three do nothing but perform onstage. In the olden days a miraculous rescue like yours would have meant conversion, radical change. You'd have had an epiphany and vowed to commit yourself to life as a monk or doing good works. But you—all you've done is make money."

Bewilderment was lending Leon a sensation of weightlessness. "We'll be finished soon. I'll do something else then. What do you want, Minh? What do you want me to do?"

"I don't know. Because I don't know you."

"But I had no idea . . . ," he protested. "If I'd realized you were unhappy I would have . . ." No, in truth he didn't know what he would have done.

He was sure it was a mistake. She'd calm down. They had been married less than a year. He would work at it, make things better, tell her whatever she wanted to know.

She spent all day in the studio and the medical office. Leon resisted the urge to search through the old self-help books or find advice online. He guessed she would accuse him of falling back into the old ways. What irony that she was waiting for him to figure this out himself, while the ghostwriter was in the study, waiting for the same thing. At night Minh crept into the room late and slipped onto the edge of their bed, leaving a slab of cold sheet between them.

On Saturday he found her packing clothes in the apartment. She had changed everything about the rooms since she'd moved in. What had been spare, book-lined rooms with white walls and unexceptional timber furniture had become shades of cream and avocado, overstuffed reading chairs and vases of flowers from the garden, the aroma of chili oil and lime and mint, music drifting through the rooms.

Leon watched her taking blouses and skirts off hangers. She smoothed her skirts out flat on the bed and rolled them into tubes that tucked into the gaps in the suitcase. Her shelves in the bathroom were already empty.

"I'll move to my old garden cottage until the shows are finished," she said.

"Don't, please." He moved behind her and put his arms around her waist. "Stop packing."

She pulled a tissue from her skirt pocket and blew her nose, then began to shake out each blouse and hold it against her body in order to overlay the sleeves into the bodice and scroll it into a neat bundle.

"I'll learn. I want to be the man you love."

He still didn't believe she would go until she lifted her framed sketch of Maisie and Maximus off the wall.

She zipped the suitcase shut, and Leon found himself falling to his knees. Minh sat on the bed, refusing to meet his gaze. His knee slipped, and he fell forward, then pushed himself up and walked ahead on his knees until he was resting his hands on Minh's legs. His throat swelled with tight swallows. He had never known emotion could inundate the body this way. Even when his father died and he watched the coffin slide away at the funeral and heard his mother beside him heave a sob into her tissue-crammed hand, he had not felt his whole body spasm with desolation as he did now. His blazing skin, his aching head and sore cheeks, the watery rush to his nose and eyes compensated for what his metal heart could not do. He begged Minh to stay. He took her hand and laid his damp cheek on it.

Minh brushed the hair from his sweating forehead. "I didn't know you could be like this."

It was all Leon could do to breathe. "Love," he whispered between gasps of air.

After a wait that nearly emptied him of hope, she agreed to try a little longer.

"It was you who wanted to be a husband," she said. "Can you do it?"

35

A T THE SHOW in Paris, when Leon began to recite his story and the crowd scrambled across the room to his booth, a small man remained behind and moved closer to Kathryn's booth. Leon noticed the lone spidery creature pressed up against the glass, staring intently at Kathryn, so he moved his foot to the alarm button and pressed. He delivered his monologue as he kept an eye on the two of them. The man stood motionless in front of Kathryn. Inside her booth, transfixed by his stare, Kathryn quivered like a plucked guitar string. She seemed afraid until she jumped off her stage and ran toward the glass. When she reached the place where the man was standing, she slammed her hands flat against the glass wall. He fell back.

Her mic was off—Leon's voice was coming through the speaker system—but the words she shouted still resounded around the space.

"If you try to contact me, speak to me, come near me, even fecking think of me again, you will regret it for the rest of your life. You have nothing on me now."

Now Leon recognized him. It was her husband, the one who had exploited her, photographed her and sold the images, gone on talk shows to express his disgust at what was happening to her. The man who was still trying to extract money from Rhona.

Kathryn pressed her hands hard against the booth wall until the palms whitened and the lines were maps, and stared down her ex-husband. Leon could have punched the air in triumph. He wanted to race from his people-proof booth and call Minh immediately and tell her what he'd seen: that Kathryn was no longer afraid of her barbarous ex-husband. But Rhona, together with his performance coach, the booth shows and the dinner bookings, had trained him into a professional. He raised his voice to keep the attention of the audience while from the corner of his eye he watched the husband slope away, his arms gripped by two security guards. Kathryn banged her fist one more time against the glass behind him.

After the show, Leon asked Rhona what the guards had done with the creep.

It was under control. Kathryn had asked that he be charged if possible. If not, warned and put on a flight back to Dublin.

"When she heard he was trying to get a share of her profits, she told me to do whatever it takes to make sure he gets nothing. Which demonstrates," Rhona pointed out, "that she's stronger than she's ever been. I'm more proud of her every day."

And there it was, two days later, all over the net. Footage of the filthy demon standing at the wall of the booth and Kathryn slamming her hands against the glass. Even though ticket holders were scanned at every show for devices that could capture images. Even though they had to surrender all electronic equipment at the cloakroom before passing through the scanner. How had the paparazzo gotten so close? Who was betraying them?

Back at Overington the next week, Hap arrived to report on

his investigations. He had hired a cybertracking firm to trace the origin of the images and footage. It had taken time, but finally they had located the source, a computer that moved from place to place around the world, that used sophisticated software to dissemble its identity and the route of its transmissions. The three Wonders were sprawled in their respective chairs in the common room. Kathryn sighed loudly.

"I don't care who it was. Why do we have to have a meeting? I'm so tired of meetings. You've done your job, congratulations and toodlepip. Can't they charge him with something and be done with it?"

"Maybe it was a her?" Christos drawled from his supine position. "That would make it more interesting."

"You're not going to be happy," Hap said. "So I won't try to make it easier. The leaker is Kyle. It's been Kyle all along."

Leon clutched Minh's hand, awash with vindication and fury. "I knew it. I knew, I knew it, I knew it."

"He knew it," Minh repeated drily.

Leon squeezed her hand once again and rose from the chair. He went to the window, stared out, tried to calm himself. "I knew it," he said once more, even though the feeling of triumph was subsiding. What was the use of his having known it when he never told anyone?

"Well then, Kyle has to go." Christos shrugged. His leaked images had only ever shown him primping and preening, except for one low-light shot in which he was draped on a banquette in a nightclub in an unflattering position that revealed a shadowy layer of flab. After that he redoubled his efforts at the gym until a month later, when he could demonstrate that the flab was gone.

"You bet he has to fecking go. He was one of us! What a prick. Did he do it for money?" Kathryn jumped up and went to stand in front of Rhona, hands on hips with her fists balled. The Irish accent always grew more pronounced when she was angry. "No payout for him, Rhona. None of that golden handshake that arseholes get. He must have broken some clause in his contract?"

"Sure. He broke the confidentiality clause."

"There." Kathryn turned to Leon and Minh. "The little worm will get nothing. We were supposed to be a team!"

Rhona, seated in her favorite armchair, uncrossed and recrossed her legs. She pushed back her hair and rubbed circles on her temples with four fingers before closing her eyes. Her tiny cowgirl boots sat neatly beside her plump stockinged feet. She told them Kyle was in his apartment, waiting.

"We have to make a decision about his future with us," she said.

"What future? That traitor has no future here!" Kathryn danced backward and forward in a two-step of frustration.

Rhona sighed. "Please sit down again, all of you."

Kathryn and Leon returned to their seats. As Leon eased into his deep sofa, he noticed how worn the armrest had become. The suite had been brand-new when they arrived at Overington. Over their time together the chafing of people sitting and moving about had rubbed away the plush brown velvet pile and now he could see the cords under the upholstery material showing through like the tendons in a stressed neck. Everything was wearing thin: the furniture, the shows, the lifestyle, their relationships.

"Was it revenge?" Minh asked. Leon had told her about what he saw in Kathryn's apartment. "Because Kathryn rejected him?"

Rhona, Christos and Yuri all shifted in their seats and stared at Kathryn.

"No," Kathryn answered crossly. "It's nothing to do with any of that. The leaks started last year."

"She's right." Rhona turned the rings on her fingers, one rotation each finger. "I've talked to him. He showed me some paperwork. It's been a part of his strategy all along. He never wanted us to know it was him because he guessed you'd all react this way. But the public needs the salacious stuff too. If you're all perfectly wondrous all of the time, your followers lose interest. A touch of ugliness and bad behavior makes them crave you more." Rhona laughed. "He did say it would have been much better if one of you had been to rehab."

"You think it's funny?" Kathryn stared at Rhona. "I don't believe it. He lied to us all—even you. If we'd known what he was doing none of us would have cared. But he lied."

"You would have cared. You three would have wanted to pretty up the shots, make yourselves look better."

"No, we're smarter than that. And he's a slimy liar. Why do you want to keep him?"

"Come on, face it, until now you liked him. His strategies work, we're doing better than I dreamed. I know you're all tired, but we're nearly there. We only have five more shows. And Kyle has said that's the last of the leaks. There have been enough, he won't do it anymore. He'll be focusing all his efforts on the finale now."

No one knew before this whether Kathryn could cry, whether the treatment that triggered her wool growth had also affected her tear glands. She'd sat dry-eyed through movie screenings that had every other one of them dabbing madly at their eyes with tissues; she'd broken a toe once by tripping on a paving stone in the grounds and not shed a tear; she'd rehearsed her routine until she was so exhausted she collapsed. This was the first time Leon had seen the giveaway of fast blinking and sniffing.

She turned, swiped her eyes as she faced away from them. "I'm worn out. I can't wait till this is over, Rhona."

36

IT HAD BEEN an uneventful booth show, the third from last, in a newly built venue next to a shopping mall in the Brazilian capital. Eight hundred audience members already fizzing with excitement from the circus, charging around the booths, dropping their sweets and popcorn and drips of sauce and trampling them into the sawdust floor. To the Wonders it was the same old show, same old music, same old awe and astonishment. In the final scene, Christos cut short his performance by thirty-two seconds and left the tech fumbling with the sound and lighting and projections to bring the show to a close without its being obvious that they'd messed up. Back in the dressing room, Kathryn stomped around on the glossy parquetry.

"Call yourself an artist, Christos? You think these people don't deserve a proper performance? Or do you only care about some art collector in fecking Soho?"

"I don't care about any of them. And you don't either. You hate them. You said so last night. You said they are stupid shits who'd pay to see a turd if it was celebrity endorsed."

Leon laughed. He loved Kathryn's smart mouth—when it wasn't used on him. That was exactly what she had said the night before at the rooftop restaurant in the hotel as they looked out over the sleek modernist buildings of Brasília. They were squabbling and toying with their food. They had seen enough of the world, at least the world they inhabited, one of vectors and passages and windows. Enough of bird's-eye views from the top floors of hotels. Enough of countries where the language meant nothing and the food tasted too fruity or too fatty or too thin or of nothing but dusty old spices. And enough of each other.

Christos had thrown four tantrums in a month about trivialities: whole milk instead of half-and-half; the width of the seats on their private jet; Yuri's failure to master English grammar; Kathryn's noisy heels on the floors at Overington. Furious, Kathryn had ordered forty pairs of wooden Swedish clogs delivered to Christos's apartment. Christos responded by hiring a bouzouki orchestra to play in the common room for five hours. When Rhona arrived home to find Christos and Kathryn shouting at each other over the music, she joined in the yelling herself. After a house meeting, where she once again explained the penalties in the fine print of the contracts that meant that early departure or expulsion from the Wonders would result in a massive depletion of percentages, they settled into an uneasy truce.

At night Leon and Minh lay in the quiet darkness whispering about what was to come for each of them. Minh wasn't worried about Christos, who reminded her of the spoiled proud boy children of her neighborhood when she was growing up. "Those little kings," she said to Leon. "Someone always picks up after them."

But Kathryn was her best friend, and as the end of the Wonders drew closer, Minh had begun to talk about Kathryn's plan.

What was the point of buying a Caribbean island if you had to live on it by yourself? Kathryn's wool had lost its glossy sheen. She often finished dinner early if they were dining together, or got up and left the room in the middle of group conversations. Between shows she threw herself into long bouts of reading where nothing could penetrate her concentration. She was the most famous woman on the planet, and she was preparing to become the most alone.

Over their time together, Leon had gradually learned something of how the scar lines streaked through Kathryn like damaged nerve sheaths. He was better at avoiding the sensitive places, the words, the emotional bruises that made her flinch. He had grown used to her sharp edges, her funny lines—"Don't try to fool me, Leon, I can see right through you." She had always been determined to puncture the fast-inflating bubble of their self-importance. "We are the humans where you can see the seams. It's like looking at those deep-water fish that are transparent and have odd protuberances from their heads." When she'd said that, Kathryn had glanced slyly at Minh, then put on a fake posh accent. "Protuberances, there's another one of those wonderful words. Like Christos's wings. Do you think he'd appreciate that title—the Magnificent Christos and his Protuberances." The three of them split into laughter.

"I want to ask her to come with us myself," Leon had said to Minh before the Wonders left for the South American tour. "She knows you want her to. If I ask, she'll know we both do." Kathryn's whole life had been shot through with threads of pain and betrayal—perhaps their home could be her sanctuary.

In the dressing room of the Brazilian auditorium, Kathryn swiveled on the parquetry floor, soles scraping with the resin Yuri had put on all their shoes to prevent slipping.

"Well, they pay to see us, and we are celebrity-endorsed turds. So fuck you, Christos. Just shut up, will you?"

As she disappeared into the bathroom to clean off her makeup, Christos and Yuri snapped shut their equipment cases and called the escort guards. Leon quickly changed into clean clothes and packed his costume into a pull-along suitcase.

"Let's go!" Christos shouted through the bathroom door at Kathryn. "Hurry up!"

Leon was impatient to get moving too. Tonight they would fly home to Overington, where the final plans for the house he and Minh were having built in Australia would be waiting.

Kathryn emerged from the bathroom with a shiny face, wearing her velvet traveling cape. She handed her bag to the security guard and wheeled around to face Christos.

"Oh, you're still here. Shouldn't you be striding ahead in the vanguard of the art movement?"

The group of six headed out of the dressing room and along the corridor. Christos and Yuri hurried alongside the guard at the head, Leon trundled his case along in the middle and Kathryn and the rear security guard walked behind. The head guard opened a door in the wall and they slipped into a service corridor, descended two flights of stairs and found themselves in a winding tunnel that ran below the shopping mall. At regular intervals they passed cleaning stations and other tunnels leading further into the bowels of the complex. Leon had his head down as he followed Christos and Yuri, pulling the case behind him and hearing the irregular rumble of the wheels as they rode the bumps of the concrete flooring. His signature tune was repeating relentlessly in his head, and he tried to oust it by humming snatches of pop tunes from his teen years. Anything to get rid of that melody. It was only after minutes of trying song after song that he realized he could no longer hear the clicking of Kathryn's heels behind him.

For a moment everything became supercharged. He smelled a whiff of cleaning fluid and another of cooked meat. He heard the distant clatter of a cleaning cart and voices from a corridor far away. He noticed how dimly lit the space was. A chilly draft curled around his ankles. He turned and saw only an empty tunnel behind him.

"Kathryn?" he called.

The concrete whispered with a sound like falling scree. Kathryn didn't reply. He called her name again, and his voice rattled around the walls. They had turned a corner about three hundred feet before. Leon dropped the handle of his case and ran back. He turned the corner. Nothing. He pressed his hand to his chest. Running without warming up made him instantly breathless and panicky. He called Christos and Yuri.

Further inside the tunnel, beyond another bend, they found the security guard slumped unconscious on the floor near a junction, a hypodermic sticking from his leg. Three more corridors led off from the junction.

There was no sound apart from the clanking and rumbling of the workings of the complex. Leon found himself gasping for breath. Yuri was silent and wide-eyed, staring at the guard on the floor. Christos strode from entrance to entrance in each tunnel, calling Kathryn's name. The remaining security guard had run off along one of the corridors where he thought he had heard a cry. No one else had heard it. She was gone.

The message came later that night. It told Rhona to go home to the US, to wait for instructions, to tell no one. Kathryn had been taken.

37

LEON PRESSED THE *Play* arrow again.

The room had a low ceiling and scuffed cream paint-work. A metal-framed camp bed was pushed against the rear wall. A kitchen chair with turned legs and a brightly patterned orange-and-yellow flat cushion sat at the end of the bed. Under the bed was a green plastic bucket. A soiled pillow and rumpled sheet lay on top of the bed. Leon looked at that sheet and he felt terror that Kathryn would think of how to use it to escape from hell.

The room was shadowy from the poor lighting.

Kathryn sat on the bed, head bowed. She was draped in a length of dirty red brocade curtain material that might have been torn from a decaying mansion. A dull gleam at her ankle indicated a manacle attached to a chain that led to an eyebolt in the wall beside the camp bed.

A voice spoke from behind the camera. "Tell them you are being treated well." The voice was electronically transformed into menacing digital dictation.

She didn't respond. The camera operator zoomed the camera in spasms until her bowed head filled the frame.

"Look at the camera."

She didn't move. A black object appeared in the frame, pushed past her shoulder and prodded her neck. She convulsed. The brocade covering fell from her head and shoulders. She couldn't have lost weight in such a short time, but her shoulders seemed bony and fragile under the wool.

Kathryn looked up after she had been shocked with the electric prod. Her eyes were heavy lidded and bloodshot and focused on a point behind the camera.

A male voice, accented, from another part of the room. "I thought you would have horns under that hat."

"You're a fecking idiot."

The robotic voice from behind the camera told the other speaker to be quiet, then grunted. It grunted as if the owner of the voice was exasperated by this woman he had kidnapped and was holding captive. When Rhona heard that grunt as they watched the footage for the first time, Leon saw her face shift as if a magic cloth had been smoothed across her features. Her rage and fear and helplessness froze into an icy mask.

On the screen, two men in loose gray cloth masks moved to stand either side of Kathryn. The scraping and shuffling of their boots on the concrete floor gave the scene an incongruous atmosphere of banality. One of them accidentally brushed Kathryn's woolly shoulder with his hand and he recoiled, shaking his hand and wiping it against his trouser leg.

Someone off camera passed the two hooded men, or boys they might have been from the way they moved, a pair of rubber gloves each. As they snapped the thin translucent gloves onto their hands, a puff of white talc rose from their wrists.

Kathryn stared ahead. She was motionless except for her

shuddering, which had been intensifying over the course of the footage and was now causing the metal feet of the camp bed to jitter against the concrete floor.

The gloved hands took hold of her upper arms and lifted her to a standing position. Still she refused to look at the camera. The camera panned up and down her body. Her feet were bare and childlike. Leon rarely saw her in bare feet. She always wore those frivolous slippers or high heels.

"She is not harmed," the robotic voice said.

This was the ninth time Leon had watched. Each time he saw a new detail. The eighth time he noticed a flicker of the light, not enough to be called a shadow. The almost imperceptible flicker hinted at more people moving around the room out of the camera's visual field. On this ninth viewing he became aware that the man on the right had a way of standing that made him look as if he had himself been beaten. A closure of the shoulders. A hollowing of the chest. The chin thrust toward the breastbone. He imagined that if he watched the film enough times, he would hear a noise, or see a blur of old writing on the wall, or recognize the pattern on a woven blanket. There would be a sign belonging to a small town or a foodstuff that identified a specific region. The reprieve that always happened on TV.

When he finally went to bed, he lay dreaming about how this would happen, then pulling himself up, then drifting into reveries of detection and rescue. Each time he caught himself fantasizing about discovering a clue or working out a pattern that could reveal her location, he writhed in shame, twisting the sweaty sheets around his thrashing legs in the dark, waking Minh and apologizing and trying to lie still even though he wanted to shout and rip holes in the sheets. He lay rigid in the long dark of the night wishing he had turned around during the walk through the underground tunnels of that shopping center. Wishing he hadn't been humming to himself, hadn't been caught up, as always, in his solipsistic meanderings. Hadn't he learned from Minh that the story of his life did not always revolve around him?

Minh cried as she told him the next morning that she had dreamed Kathryn was nearby, and that Minh was following the high sharp note of Kathryn's keening out from the tunnels of the center, through the streets and alleyways of a dark city.

"I can't stand it," Minh said, sodden with tears. "I can't stand thinking about what's happening to her."

Christos called his family in Greece every few hours. His grandmother, in particular, had fallen for Kathryn's charm. He told them Kathryn hadn't been found yet, without giving any details. "I asked them to pray," he said. "Pray harder. Pray every minute of the day."

Hap was in control of finding Kathryn and getting her home. He wouldn't allow Rhona to call in the police or the FBI. "If it's religious, if it's ideology, if it's some lunatics with an agenda, then the FBI is already useless because they didn't see it coming. If it's money, we'll pay. That's the right thing to do because it will be a clean transaction. Kidnapping's an international business run by professional criminals. We need to adhere to the process. All we have to do is pay the money and she'll be released. It happens all the time. But if someone has a point to make, if they're going to use her in some campaign . . ." He looked at the floor.

Rhona touched his arm, and he laid his square cheek on the top of her head.

Minh turned to Leon. Hap and Rhona an item? They'd had no idea.

38

LEON'S FIRST GUESS was the disability rights people, the ones who had been wheeling and limping and trudging around the boundary of the grounds for so long, appearing on random days, scrawling their accusations on the footpath in chalk or spray-painting them on the hedges so that the words appeared as speckled artworks that faded as the leaves died and fell to the ground.

Hap said no. "What would a kidnap do except give them bad press? Think again. What else have you heard? Who are you afraid of?" He punched the room with his questions, and the air gave way. "Could it be the husband? He's greedy and stupid. Lethal combination. Or a madman on a mission? You might have seen him in a crowd or from a car. Think. Anything unusual? Anyone?"

Kyle, Leon realized, *that's who I used to be wary of.* Kyle sat on the couch beside Rhona. He was pale and uncharacteristically mute. He looked old. As old as his age. And Leon began to wonder whether he had been harsh, whether he had taken a set against Kyle only because of his confidence and charm and all the other traits Leon lacked. Perhaps Kyle was simply a hopeless man, another of the many besotted men who loved beyond reason the uncanny bewitching human who was Kathryn.

After Hap left to get his team together, they talked for hours, hysterical and babbling, trying to find solutions, posing ludicrous rescue scenarios. They subsided into silence, hollowed the building with despair. Started up again with the what-ifs. Hated themselves for it.

Christos was nursing a brooding rage at Hap. Even though it wasn't Hap's men who had failed Kathryn but hired security from the complex, Christos still blamed him. He tried out different accusations: "Hap hired those men—it's his fault." "He didn't hire enough men." "He was doing nothing at home while Kathryn was being taken." The others wouldn't agree.

Time jerked along in unpredictable increments as the residents of Overington wound down with tiredness and anguish. Leon, Minh, Christos, Yuri, even Kyle: they had become clockwork people whose mechanisms hadn't been wound. Their movements were torpid, their speech semicoherent. By the next morning they could barely form words.

Except for Rhona. Rhona blew a tornado through room after room, shouting on the phone to insurance agents, banks, Hap, her old friends. Even though there was no news, she still burst from hugging Christos to kissing Leon or Yuri or Minh, clasping hands, taking faces in her hands and speaking so close that her breath warmed them. "She will be all right," she told Leon. "She will be all right. I know she will."

Hap was running teams searching all possible worlds. One team churned through computers and databases looking for anomalies in Kathryn's online following, in the patterns of the lives of thousands of potential suspects who wrote about her, posted information or pictures, set up fan pages. Others were in the field, sniffing along the concrete of the underground passage where she was taken, grilling bystanders and security guards. One more group worked the electronic routes that the kidnappers' messages had traveled. Hap's day was spent walking around the garden talking into his headset, occasionally pulling a screen from his pocket to see what had been captured on video. Every now and then Hap and Rhona would collide on their pacing routes, and they would embrace wordlessly before moving on, back to work on their communication devices.

"It's those fucking Muslims." Christos swam out of his apartment every now and then with a new theory. "Remember the letters? Remember the imam who put the death sentence on her? Said she was Satan's ultimate weapon of enticement?"

"I think the Christians have her. No offense, Christos. I mean the crazy ones." Minh lay limp on a couch in the common room, a damp cloth over her forehead. "I don't know why they haven't arrested that nut who runs the TV station, the one in the South. He funds the abortion clinic bombers. He's the one who called her the Princess of Darkness, got himself on all the talk shows with his ravings about the apocalypse."

Where was Christos's god now? Some journalists had accused the Wonders of acting as if they were gods, strutting around the world stage, known by almost every person on the planet, celebrities of a higher order than had ever been seen. *Do these false gods believe they are immortal?* one Christian broadsheet demanded on the front page when the Wonders first went global. *We shall soon see.*

Later that night Leon sat in the rickety pavilion in the old monkey enclosure where Rosa had originally been housed. He sipped his whiskey and stared at the shadowy palm trees clacking their fronds together in the breeze. Minh was inside sleeping. When Hap passed by, Leon caught his attention by waving the whiskey bottle and miming taking a swig. Hap refused the offer with a shake of his head. His headset blinked blue, and he tapped it and moved off, his voice sniping under the whisper of wind.

39

THE RANSOM DEMAND came at eight the next morning through Kathryn's fan site. The money was to be delivered to a designated spot in the highlands of Colombia in twenty-four hours' time.

An hour later Rhona called the house together for an update. "It's ready. The insurance company had already prepared cash in case it was going to be ransom."

Minh laid her head on Leon's shoulder. "She's coming home."

Hap was in his usual stance next to Rhona. He had become her suit of protective armor. She was tiny beside him. "This is good news. Great news. If it's simple K and R, Kathryn will be home safe in no time."

"Kidnap and ransom," Rhona said slowly, as if the words were exotic foods she was tasting for the first time. "It sounds like a TV show. Not real. None of this seems real."

"So now we should call the police?" Christos had been arguing for the police all along.

"Now would be the worst time. They want to catch the kidnappers. We want Kathryn back. Two different and opposing objectives." Hap muscled across the room to Christos, who was glowering in the corner. "Don't try to be a hero and call the police. You'll cause chaos and Kathryn will die. Is that clear?"

"But they can find out where she is!" He wore a T-shirt and jeans but when Christos stood at his full height, Leon half believed he could see the shadow of wrathful angel wings arched above him.

"Sure, and shoot everything that moves while they try to rescue her. Don't make me lock you up till it's over, Christos. My objective is to keep Kathryn alive. If you threaten that in any way, I'll shut you down until she's safe. We've hired a professional K and R negotiator. They've done this in Colombia plenty of times. This is the first take of an international celebrity by one of the gangs but it's the same deal. We pay, they release her. Now butt out and pray some more."

Hap asked what the proof-of-life question should be. What piece of information did anyone know about Kathryn that only she could answer?

"Can't we just give them the money?" Rhona said. "They can have it now, whenever, however much they want."

Hap said no. "We have to demand proof of life or they'll think we're up to something, some trick to avoid paying. We have to follow the procedure. They're professionals who expect us to play this a certain way. Now, please, try to think of questions only Kathryn could answer. We have a live video link in half an hour."

Minh suggested the question. "What was your nickname for your brother when you were little?"

She told them how, weeks before, Kathryn had charmed her with this story. Kathryn used to call her brother, the seasoned criminal at fourteen, Wolf. Kathryn was the lamb and he was the wolf. And then she grew into a sheep. Minh's voice wavered. "She was making those jokes about herself, feeling safe enough with us to do that."

"She is the Lamb of God." Christos's belief in god seemed to have been reinforced by this nightmare. Leon had watched him crossing himself and praying under his breath the way his yiayia had when she visited Overington. When the footage of Kathryn in chains played at Overington, Christos told Rhona to have faith. She smiled sadly at him as though he was a child full of hope that the fairies were living at the bottom of the garden.

An hour later, Hap came back to confirm that Kathryn had come on-screen and answered the question.

"How was she?" Rhona grabbed Hap's arm with both hands. "Did she say anything to us? I wish you'd let me see her."

"It went smoothly. No heroics on her part, which is the best outcome possible. I asked the question, she answered, they shut off the camera. All good. It's all good."

After that Hap stopped reporting in because each time he walked into the room where they waited, all of them surged forward, their terror so palpable the room itself seemed to swell and subside like a panicking heart. Half an hour later they scattered to their apartments.

"I've never worried much about it, Leon, but now I feel I need to know," Minh said as they huddled on their bed, too anxious to do anything but wait, try to drink tea or water, try to get something into their aching stomachs. It was eleven o'clock, twenty-one hours till the deadline.

"What is it? Can I help?" He spoke through gritted teeth, using all his energy to suppress the desire to pick at his skin. When he had sat outside drinking whiskey the night before while Minh slept for a few hours, the mosquitoes had sucked at him, and today he was covered in swollen bites. Minh had given him an antihistamine that was supposed to take away the itch, yet as he sat on the bed, spine pressed against the headboard and arms hugging his knees to his chest, he was giddy with the raging urge to scratch the skin off his body. It was almost, but not quite, enough to shift his attention momentarily from Kathryn.

"Is there a god?" Minh asked. Her parents were Catholic in name but had never had any time to do the rituals of church or make offerings with the community of the parish. Minh grew up with a couple of books about Jesus and her dead grandmother's ugly wooden rosary that she kept tucked at the bottom of her jewelry box. She was thirteen before she found out it wasn't a necklace.

"The day I asked my mother about god, she went quite red," Leon said. He was nine. A boy at school had been telling him how god made everyone and would punish people forever in damnation if they sinned. "Of course there's a god, darling," Leon's mother answered, still with those high pink spots on her cheeks as if she had been caught out neglecting an elderly relative. "He loves us all and"—her eyes rolled briefly skyward as she wiped her hands up and down the thighs of her tight blue tracksuit pants—"and he lives in heaven. Do you want to learn more about him? I could enroll you in Sunday school."

Leon didn't need to say it. God was irrelevant. Kathryn's kidnap wasn't about a god. It was about money. Everything was about money now. There were people who tried to make out that the value of human life was about god or justice or truth. But they relied on money to propagate their message. In the end, it was as though this medium of exchange had become a true organism: purposeful, amoral, determined to reproduce itself at any cost. And because humans made it, the cost rebounded on its maker. Leon could see it now. The cost of money was humanity.

Who were these kidnappers anyway? What kind of person would choose to make a living by stealing other people?

"What do you think the kidnappers are doing now?" he asked Minh. "Are they watching TV? Are they talking to Kathryn? Are they eating lunch?"

"Don't, Leon!" Minh's voice was hoarse from crying. "Don't talk about them like they're human."

40

SUSAN AND HOWARD had given Leon life. Medical pioneers are people who take risks in order to make possible what has been impossible. The risks they take mean that the survival rate of their patients is low. They operate on people others have given up for dead. They operate on people who would have died without them, and often the patients still die.

When Susan approached Leon, he was the walking dead. He was eleventh on the list of people Susan had called. Her phone call was courteous, brusque. She told him she was working for a medical-technology company that offered an extremely high-risk procedure for patients who had no further options for treatment. She said he would have to sign a waiver that his family would not sue if he died during the procedure or as a result of the proce-dure. She said the treatment would be lengthy, lonely and pain-ful, but that it would cost him nothing in terms of money.

Only when they met did she tell him that she was the sur-geon, that her husband was the engineer, that the whole venture was illegal, that Leon would probably die and that his family would never know what had happened to him, because he would have told them that he was leaving for palliative treatment overseas and could not be contacted.

But he was going to die if nothing happened. What did he have to lose? He couldn't understand why the other ten people had refused.

"Because they want to die close to their families and friends, Leon. They were happy to take the risk of the procedure, but when I told them they would have no contact with the outside world during treatment, during which they could well die, they backed off." Susan tilted her head as she spoke, as if she was surprised Leon hadn't already understood this.

At last his solitary nature, his fearfulness with people, his propensity to spend time alone with his books, had come into its own. He was the only one who was happy to walk away from his life. It was the first real risk he had ever taken.

That conversation had come back to him when Hap called him alone to the screening room.

More footage had been uploaded. A bruise shaded Kathryn's cheekbone purple and yellow. Her lower lip was split. The wound gaped open, no longer bleeding but still raw and swollen.

"I need to discuss something, Leon. I'm extremely concerned."

Leon wiped his forehead. Surely someone else should be here.

"I need to talk to someone because I think this kidnap isn't what it seems. Or else it is what it seems but they've taken on more than they can handle. They're insisting we bring forward the time of the trade and they only put up that footage because we said no deal without proof she was still alive. Professional kidnappers never damage the goods. Kathryn shouldn't be injured. I need to ask the Wonders' permission to take radical action, and Rhona's gone into some kind of overdrive. The insurance company has asked me to stop her from calling them. She's not thinking straight. The thing is, Leon, this kind of action can have consequences. Sometimes, despite our best men and our best plans, the hostage doesn't survive the rescue attempt."

"I can't make that decision, Hap. It's not up to me. Ask Christos." As if Hap could. Christos was already furious with Hap, wanting to blame someone and finding only him. Leon couldn't stop the words coming. "No, sorry, of course you can't ask Christos. But, Hap, I'm not the right person to ask. What about . . ." Leon had been about to suggest Hap speak to Minh. After all, Minh was the one who wrapped her steady trust around people, who settled things down in tense times. But if Hap went to Minh because she was the only one with enough moral fiber to make a decision, what did that say about Leon?

"Okay, forget it. I'll deal with it." Hap opened the door for Leon to leave.

Clockwork Man. Rhona had been right all along. Leon's expertise involved reading, searching the Internet, learning everything secondhand. Finding things out about people not to help them, not to improve their lives. Simply so he could pretend to know them, to pretend he was closer to them. All the jokes the Wonders had made about the people who came to see them being voyeurs, and here, at their heart, was the man without a heart, the ultimate voyeur, who watched the world through screens, exactly as Minh had said. During the time when he was going to die, he took a risk because he had nothing to lose, not even life. Now that he was alive, wealthy, famous and loved, he had turned into a weak brace-wearing man who ran from bad news.

The indigestion that had plagued Leon since the operations burned up his throat in a fiery tide and flooded his mouth. He raced to the apartment, and when Minh got back from her walk, she found him hunched over the toilet bowl, waiting to vomit.

After he had lain down, Minh came into the bedroom and sat beside him on the bed. Her weight tipped him in her direction. He closed his eyes.

"Can I do anything?" She ran her hand along his thigh, encased in its tube of stiff denim cotton. "Do you want an analgesic or some tea? Hap told me that we have a meeting in thirty minutes. He wants to tell us something about Kathryn."

Leon rolled over so his back was toward her. "I don't need drugs. I'll be ready for the meeting." He needed to think. How to become stronger, a braver man, a true man.

At least he had learned something. He was no automaton. No machine could experience shame the way he was experiencing it. No matter how smart or trained or wired or bioengineered, machines could never replicate the uniquely human emotion of shame.

At the meeting, the common room was dimly lit, but Leon could still see how reddened the eyes of Rhona and Yuri were, how rigid the face of Christos. Kyle jigged at the side of the room, unable to stand still while talking to someone on the phone. Minh stood behind Leon, her arms wrapped around his waist, her head resting on his right shoulder blade. The staff gathered at the door leading to the kitchen to listen as Hap reported the latest.

"We've brought the handover time forward to midnight. That's the earliest we can reach the handover location. It's remote. The kidnappers say they're worried about tip-offs. I don't like it, but it's not unheard of. There are other worrying factors, but there's probably no time for anything else now except to do the trade as soon as we can. I wanted to keep you updated."

Rhona sagged into a chair. "Does this mean we'll have her

back sooner? Isn't that a good thing?" Her eager voice was far from her usual authoritative tone.

"It's an earlier handover. We can't be sure exactly what it means." Hap gave Rhona's shoulder a brisk massage before he bent down and whispered in her ear.

He strode off, leaving Leon wondering whether he had shared his concerns about Kathryn with anyone else. It was improbable he would have gone to Christos, who was already incandescent with fear and fury, flailing around trying to find a reason to blame Hap. In the last couple of hours, Rhona had folded in on herself. She had stopped hurrying about, stopped calling people on the phone, stopped everything. Minh wept and wept, a mound of damp tissues rising beside her. Yuri sat silent and shrunken in the corner.

Kyle paced from room to room, plugged into various communication devices, dealing with interview cancellations and trying to build a story that Kathryn was indisposed with the flu. No one was supposed to know Kathryn had been kidnapped. If it got out, who knew what would happen. What would the crazies do? What would her fans do? What would the religious groups who had been calling for her death do? It was impossible to imagine the madness that would manifest after that kind of announcement.

As the hours to the deadline juddered along, Leon walked the house and the grounds, encountering each person maintaining their own vigil. Kyle insisted on having TV and online media streaming all the time.

"Can't you turn that off?" he asked Kyle.

"And then? Do what instead?"

Leon found the relentless drone of newscasters insufferable. He hunted out an old pair of earphones and a music player loaded with Minh's music, and kept walking with Beethoven scouring his brain, scratching away the fear, the self-recriminations. Minh had gone to her studio, where Leon knew she'd be methodically cleaning every brush, every palette, every water glass. Leon found Yuri sitting on a stool by the bear enclosure, singing into the darkness. He pulled off the earphones. He had never heard Yuri sing before. It was a melancholy air, the words in a language he couldn't understand.

Back toward the house, Leon stopped to watch the great sleeping bodies of the elephants. Perhaps the faint music of Yuri's song had entered their wide ears because they shifted position, eyes still closed, and twined their trunks together.

He put the earphones on again. The screen of the player said that this symphony was by Mahler. In the kitchen he found Christos sitting beside tiny Vidonia, who had decided to stay through the night. Leon took his place on a stool beside them. He accepted a small cookie Vidonia offered. The dry floury lemon crumbs melted slowly on his tongue. The music in his ears was so dense he felt separated from the world around him, immersed in a sea of sound. Christos picked up his phone, and although Leon could hear nothing but the music he imagined Christos was ordering more candles lit in his village in Greece, more prayers offered.

He left Christos and Vidonia and walked back to Minh's studio. She had finished cleaning her equipment. She stood before a large bare canvas. Leon pulled off the earphones.

"Are you going to paint her?" he asked.

"I don't know," she said. Her hair, the hair he loved to touch, usually thick and glossy, hung in strings around her face.

She didn't know about what Hap had said either. Leon knew he should tell her, but he couldn't. He put the earphones back on and drowned himself in the music.

At one in the morning, Hap brought the news they had dreaded.

41

THE K AND R negotiator arrived at Overington, disheveled and sweating from the journey, his gray hair oily and a brush of stubble rasping against his hand each time he rubbed his face. It was not his fault, everyone knew that, yet he was the one who had seen Kathryn dead, and that made him ugly and despicable.

Hap sat, legs apart, face in hands, while the negotiator explained what had happened. Leon could barely breathe. No one wept or spoke. They had all cried themselves out. The air in the room was curdled from the rank breath of people so wretched they could not eat, could not sleep.

The negotiator told them that when he arrived at the exchange location, loaded up with the ransom, a truck was waiting for him. Inside the cab of the truck were three figures. It was midnight. Normally the negotiator would not do a trade in the dark—he needed to see that the kidnap victim was unharmed—but the spokesman for the kidnappers had sounded jittery and was pressing for the trade to happen early. Hap and the negotiator had decided that if the kidnappers were that anxious, it would be better to get Kathryn away as fast as they could. The damage to Kathryn's face was worrying too. So the handover had been brought forward to midnight from the original time. It was essential that the kidnappers not be panicked or believe that the police might be involved.

"Damage to her face?" Rhona said, looking to Hap.

"There was no point showing you the footage. You would have worried even more," Hap said, without glancing at Leon.

"Why didn't you go in and rescue her then?" Christos sat up. "You knew it had gone wrong? So many times I begged you to—"

"We tried. They'd already left when we got there. Moved to another location. We found one of them shot through the head, an execution. Go on," Hap told the negotiator.

Leon had to stand up. No one noticed except Minh because they were all immersed in their own grief, but he had to move. His whole body was knotting up. What Hap had feared had come true. Something had been wrong, but Leon had lacked the courage to authorize Hap's intervention. At least Hap had taken the initiative without authorization. And yet . . . When the negotiator began to speak again, Leon had to pace around behind the chairs to ease the contraction of his muscles.

"Two men got out of the cab of the truck. They were a hundred yards away, two twitching shadows. The third figure stayed in the truck and I couldn't see whether it was Lady. We switched on the floodlight attached to the roof of our van, but it didn't do much to illuminate the inside of the cab."

As he listened to the negotiator talk, Leon felt as if his mind was rolling over and over, a great wave traversing the ocean. He moved to perch on the edge of the sofa, holding Minh's sweating hand in his tight grip. Her head was bowed as if sorrow had weight and was dragging it down.

"It was a cleared area near a new plantation. I had an armed man hiding in the back of my van as I always do. That's normal procedure. I've done it plenty of times, and the exchange happens like a business transaction. But Hap and I both knew something was bad when we saw the bruises in the footage, right, Hap?" The negotiator looked to Hap, who gave a slight nod, turned away. His face was gray and lumpy, a piece of pummeled lead. The negotiator went on. "Professionals wouldn't harm a hostage; that would be stupid. They get their ransom for undamaged goods. So I was already cautious. I'd made special arrangements to have a dozen armed men hidden around the exchange location, just in case. Something smelled wrong.

"So after they had gotten out and were standing beside their vehicle, I lifted the case off the seat beside me, thought better and put it down again, got out of the van, and started walking toward them. I've done this twenty, thirty times. Never for this much money, but always the same routine. We meet halfway in the no-man's-land between the cars. I make sure the hostage is okay, then we do the swap. But they set off from their vehicle without bringing the hostage, and I knew right away." He paused, took a sip of the coffee sitting on the tray beside him, patted his face again with his hands as if to wake himself up.

"I guess I'm trying to say to you that it was probably all over before we even finalized the meet. It was Lady in the cab of the truck, but . . ."

At a signal from Hap, the negotiator went on. "When we met in the middle of the no-man's-land between the cars, I could see one of the kidnappers was trembling, and that's when I was one hundred percent sure. He was young, skinny, grubby, and obviously terrified. I told them to get Lady from the truck and bring her to me immediately or no deal. Normally I would have had the money in my case under my arm, but being already suspicious, I'd left it in the van to give myself a bit of leeway. 'Bring me the woman and I'll get the cash,' I said to them. The young one pulled his gun and aimed it at me. The kid was shaking so badly he could easily have shot me by mistake, and his friend saw that and grabbed the gun from him. It was stupid and frightening and the air was thick with panic. These weren't professionals, or if they were, something had happened and they were reacting very badly. It had to be the worst thing possible."

The negotiator had whistled to his friend in the car, who jumped out and aimed his high-powered rifle at the kidnappers, who in turn ducked and raced, bent low, to the truck. The negotiator saw that when the first man jumped into the driver's seat, the third shadowy passenger who had been left in the cab slumped to the side. It had to be Kathryn, and she was clearly not conscious. The negotiator gave a silent signal to the men he had planted around the site, and when the truck took off and screeched in a U-turn to escape, it was met by a row of four masked men aiming guns at the driver. They dragged the kidnappers from the truck, but it was too late. Kathryn was already dead.

42

AFTER THE NEGOTIATOR had arranged to have Kathryn's body transported to the US, and before the police became involved, the negotiator's team took the kidnappers to a safe house in Colombia to interrogate them. The story they heard was of men faced with a phenomenon that unseated all their assumptions, the effect Kathryn had on everyone.

They would have taken any one of the three Wonders, the men said, but Kathryn had been lagging behind, easy to pick off. Everything had been calm and professional inside the plane that was flying them under the radar. Kathryn was hooded and silent. Her captors stayed alert and tense until she was secured in the house in the mountains.

Once they removed the hood and her cape inside the small room where she was imprisoned, they couldn't stop staring. For the first day, she said little and didn't resist their furtive touches of her wool. Then for no reason, they said, she began to laugh. They were already unsure, afraid they might have made a mistake in taking someone so high-profile. One of the men smacked her when she spat at him. They slipped into an uneasy quiet, taking turns to sleep while the leader put together the ransom demand.

After the demand had been sent, Kathryn heard them talking about the ransom. She laughed and told them they should have asked for more. She told them they were stupid and amateur. One of the men brought out a bottle of rum to calm everyone down. He passed the bottle around. Soon they moved on to another bottle.

There were two kidnappers on guard and two sleeping when the cattle prod, which had only been used once for the first recording, was retrieved from another room by the youngest, most inflamed gang member. The noise of his drunken shouting woke everyone. He waved the prod in front of Kathryn as the others urged him to settle down, to remember why they were there. "She can't feel it," he said to them, circling her like a man with a burning brand edging around a tiger. "Look at her, she's not human. She's an animal. They don't feel the things we do. See?" And he jabbed her with the prod.

The others watched as Kathryn jerked about under the electric current, then fell to the floor. One nudged her with the toe of his boot. There were now five men in the room. Three were trying to talk the other two into settling down, reminding them that this was business, that Kathryn was their meal ticket. The first young man edged around her, leaning in to look closely at her head, her pale ears. When his boot accidentally contacted her buttock her body jerked involuntarily even though she was unconscious. He jumped back, startled, then kicked her. She lay motionless.

"See?" he slurred. "It can't feel anything. It's a dumb animal."

After a few seconds she woke, still shackled to the wall next to the camp bed in the small dank room in the mountainside jungle. When the leader saw the facial bruising that had been hidden as she lay on the floor, he recognized they were in trouble. He had her lifted back onto the bed and tied her into a sitting position. He got on the computer and made the demand to bring forward the ransom handover, and he uploaded footage to prove she was still alive. The drunken man who had kicked her was locked in the room next door. But it wasn't long before the drunk broke out, propelled by lust and a revulsion at his own urges, and wrestled a gun from his fellow kidnapper.

"If they had taken one of you men," the negotiator told everyone at Overington, "everything would have been different."

Kathryn's body was flown to Overington. There was a quick private service. Rhona, who had been gifted with power of attorney for each of the Wonders when they signed up, ordered that Kathryn be cremated so that no one else could violate her body.

43

THE PROFESSIONAL COUNSELORS failed to come up with a single consolation that Leon hadn't read in a self-help book. The household at Overington stumbled through the next few days, trying to avoid speaking about Kathryn, trying not to imagine her last moments. All they could manage was a sorrowful mask, behind which lay the immovable glutinous gray mound of their grief.

Rhona, when she finally emerged from her room, leaning on Hap, called a meeting. She asked them to bring everything personal from Kathryn's quarters. She wanted to touch Kathryn's things, hold them in her hands, sniff them and think about Kathryn, before the distant relatives who had swarmed out of nowhere when Lady Lamb went global came to lay claim to everything from the dead woman they used to despise. And who had shunned them in return.

All morning Leon and Minh carried the cosmetics and medicines and perfumes and trinkets and ornaments piece by piece from Kathryn's quarters to the floor in the common room.

Christos and Yuri brought out the capes and cloaks, the *ao dai* and the saris, the shoes. Kyle brought the jewelry trees, walking so slowly and with such a somber face he could have been a priest holding aloft burning candelabras at a requiem mass. When everything was piled in a messy heap on the carpet, Rhona pulled her chair next to the mound and lifted objects with care. She turned them over, examined them, pressed them against her face, rubbed them between her palms.

There were many cloaks in the pile. At first Kathryn had balked at wearing anything over her wool, but she came to love the cloaks. The drama of the cloak as it furled around her. The privacy against the gaze of the curious. Cloaks of rich ruby red and gold. Sea blue-green woven with alternate threads of silver and color that caught the light when she moved. Satin and silk and cotton and rayon. Some were patterned with paisley swirls and others with traditional tartans.

Christos was the first to pull on a cloak. He chose a midnight-blue velvet. Too short, of course, and not wide enough. But the neck had a long drawstring of silk plaited cord that he tied in a loose knot at his throat. He drew the cloak in close, covering his arms. He pressed his cheek to his shoulder and breathed in deeply.

"I can smell her."

Yuri picked up her most fantastic cloak, the one she wore to impress at parties. It was the padded silk of a Chinese emperor's robe, hand-embroidered in scarlet and gold and green with the scene of a palace on a hillside and the sun rising behind it, peasants working in the fields below, their conical hats tipped against the sun's rays, pantaloons puffed out above the shimmering silver of the watery rice fields. Yuri draped it over his shoulders, and his knees buckled a little under the weight.

Rhona swung a flimsy ivory silk and antique lace cloak across her shoulders. She was too short, and it dragged behind her on the ground. Hap shook his head, but she stared at him until he relented and picked up a denim cape, short, more of a swing jacket, and draped it across his shoulders. It made the others laugh, seeing him embarrassed in such an incongruous piece of clothing when they had only ever seen him wearing fatigues. Minh ran, still laughing, to the pile and took a cloak made of colorful braided plastic from the rubbish dumps of the Philippines that Kathryn had commissioned and paid fifty times what the makers asked.

"Kyle?" Rhona asked. He was in the corner of the room, away from the others. After the revelation about the leaks, even though he had continued to work for the Wonders, he had distanced himself, spent even less time with the household than before. "It's okay. Really, hon. You know, Kathryn told me she was sorry she couldn't be what you wanted. She'd forgiven you for the leaks. We all accepted, in the end at least, that they had worked for us."

Kyle turned his face to the wall beside him. He lifted his hand to his brow. His Adam's apple was bobbing up and down.

"Oh, darling." Rhona picked up a pea-green velvet cloak and took it over to Kyle. She arranged it over his shoulders and pulled it tight so it swaddled him while he stood passively, hunched over, weeping. Leon felt the familiar rise of a swollen sob in his chest. How badly he had misjudged Kyle. Kyle had been devoted to Kathryn from the first moment he met her. It was as simple as that.

"What about you, Leon?" Minh grasped his arm and led him to the pile. The plastic braid of her cloak rustled as she walked. Leon had a sudden memory of Kathryn striding in front of him into a New York penthouse where a private show was to be held. The cloak hissed and crackled as she moved, and when they reached the doorway where a servant in white tails was bowing as he held open the sturdy oak door, she turned to Leon and laughed. "Should I tell them that this cloak came out of a garbage dump?"

Minh pulled an olive satin cloak from the pile and brushed it straight before holding it up against Leon. "No, makes you look too pale." She rummaged deeper into the pile. "How about this one?"

The cloak of synthetic fur looked like a mangy pelt—the shabby trophy from a hunt of the colonial era. Another of Kathryn's jokes.

Leon still hadn't told Minh about the time he should have listened to Hap and urged him to act on his fears. She had heard many times the story of how Leon and Christos raced out of the entertainment center instead of staying with Kathryn in a tight safe group as Hap had ordered them to do. But it was always Christos telling the story.

Maybe he could have helped Kathryn, maybe he could have saved a life, maybe he could have changed something for the better, maybe he could have become a better man, maybe his actions would have ruined everything. He didn't know. But he did know that he hid these things from Minh because he was afraid they would diminish him in her eyes. A cascade of shoulds tumbling back to his childhood.

Leon took the scrappy cloak and lifted it to his shoulders. The Velcro straps barely met around his throat. He tore the Velcro away, tossed the cloak onto the pile and took a few deep breaths before bracing himself and choosing a pale green cotton cloak that settled loosely around his shoulders.

"Now what?" he said. He was unworthy of wearing Kathryn's cloak. He would have to tell Minh what he had done. Minh reached over and touched his arm. Leon placed his hand over hers and changed his mind for the hundredth time. He could never tell her. He must never tell anyone.

Christos slammed a fist on the table. "Now nothing, Leon. Think of Kathryn. Honor her."

44

SHE HAD CONTACTED Leon and asked him to meet her in Manhattan. At first he didn't recognize her. The gray hair that used to hang over him as she examined his chest was clipped close to her scalp. She wore an oversized scarlet shirt and a teal scarf on top of white linen pants. Back in the basement she was always in black pants and a pastel shirt covered by the lab coat that had grown more stained and threadbare as the year of Leon's surgeries wore on. Here in the diner she stood when he moved toward her. He quickened his pace. He wanted to push forward and embrace her, and yet it wasn't her, it was a new Susan, and he had to respect that.

"Leon, I'm so sorry about Lady."

Her hand reached out and without thinking he took the hand and shook it. They stood beside a booth in the diner on Seventh Avenue. When Leon went to kiss Susan on the cheek she pulled away and made out to be adjusting her clothes before she settled into the booth again.

"It's a tragedy. I truly am so very sorry," she said, once they were sitting facing each other. "It unsettled me in ways I hadn't imagined."

An old-fashioned chrome-and-red-vinyl bar ran the length of the diner, opposite the booths. Glass domes covered muffins and pieces of pie. A waitress came over with her pen and pad poised, and listed the lunch specials in a monotone. They ordered the soup of the day.

"Susan, I . . ." Leon wasn't sure what he wanted to say, even though he had been fretting about it all the way down from Overington. He had asked the driver to turn down the radio to give him space to think. Now he wished he had made notes or rehearsed the conversation the way Minh suggested. "Thank you for contacting me. I wanted—"

"I shouldn't have ordered food," Susan interrupted. Behind her another waitress was reciting the specials to a pair of customers. "This isn't social. Leon, I've contacted you because I have to make a confession."

He could see their soup coming. Two big steaming bowls of crimson tomato soup carried precariously by their bored waitress. She landed the plates on the table and pushed them toward Leon and Susan. The soup rocked inside the bowls.

"I want to give you money," he said. "However much you need. To make hearts for people who can't get them. I'm very very rich. I'll be rich for the rest of my life."

Susan dropped her forehead to the V of her hand and rested her elbow on the table. She was silent for a moment. Leon took a breath, ready to persuade her, but she spoke first.

"When we sent you off with the new heart and I took Howard to the coast for his last few weeks, I was so angry, Leon. Angry at Howard's final year spent in a basement, hiding, working madly. Angry at his ambition, at his stubbornness, even at you. I spent a year watching him deteriorate. You know we did what we did because he was dying."

"I know," Leon said. "I know and I'm more than grateful."

"Yes, but you don't understand. After he died, I decided that we had wasted that time. Sure, we saved you, but one life? One life in exchange for our last year together? I wished we hadn't known he was dying. If we hadn't, he would have worked at a normal pace, thinking he had years to complete his project. We could have spent our time like normal people. We could have drunk wine and swum in the sea and traveled. But no, he had to finish that work because he knew he was dying. So I decided, Leon, that it was better if people didn't know they were dying. That no one should know how much time they had left." She paused.

The hollow deep rumble of traffic and the hooting of horns washed into the diner as a man held open the diner door and spoke a few words with an acquaintance passing by. Leon leaned forward to hear better as Susan went on.

"Then Lady Lamb and the whole kidnapping thing. It was so shocking—taken in her prime. And, Leon, I realized I was wrong. I thought about how young you are. You do need to know. It has to be your choice how you spend your remaining time. The problem is the battery. Inside the heart, sealed in there, is a battery that will run out. We had no choice. At the time we had no other way to power the heart, and the design didn't allow an external battery, so we used Howard's experimental metabolically recharging battery. It has a limited life."

When the man crossed back to his seat at the counter, the tide of noise receded with the slowly closing door.

More I would, but Death invades me, Leon remembered. "How long?"

45

THE IRONY DIDN'T escape Leon. What use was being a Wonder when after all the suffering, the surgery, the pain, the training, the struggle to become something more than human, you simply died like everybody else? Kathryn had died, and he would follow soon enough. Maybe one more year, maybe, if he was lucky, three or four. The hype of the Wonders had made him feel immortal. What a fool.

After Kathryn's death there were some celebrations: the fundamentalists who had feared and loathed Kathryn called it a triumph that someone had assassinated her and held religious services to give thanks. The rest of the planet mourned. The data world and the real world were swamped with images of Lady, poems to Lady, tributes, TV specials rushed out with montages of footage and hasty interviews with people who hardly knew her, instant books and magazine articles and rambling online posts and conspiracy theories and flowers, flowers everywhere.

At Overington the road was blocked for a week by the vigil

of mourners and onlookers and the flowers piling up until they began to rot underneath, and the stench became so bad that the local authority sent in a bulldozer to clean up. Leon caught a whiff of the sickly sweet putrefaction one day as he sat beside the open window. People were milling around outside, weeping, calling out "Lady" as if Kathryn could hear, still tossing bouquets and dolls and heart cushions onto the fetid overblown mounds along the fence, just as they had years before when that English princess died. What drove them to be so incensed with grief for a woman they had never met?

Three weeks later, news broke of a young actress's botched breast surgery. Her televised sobbing pleas to young women to love and respect their bodies blanketed the media. The herd swerved and galloped after her, leaving Kathryn's memory behind. Bookings at plastic surgeons soared, even as the images of the actress's mutilated breasts were beamed around the world. The fans who had bought skintight suits modeled on Kathryn's wool dropped them off at charity bins until the charities said they would not accept any more, and a month after that, Kathryn and the other Wonders' paraphernalia was being carted in truckloads to landfills.

During this time, Leon and the remaining house members drifted around Overington in a lethargic stupor of misery. The air began to gather an autumn chill as the building louvers rotated with their slow solemn fanning. Maisie and Maximus ambled through the grounds on their daily constitutional and Agnes kicked up her heels with two new ponies that had been sent by a retiring television trainer. Rosa the chimp had a new companion as well, a pet chimpanzee confiscated from a convicted drug dealer who had arrived at Overington half-starved and fearful. That gave Yuri a task to keep him occupied and not thinking constantly about Kathryn—the rehabilitation of the new chimp and the appeasement of a jealous Rosa. After a few weeks, Christos buried himself in planning for his next project. Rhona and Hap took a vacation in Italy.

Leon and Minh took over the kitchen and the common room. They cooked and ate and read and talked and held each other. Minh sometimes asked what Leon was thinking. He couldn't tell her, not yet.

In the time that fame had untethered the Wonders from the earth, they had drifted in a layer of high atmosphere, insulated in their private jets and penthouse rooms from the ordinary human world.

Death ended that. The loss of Kathryn made everything seem worthless, pointless. With the passing of the days, reality dawned on Leon, the image in a telescope sharpening with each turn of the focus ring. They were normal people with tricked-up bodies and a whole lot of money. The only one of them who had profoundly changed had been Kathryn. She was a mistreated woman in an unhappy marriage who was destined to die of a horrific disease. When she was cured of the disease and the wool grew, after she had escaped the torments of her husband and been rescued by Rhona, she metamorphosed in other ways. She said that her wool had nurtured her instead of being a reminder of her affliction. The wool curled tight against her skin in an elastic layer, stronger and more resilient than skin, continuously growing, twisting, tightening against her body in a snug caress. "I am strong, Leon," she said once. "I used to be weak but now I am strong and solid. I'm not afraid to be alone anymore." She was not afraid to be alone, but neither was she alone. She loved her family at Overington. They loved her. Minh may have taught Leon how to love a woman, Christos may have named family as the thing that mattered most, but it was Kathryn, he had come to understand, who had brought them together as family.

And he had married Minh under false pretenses. He had promised her a lifetime together, thinking that a lifetime was long.

As the weeks trudged on, the more the Overington team tried to melt into the background of the celebrity culture, the more rogue journalists pursued them for a "one month after" or "how are they coping now" story. So while everything was being prepared for the full retirement of the Wonders, on balance it seemed easier to turn up to an occasional opening or event than to hide away and be hunted. Tonight it was a charity event at the Mandarin Oriental to raise money for clinics in Africa. Minh and Yuri were already inside, having entered by the mortals' door.

Rhona escorted the Wonders, as usual, down the carpet in the center of the golden ropes that kept the public away from the stars. Behind her came Leon and Christos. Between them a terrible absence where Kathryn should have been. Leon and Christos walked closer together, as if to fill the gap, but the space between them ached like a phantom limb. Studio lights were trained on the carpet. On the flank, in a special area set aside for interviews, camera operators and interviewers with microphones of all shapes and sizes shifted from foot to foot and peered anxiously as each car pulled up at the curb. They called names and greetings and enticements as the celebrities stepped out of the vehicles. "I heard you're in love, Jennifer!" "We're running a whole show on your new movie, Eve!" "Kevin, Kevin, over here." On the other side of the carpet the paparazzi also were shouting and screaming names, and buoying them up on a raft of noise below was the bubble and chatter and cheers of the crowd of onlookers.

Most of the people lining the walkway into the hotel were there to see aLiNa, the music sensation famous for her outrageous costumes, but they clapped politely as Rhona led her two fading stars down the red carpet. Hap stood guard near the entrance. He had four other men hidden in the crowd just in case. A lone deranged fan was out there. She had made clear that she planned to destroy first Christos, then Leon. In the woman's feverish fantasies, she believed Leon had killed Kathryn to steal her heart of flesh. The madwoman was threatening to cut out Leon's heart and use it to bring Kathryn back to life. The only thing that stood between her and the mechanical man who had stolen Kathryn's heart was Christos, winged guardian demon of the heart thief. Without her heart, Kathryn could not enter paradise, where she and the fan, who would commit suicide to be with her once she had recaptured Kathryn's heart from Leon, could be together at last.

"Valentino!" "Angel!" Only one of the show hosts in the interview arena wanted to speak to them. She waved a thin tanned arm in their direction, the fat microphone in the shape of a giant licorice ice-cream cone at the end of it. Rhona turned and nodded to Christos, who sighed and walked reluctantly to the side, where the anchor was already gushing into the microphone about the bravery of the remaining Wonders and their gradual reentry into society after the tragedy. Leon hung back. It had always been this way. Despite all his media training, he was most interesting with his shirt off, fine with rehearsed pieces but too reserved to master the unscripted interview.

While Leon and Rhona waited, aLiNa's car arrived. A shadow of disappointment passed across the face of the anchor interviewing Christos, who had missed her chance at snapping up the big drawing card of the night, but she carried on gallantly. Leon turned to watch aLiNa sashay down the carpet in a dress made of plastic soft-drink bottles. The outfit had a train of bottles three feet long that made the sound of lightweight trash chittering over the footpath on a windy day. aLiNa walked along the carpet, smiling and signing a few programs and body parts. She waved at Leon as she passed.

"Hey, Valentino, can I see your heart one day?"

"Sure."

aLiNa was only nineteen, a child still. Leon hoped she wouldn't fall prey to the disease that brought down so many celebrities who came to it young, the gnawing emptiness that drove them to drugs and rage and a fickle hubris that made them feel alternately invincible and worthless.

Rhona tapped Leon on the shoulder. "Come on, hon, let's go in."

He saw the woman as he swung around. She stood at the rope directly behind Christos, grinning furiously. That's what caught Leon's eye, the mad grin. He stared at her, at the same time wondering why he felt he needed to stop and do that. The woman's glance shifted to Leon for a moment, and her eyes widened before her focus looped back to Christos. Even as her hand moved to her bag, Leon understood. She was so close to Christos, an arm's length away behind the rope, that there was no time for Leon to call out to Hap or Rhona, or to do anything but lunge toward her.

46

HE WOKE TO the familiarity of rough cotton sheets, antiseptic smells and the beeping of medical equipment. In his confusion and pain, he imagined he was in the basement again.

"Susan," he called weakly, and an arrow streaked from his belly to alert the vigilant pain homunculus in his brain.

"Darling, it's me, Minh. Can you hear me?"

Knowledge came to him in pinpricks. He was alive, he had been one of the brightest shining stars on the planet, Kathryn was dead, Minh was here beside him.

When he tensed his muscles to move, the pain became impossible, and he cried out.

"Don't move, Leon. You need another few days of healing before you'll be able to move easily." Minh's warm hand took his.

He opened his eyes and squinted against the cool glare of hospital light. More images came to him. The knife of the would-be assassin emerging gleaming from her handbag. Christos talking to the TV anchor, unaware of the danger behind him.

"Christos?" he croaked.

"In the private waiting room with Yuri and Rhona. You saved him. Got a hole in the belly for your trouble. But you'll be fine." Minh lifted Leon's hand and held it against her cheek. He felt a twinge of pain as his arm pulled away from his side but he disguised the wince with an attempt at a smile.

"Minh," he whispered.

"Yes?" She dipped her head so that her ear was close to his mouth. Her hair tickled his lips.

"I'm sorry."

She pulled back, gazed into his eyes. "Sorry? What for?"

"For not being enough."

She laughed, that musical laugh that had always made him want to laugh along with her. "You're plenty for me. And a hero too."

Leon turned his face to the side. So he had saved Christos. At least he had been able to perform one act worthy of a life. But that would never make up for his weakness over Kathryn. One day he would tell Minh. One day soon. Because he had to do everything soon, and he had to tell her why.

47

CHRISTOS AND YURI had booked their flights to Malaysia, where Christos would begin work on his final project.

Minh still wanted to move to Australia, into the house they had commissioned. She needed to get away from America and her family. Her mother in Orange County called every day, begging her to come home and leave the dangerous group of people she had taken up with. Now Kathryn was gone, and since she had died in such a sordid and spectacular fashion, the Wonders had stopped being glamorous. The media were bleeding pity for the two remaining Wonders and their disabilities. They were true freaks now. Freaks in danger of being captured and caged like animals, and in Leon's case, experimented upon. In danger of being seen as less than human, they who had been the überhumans. Were the demonstrators who had haunted Overington for so long pleased that the Wonders had lost their shine? Or did this make it all worse? Had the whole sorry mess dragged them even further down in their struggle for equality?

THE WONDERS

Christos was frantic to get out of the spotlight and refine his next artwork for a year or two. Once the furor had died down and the Wonders were forgotten, he could emerge in his new form, the Illuminated Human.

Rhona would stay. She would bring in more animals, reestablish the sanctuary, take in abused animals from overseas to fill the space. Circuses with performing animals were becoming rare in North America, but Chinese bears were still being milked for bile, a tube running into a raw wound in their side, the cages that held them rusty and filthy. Bearbaiting was still a pastime that drew thousands in Pakistan to watch clawless tethered bears being set upon by trained attack dogs. Dancing monkeys would be rescued from India. Exotic pets from the wealthy of the first world. She would take in abandoned panthers and snakes and simians that people had bought as illegal pets to add glamour to their homes. Leon listened to her talk about how she would hire trainers to pacify the wild animals and keepers to look after the damaged ones. "Except that they're all damaged," she said. "I'll get them special care. Like you all had."

"We're not animals," Leon said.

"We are all animals." She pointed her finger at him. "We are all animals."

Kyle was already working for a US presidential candidate.

Once their decision had been made, it took a month for Leon and Minh to pack and leave Overington. Rhona set up the transfer of the money. They moved into the house they had designed and had built on a property near the Grampians in Victoria. Leon grew a mustache and beard, and they hunkered down in their hideaway until they were sure no one was looking for them anymore. And he told her everything.

"You don't know how long? Susan doesn't know?" she said.

Leon shook his head. "What do you want to do?"

Minh looked out of the window to the land beyond, the sharp morning light cutting tree shadows into the pasture, the feral rabbits feeding before the sun burned away their camouflage.

"This," she said.

"I want to grow things," Leon said. "I want to grow plants and animals. Life."

Six months later, a journalist called. She talked fast and hard about a piece she wanted to write, profiling Leon and Minh. It would be about them after Kathryn's death, what had happened for them, how they had adjusted to life after the Wonders. Her insistent voice was an aural foot wedged in the door. When Leon realized what was happening, that the media had tracked them down, he was convinced his heart skipped a beat. How odd, when of course his heart did not beat at all.

Back during their trip to their new home the same thing had happened. He had been holding his passport and his customs declaration and immigration form. He and Minh were on the last leg of the arduous trip to their new life in the shadows. With Hap's help they had planned a labyrinth of subterfuge to get Leon's heart through private-security screening and lose the media who were trying to track them. They had been through countless hot sheds that served as airports with nothing but a vending machine and a ticket counter. At immigration control in Melbourne, a woman at the desk was examining people's identity documents and deciding whether these people were honest and true enough to enter the country. Leon looked down at his passport in his hand, open at the page with his picture and date of birth. The passport expiration date was five years and four months away, and with what he imagined to be a skip in his chest, he wondered if he would live that long.

The adolescent boy who was once Leon, mired in the world

of facile self-help books, used to look out to the forsaken Canadian Forest beyond his backyard and see only an unkempt wall of nature pocked with burned-out cars and fallen tree limbs. After the age of ten he never set foot in that bushland. "Go and play in the forest till teatime," his mother would say, but he turned in the opposite direction and headed to his dank room.

He could never see past the wall of trees. If he had gone down the hill and jumped the fence and walked, slowly, between the grass trees and the paperbarks, if he had stopped and bent over to gaze at the leaf litter or stood still long enough for the creatures of the bush to forget he was there, he would have seen the world that existed beyond the wall. Forest dissolving into beetles weaving through the humus, dangling webs of long-gone spiders, the whisper of life traveling through the understory, shocking green spikes sprouting from the ground that years later would pierce the clouds above the trees. The density of his vision would have cleared from a mass of gray and green and brown to florets of orange lichen between strips of peeling bark. A darkening shadow under a tree into the resting place of the brown-faced wallaby. The sky would have become a filtered high blue that stung his eyes. If he had been able to see and smell and hear these things that lived around him, perhaps his heart could have cured itself.

Leon and Minh walked sometimes to the boundary of their property. The cleared paddocks with their neat fences and cropped grass gave way to bush. They would open the gate Leon had specially built and trace their way to a nearby path worn by kangaroos. The path tracked from the boundary line of their property to a small seasonal pool at the foot of Mount Sturgeon, which rose to fill the view, its jagged profile delineating the sky from the land. Around it the land was flat, as though this single mountain had burst through the earth like a fist only yesterday. Each time Leon looked at it, he could imagine it surging up out of the land at dawn and sinking into the horizon each night.

There were times when he followed the path to where it diverged into many different paths that could probably only be followed by scent or instinct. At that point, where his feeble human senses gave out and he was left staring wide-eyed at a world of which he could only sense a tiny part, the shadows of the bush, the scratchings and rustles, the smells of rotting and renewal, the tickle of invisible skeins of web against his bare calf—all these things caused even his steady mechanical heart to feel as though it had swelled to an enormous size and was full, in the way of a normal joyful human heart of flesh.

He had thrown away his old self-help books. The one he was writing with the ghostly ghostwriter had been abandoned long before. He walked instead, and listened and sniffed and watched the world that went on, that had gone on all the time the Wonders were parading around the planet as if they were important.

These days it was the small things that made him ache with happiness. The thump of the kangaroos that leaped to safer ground when they heard his steps. The soil so rich it stuck to his fingers when he grasped a handful to smell the moisture. Minh's tired smile after a day at the clinic in town. The earthy taste of beetroot soup made with the crop they had grown in their garden. Standing at the window and watching the weak winter sun slant across bright green fields in the late afternoon.

On the wall above the fireplace hung an enlarged framed photograph Yuri had taken one afternoon of Kathryn dancing across the common room at Overington in her scarlet high heels. Splendiferous. Written underneath:

THE WONDERS

Gave thee clothing of delight,
Softest clothing, woolly, bright;
Gave thee such a tender voice,
Making all the vales rejoice!
Little lamb, who made thee?
Dost thou know who made thee?

ACKNOWLEDGMENTS

M Y DEEP GRATITUDE goes to Alison Ravenscroft for her un-swerving encouragement during the writing of this work. Fran Cusworth and Kelly Gardiner read an early draft and I am grateful for both their feedback and their company. Peter Dil-lane corrected some of my medical slips (no doubt I inserted a few more afterward) and Jan O'Reilly picked up my proofing fails (again, except for the ones I probably added later). Many other people have also been stalwart friends and supporters—I feel lucky to be a part of Australia's generous literary commu-nity. In addition, the support of Arts Victoria and the Australia Council were vital to the creation and development of this work. Finally, I wish to thank my wonderful editor, Sarah Branham.

ABOUT THE AUTHOR

PADDY O'REILLY is an international award-winning writer of novels, short stories, and screenplays. Her most recent novel, *The Fine Color of Rust,* was short-listed for the ALS Gold Medal. Her debut novel, *The Factory,* was "Highly Commended" in the FAW Christina Stead Award for Fiction.

Her short story collection, *The End of the World,* won a number of national and international story awards, including The Age, the Glen Eira My Brother Jack, Zoetrope All-Story and the Commonwealth Broadcasting Corporation. *The End of the World* was chosen as one the year's best books in various publications, from *Australian Book Review* to *The Financial Review.* It was short-listed for the Queensland Premier's Literary Awards and commended in the Victorian Premier's Literary Awards.

Paddy has been an Asialink writer-in-residence in Japan; a fellow at Varuna, the Writers House retreat in Australia; a writer-in-residence at the Katharine Susannah Prichard Writers' Centre in Perth, Australia; at the Kelly Steps Cottage in Tasmania; The Lock-up in Newcastle, Australia, and a full fellow at the Vermont Studio Center.

She spent several years living in Japan, working as a copywriter and translator, and now lives and works in Victoria, Australia.

Get email updates on

PADDY O'REILLY,

exclusive offers,

and other great book recommendations

from Simon & Schuster.